"I'm willing to help you. I'm willing to go to the mat and pre[...] **run the risk that w**[...] **the front line of da**[...] **wrong. I do care al**[...] **I care about them and their families."**

"So you will help?"

"On one condition."

His mouth opened slightly before snapping shut once more, his lips compressing into a firm line. As if outside of herself, Arden saw the moment with stark clarity.

Ryder knew what she was going to ask and Arden knew it. Knew it with the same sureness as when a storm was coming in or when a mare was about to foal.

With nothing to lose, she leaned forward.

Because she also knew he was desperate enough not to deny her what she asked.

"I want to know the truth of who you're really after. And what's really behind this operation you're so hell-bent to run."

* * *

We hope you enjoy the Midnight Pass, Texas miniseries

Dear Reader,

Welcome back to Midnight Pass, Texas. The Reynolds family has dealt with their fair share of danger over the past year and the three Reynolds brothers—Ace, Tate and Hoyt—believed it behind them. But the fresh wind blowing into town just ahead of spring has brought even more trouble, and it has set its sights on their little sister, Arden.

Arden has buried her personal pain, determined to erase her sad past. With it, she's focused on the family ranch, her new niece or nephew coming any day now and her business in town: running a well-respected yoga and fitness studio. What she isn't counting on is a romance with charming FBI agent and K-9 expert Ryder Durant.

As Arden comes to realize Ryder is more than what's on the surface, she allows him to unearth the quiet secrets she's been carrying so close to the vest. But just as she's about to let him in, their world goes sideways. A threat no one saw coming has been biding its time in the Pass.

And now he's prepared to strike.

I'm so excited to share Arden's story with you. And if you'd like to go back to the start of the series and read all about her brothers' HEAs, Tate's story begins the fun with *The Cowboy's Deadly Mission*.

Best,

Addison Fox

UNDERCOVER
K-9 COWBOY

Addison Fox

HARLEQUIN

ROMANTIC
SUSPENSE

HARLEQUIN®
ROMANTIC SUSPENSE™

Recycling programs for this product may not exist in your area.

ISBN-13: 978-1-335-75959-7

Undercover K-9 Cowboy

Copyright © 2022 by Frances Karkosak

This edition published by arrangement with Harlequin Books S.A.

For questions and comments about the quality of this book, please contact us at CustomerService@Harlequin.com.

Harlequin Enterprises ULC
22 Adelaide St. West, 40th Floor
Toronto, Ontario M5H 4E3, Canada
www.Harlequin.com

Printed in U.S.A.

Addison Fox is a lifelong romance reader, addicted to happily-ever-afters. After discovering she found as much joy writing about romance as she did reading it, she's never looked back. Addison lives in New York with an apartment full of books, a laptop that's rarely out of sight and a wily beagle who keeps her running. You can find her at her home on the web at www.addisonfox.com or on Facebook (www.Facebook.com/addisonfoxauthor) and Twitter (@addisonfox).

Books by Addison Fox

Harlequin Romantic Suspense

Midnight Pass, Texas

The Cowboy's Deadly Mission
Special Ops Cowboy
Under the Rancher's Protection
Undercover K-9 Cowboy

The Coltons of Grave Gulch

Colton's Covert Witness

The Coltons of Mustang Valley

Deadly Colton Search

The Coltons of Roaring Springs

The Colton Sheriff

Visit the Author Profile page at Harlequin.com for more titles.

For those who never give up hope.

And for those who have, may yours find its way back to you. You are stronger than you know.

Chapter 1

"We want to set a trap."

Arden Reynolds stared at the attractive stranger sitting across her warm, peach-colored kitchen and wondered if the world had lost its mind. Or maybe just her corner of it.

Her brothers and their wives had taken up positions around their solid Texas pine table, but in the subtle gesture of respect she'd received from the women who had come into her life over the past year—each a sister now—Arden sat at the head.

And listened to the most outrageous scheme of her life.

"What sort of trap?" Ace, her oldest brother and de facto head of their ranch, Reynolds Station, finally spoke up.

"The vastness of your land and proximity to the Rio Grande makes you an easy mark for drug trafficking.

We've watched patterns for the past few years and every four to six months, one cartel or another works up the courage to try passage through your land again."

"We know." Tate spoke up, her brother's own experiences with discoveries on their property still obviously fresh in his mind, even after a year. "It's why we now make a significant investment in security here in our little corner of paradise."

The stranger didn't miss the sarcasm but he did deftly ignore it. "That's where the FBI can help."

"Why don't you map it out for everyone, Ryder," Tate's wife, Belle, finally spoke up. Her role as one of the leading detectives for the Midnight Pass Police Department had given her a front-facing opportunity to observe the increasing presence of the Feds in their small Texas border town. Although she'd been vocal about her frustration with some of their tactics, in her more private moments she'd admitted the help was welcome.

And, unfortunately, necessary.

Arden considered Ryder and had to admit *stranger* wasn't quite the right term. Until this evening she hadn't known Agent Durant's last name, but she had seen him around town. The prior fall they'd spoken outside the town coffee shop after one of her yoga practices, an introduction fraught with some sort of unspoken joke only Ryder seemed to understand. At least his trained K-9 dog, Murphy, had been friendly.

Then Belle had introduced them briefly at the New Year's Day festival on the town square. Agent Durant had been busy with Murphy and the ready attention the chocolate Lab received from eager children. The steady stream of visitors had kept him from doing much talking or visiting.

But she'd noticed him.

He was hard to miss. Tall and rangy, he was a man who garnered a woman's attention. Add on the dog, and he was damn near lethally attractive.

Shame he seemed well aware of that fact, Arden lamented to herself.

"As I said, we've been following the various paths in and around Midnight Pass. Even with federal presence, it hasn't deterred the drug trade from moving back and forth over the border."

"Why's that?" Although she still chafed a bit from their initial meeting, Arden asked the question of the agent in all sincerity.

"Excuse me?" Ryder asked.

"Why is that? You'd think a federal presence would be a mighty large deterrent. The Pass is an easy transfer point but these are rather intelligent criminals and the Texas-Mexico border is long. Yet they keep traipsing back and forth over the border right here in our town. Do you have a leak?"

"Arden." Ace's voice was low, but she didn't miss the subtle note of warning.

Ryder cocked his head, his dark gaze direct and unyielding. "Why do you ask that, Miss Reynolds?"

"The very last thing the cartels need is to get caught. Why risk it with the Feds so close if not for some additional benefit?"

"We run a tight operation." The agent kept his smile firmly in place.

Although she had no reason to keep taunting, Arden pressed him further. This man was here, in her home, asking her and her loved ones to set a trap for ruthless criminals.

Was it so far-fetched to ask him to assess his own house? Or his proverbial one, at least.

She'd been blessed with her mother's spunk in spades, and when her three older brothers wore nothing more than resigned looks, she pressed on.

"You say you run a tight operation. Yet we still have a problem in Midnight Pass. Seems rather shortsighted not to consider the reasons why."

Ryder Durant liked fiery women. He'd never understood men who looked for passive females and had no desire to change his mind on that count.

But damn, he'd be lying to himself if he didn't admit that Arden Reynolds was quite a piece of work.

An incredibly attractive one, too, with her slim frame and lush hips and that long flow of red hair that spilled over her shoulders. She wore what he'd come to think of as something of her standard uniform—yoga pants and some sort of stretchy top that did nothing to hide more curves. He'd seen her around town a few times since arriving in Midnight Pass the prior August and had been intrigued by her from the start.

But there was something about sparring with her in the middle of her kitchen that had his interest shifting from intrigued straight on to attracted.

Murphy loved her. His K-9 was a good working dog and a sound and trusted partner, but he was tentative in how he warmed to others. His training had ensured he knew duty first. But there was sheer adoration in his chocolate Lab's eyes the first time those dark orbs had settled on the attractive Miss Reynolds.

Nor had he missed how Murphy had taken up a spot in the corner of the kitchen, in direct line of sight to Arden.

"The Bureau is sound," he finally answered. "We take care of our own."

As answers went, it was rather weak and evasive, but he wasn't about to give the woman any runway for her speculations. Add on the fact that she'd keyed in on something he'd worried about himself, vague and ambiguous was all he was prepared to give at the moment.

It did gnaw at him that things seemed different since top agent Noah Ross was transferred to a new post around the same time Ryder was transferred in. Ross had a stellar reputation and with his reassignment to the larger Bureau office in Dallas, Ryder couldn't help but feel that he was fending for himself down in Midnight Pass.

"Can you be sure about that, Agent Durant?" Arden's sister-in-law Reese spoke up. "Even the most stalwart can lose their way."

Ryder knew there was more to Reese Grantham Reynolds's question. Yet she'd sat through his pitch anyway. Her back had remained straight and her attention had never wavered as she gently soothed circles over her pregnant belly.

Reese and, Ryder suspected, everyone else gathered around the table, understood the stakes. But he needed access to their land for what he had in mind.

In the quiet that came after Reese's statement, Belle took the opportunity to shift the conversation. "No institution is infallible. But for the moment, let's rule out an internal problem there and consider Agent Durant's proposal to us." Belle turned her full attention toward him. "What's involved?"

Although he had the briefest urge to spar a few more rounds with Arden, Ryder focused on the question. Belle

Granger Reynolds was a good detective—she'd proven her commitment to upholding the law and working collaboratively with his office whenever necessary—and he appreciated her partnership.

"Not much from any of you. This ranch is a place of business and we're not looking to interfere with that. We need to find a way to cordon off the acreage at the southern end of the property, yet continue to make it look like there's work going on. Two of my colleagues and I would pose as ranch hands and work that end of the land as our focus. We can disguise surveillance equipment within what looks to be regular fence posts and set up a perimeter."

Reynolds Station was nestled in a prime location near the border. The land in and around Midnight Pass had been named as such because of the ravines and gullies that allowed passage over the Rio Grande. The Reynolds property sat at the apex of that, with some of the easiest passages across the border.

It was why the bad guys kept trying.

And it was why he was determined to shut them down once and for all.

"My wife and I are about to have a baby. I have no interest in inviting trouble right here onto our property." Hoyt Reynolds had been quiet up to now, the stoic rancher never moving far from his position behind his very pregnant wife's chair. "We've all worked good and hard to get away from trouble. No sense in going looking for it."

Even as a relative newcomer to The Pass, Ryder had heard all about how Hoyt's wife, Reese, had suffered a family tragedy when her father had taken on his own brand of vigilante justice the prior spring.

Russ Grantham had been the well-respected captain of the Midnight Pass Police Department. The death of his teenage son to a drug overdose more than a decade before had done more psychological damage than anyone had realized, and it was Russ's determination to pick off drug dealers, one at a time with a dark and deadly hand that had ultimately led to the man's downfall.

"I can understand your concern, but with the size of your land and our ability to remain hidden, we are confident we can keep you and your family away from any danger," Ryder said.

It was a bold statement, but a fair one. And a promise he was determined to uphold.

"We're not interested in sitting by, unaware or uninformed of what's happening on our land," Hoyt added, clearly unconvinced by Ryder's promise.

"Hoyt's right," Ace chimed in. "We're not even going to consider this if it means we're kept in the dark. This is our home and our property. We have a right to know what's going on."

Ryder had never subscribed to the notion that the FBI's role as federal peacekeepers forgave any manner of sins. But neither could he compromise an op by bringing too many civilians in on the plans.

"The Bureau will protect your family, Mr. Reynolds."

"That's not what I'm asking," Ace said.

"But it is what I'm prepared to give."

Arden had spent more than enough time growing up with three brothers to know when a situation had nowhere to go but sideways. With that foremost in her thoughts, she caught Belle's eye and gave the slightest of head nods. Her sister-in-law caught the message easily enough and smoothly cut in.

"Agent Durant. I think you've given us plenty to think about. Perhaps we can pick this conversation up at a later time. After everyone's had a chance to spend a bit more time thinking about things."

Dark eyes the color of the gooey center of a chocolate lava cake crinkled at the corners as his mouth drifted into an easy smile. Arden would have bet a mighty sum the agent was nowhere near to feeling that carefree and easy, but you'd never know it by the simple lift of his shoulders or his easy tone. "Fair enough."

Which only put her antennae up even more. What was his game?

She didn't doubt he believed what he was saying— Reynolds Station sat on one of the most easily traversed corridors over the border—but that didn't mean federal agents regularly showed up, politely asking for a hall pass to monitor the traffic.

Which was why she finally spoke up.

"Why don't I leave you all to talk for a few minutes, and I'll take Agent Durant out to see the stables?"

Although she was under no delusion any of them were ready to say yes, she wanted a few minutes of her own with the agent to see what else she could find out. She also knew Hoyt was hanging on by the slightest thread, his anxiety for Reese and the baby his foremost concern. Continuing the discussion would only push Hoyt further toward a no vote. Despite her misgivings, Arden wasn't sure that was the best option. And while she had her own concerns, including the baby's safety, she wanted to remain open to the discussion.

"We'll be back in a few minutes." She gestured toward the door, Murphy already scrambling to his feet, his toenails clipping lightly on the hardwood floor. The sound was oddly comforting, in the midst of a dangerous and unpleasant conversation, and she smiled at Ryder's handsome companion as they went out.

It was only once they'd cleared the back of the ranch house and were headed for the large, recently rebuilt stable that Ryder finally spoke. "You take care of them."

The late winter air was cold as it swirled around them and Arden ran a hand over the sleeves of her multicolored workout sweatshirt. "Of course I do."

"But you're the youngest."

"So?"

"So isn't that their job?"

"For starters, we're family. We look out for each other. It'd be a mistake to underestimate us. Any one of us." She eyed him beside her before stopping and turning to look at him fully. "Do you have siblings?"

"Sisters."

"And what do your sisters think of your high-handed tactics?"

"They don't know." He grinned broadly. "And who said I was underestimating anyone?"

"It didn't need saying. It was all over your face and it's an even more evident trait if you assume your sisters are unaware of your attitude."

He looked momentarily chagrined so Arden pressed on, taking the small advantage while she had it. "Sort of like us."

"What's that supposed to mean?"

His lazy tone had a slight bite and Arden warmed to the idea that she was getting somewhere. "You want to run your op and you want our blessing to do it."

"I can get support from my bosses with or without your family's cooperation."

It was a gamble—Arden could see that in his eyes—and for some reason she couldn't quite identify, it broke the tension. "I think that's the first honest thing you've said since you arrived tonight."

"I haven't lied."

"You've omitted."

"I didn't lie," Ryder said with more force.

To be fair, while her mother would likely turn in her grave at the direction of Arden's thoughts, Arden couldn't fully argue with Ryder's assessment. Omission wasn't an out-and-out lie. Growing up with three older brothers had taught her early on how to keep her own counsel. To her way of thinking, people blabbed what they were doing far more often than they needed to. Her thoughts were her own business and she'd be a hypocrite if she thought anything less of the federal agent for acting the same way.

Once again at an impasse, Arden moved on ahead, tapping in the code to open the stables. They'd had a scare the prior summer, their previous stable going up in flames at the hands of an old threat to Reese, and the new security system had been one of the outcomes of rebuilding. "This is quite a setup," Agent Durant marveled as he followed her through the door.

"We spared no expense to rebuild the barn and make it state-of-the-art."

"I can see that." The man's assessment was clear-eyed as he looked around the entryway. "Cameras, infrareds. Nicely done."

"Our horses arc a part of the family. Nearly losing them was a big wake-up call."

"Belle told me about what happened."

Arden turned at that, her gaze once again finding his all-too-compelling one. "You mean you spoke to local law enforcement? Collaborated with them, even? I'd have expected you got all your information out of carefully worded reports."

"I know how to talk to people."

"As I understand it, it's not one of the traits they focus on in your training."

"Look, Arden. I'm not going to apologize for being here."

Her pulse tripped unexpectedly at his use of her name and her voice came out gruffer than she intended at the surprising pleasure. "No one's asking you to."

"Oh no?" Ryder's eyebrows lifted. "I thought that was exactly what you were asking."

Since she hadn't brought him out to the stables to pick a fight, Arden wasn't quite sure where the impulse had come from to do just that. Nor had she come here to have rioting feelings fluttering her pulse like a schoolgirl. She'd had that once and, when it ended, learned to live without it. That part of her life was closed.

Simple. Easy. And done.

But she did need to keep the agent close and she wasn't about to do it with trippy feelings and googly emotions that had no place in her life. The man could be an ally. One they'd all need to keep at arm's length, but an ally all the same. That was her focus.

"Look. I'm willing to go along with your scheme, but I need a few reassurances."

"You speak for your family?"

"No, but I can be a voice of persuasion. If I'm going to do that, there need to be some rules. And I can tell you, trying to keep us out of things is going to be a problem."

Although Ryder Durant didn't strike her as a man who backed down from much, she didn't miss the quick flare of interest that lit his dark gaze in the muted lights of the stable.

"This isn't about a stakeout at all, is it?" The idea took root and Arden quickly got up a head of steam. "You have a plan. A bigger score than catching a few stray drug dealers crossing the border."

The subtle humor that seemed to perpetually light his gaze winked out, leaving behind something she'd seen in Belle. Cop eyes. Flat. Focused. And enough banked aggression to know something dark and serious lived beneath the surface of the easygoing agent.

"I laid it out for you. For all of you."

"No." Arden shook her head, conviction rising up strong and true. "It's something more. You want to run a full-blown op. I don't know how we missed it."

"You can't miss what you aren't told."

One of the horses let out a soft whicker—Grumpy, she thought—and it was enough to break the moment. Murphy perked up his head, his attention on the interior of the barn.

The shift in momentum was also enough to have Ryder stepping back a few paces. "Look. This isn't about omission or lies or anything else. I'm not at liberty to share what I know."

"Then I guess that's a real shame for you."

"Why?"

"Because I'm afraid I can't help you."

Chapter 2

"Can't help me? Or won't?" Ryder asked.

"Won't. You just went from omitting to lying and I won't help you with that." Arden turned on a heel and headed toward one of the stalls, toward the direction of the whicker that had interrupted them in the first place.

Ryder knew the import of her words, yet couldn't stop the flames of interest from continuing to lap at his ankles as he stared at the long fall of reddish-blond curls that swept down over her shoulders. He was in imminent danger of overplaying his hand—hell, of handing over the entire deck—and already ideas of how he could bring her in on what he wanted to do played through his mind.

You can't miss what you aren't told.

He'd already slipped enough with that one. And while he wasn't going to underestimate her and assume she didn't catch the slip, she also hadn't jumped on it.

Interesting. Could she be an asset?

And there it freaking was. Even now, his mind raced with attempted solutions of how he could let her in on his plans. Which was the very last thing he should be considering, especially since she hadn't been entirely off base in her assessments back in the kitchen.

He wasn't ready to accuse any coworkers, but he was playing this close to the vest.

Yet she'd guessed that. Sensed it? Understood?

Which only made this ridiculous intrigue with her something he needed to cut off.

An intrigue, he admitted to himself, that had begun the first time he'd seen her. She'd been standing outside a coffee shop on Main Street, wanting to pet Murphy. All that glorious hair had been pulled back then, up in a high ponytail that matched the workout clothes she wore. He'd flashed from the usual work response to strangers approaching Murphy to interested in a heartbeat and a half.

He hadn't had to do much asking to find out who she was. The Reynolds family was well-known in The Pass, and Arden was the owner of Midnight Pass's only yoga studio. Most everyone in town knew who she was.

Careful, Ryder.

There it was again. That quick and ready interest that always spiked at thoughts of Arden Reynolds. He had a job to do and he needed no one's permission. Nor, technically, did he need the Reynolds family's approval. But he wanted to do this the right way. It was unfortunate for them that their land sat on a prime spot but he could and would use his authority if he needed to in order to get his way. But to have an ally...

Once again ignoring the thought, he went back on the

offensive. "What part of *classified federal operations* don't you understand?"

She turned from where she patted a pretty chestnut stallion over his nose. "And what part of a family that's already dealt with more than its fair share of trouble this past year and is now focused and happy to have a baby on the way don't *you* understand?"

That same fierce commitment to her brothers and their wives, on display in the kitchen, came back in full force.

"There is no trouble to you and your family. We're talking about a federal police presence on your land. At the outer rim of that land, more to the point. Your family won't be in danger."

Her blue eyes turned volatile and it was impossible to miss the disdain as the corners of her mouth turned down, even from his distance of about fifteen feet. "Forgive me if all I hear in that is an empty promise."

"You have my word."

"Recent history suggests that means squat."

"This isn't at all the same as recent history. Besides—" he moved a few steps closer "—you didn't have *my* word."

Arden remained cool but he didn't miss the slight shift in the horse who stood behind her, ears perking on the head peeking over the stall gate. Ryder might not be able to see her tension, but the horse felt it.

Reacted to it.

It pleased him way more than it should have.

Although Ryder had spoken with Belle as well as his colleagues, getting fully up to speed on the issues the Reynolds family had dealt with over the past year, he'd also done his own homework. And while he recognized Russ Grantham's serial killing of several drug dealers and the faceless enemy that had stalked his daughter, Reese, were horrifying, they were hardly the same.

Even Ace and Veronica's recent problems with Veronica's ex-husband were more personal in nature.

No matter how he twisted or turned it, Ryder simply couldn't see how these situations—traumatic as they were—carried the same weight as what he was proposing.

He wanted the big score. The one that actually shut down trafficking corridors and stopped drugs from entering the country. The drug industry might be a many-headed hydra, but cutting off heads—especially a large one—could do some good.

Hell, screw good. It might give him and his colleagues a chance to catch up a bit.

And it might give him a chance to redeem himself from his mistakes all those years ago.

Arden Reynolds was worried about her future niece or nephew's safety and Ryder's sole focus was making sure said child *had* a future. A safe one that didn't live under the pervasive shadow of crime.

That had been his biggest realization since coming to Midnight Pass. The town looked sweet and bucolic on the surface, but there was danger that roiled beneath the calm. He feared that the whole town would break wide-open if they didn't find a way to get a handle on it.

The sprawling Reynolds property was the path to fixing that. And, from where he was standing, Arden Reynolds was the one who held the key.

Circular arguments. Prevarication. And fear.

Whatever Arden had expected in talking to Agent Durant on her own, the fear was a surprise. He masked it well, but it was there all the same. She'd spent too much of her life around animals not to recognize the telltale signs. It was a certain look in the eyes. No matter how tough the outer shell, the eyes always told the truth.

"Your confidence is interesting, Agent Durant. You speak of history like it's not something humans are destined to repeat, over and over."

"No, I'm suggesting this isn't a matter of history repeating itself at all. Your family has had challenges, I'll grant you that, but those have all been dealt with. And call me Ryder."

"Fine. Ryder." Arden felt his name roll over her tongue and wondered why she'd never noticed how a name felt before. Those two syllables were strong on her lips, and enticing, too. Unbidden, an image of uttering his name on a throaty growl as his body pressed hers into cool sheets filled her mind's eye.

Swallowing back the sudden dryness in her throat, she ignored the traitorous thoughts. Or tried to. "Why don't you think this is the same problem we've been dealing with for nearly a year?"

"Russ Grantham is gone. Reese's troubles have been handled. So has Veronica's ex-husband. You can't repeat history that's been wrapped up and solved."

Since there was more truth in his words than she wanted to admit, Arden shifted her focus to Murphy, asking Ryder's companion his opinion. "Is he always so stubborn?"

The pretty chocolate Lab thumped his tail on the thick concrete floor of the stable, a steady acknowledgment that, why yes, his master was a force of nature.

"Ahh." Arden nodded. "I can see I've hit the mark."

When Murphy's tail only thumped harder, Ryder frowned. "Don't listen to him."

"Hit a nerve, did I?" Arden couldn't hold back the quick laugh. "Being forced to acknowledge that even man's best friend knows I have a point."

When Ryder didn't say anything more, Arden pointed toward Murphy. "May I pet him?"

"Sure." Ryder moved closer, his attention on the dog. "Murphy. Come."

The dog obeyed instantly, his training so ingrained that he never hesitated as he moved toward Ryder, taking a place at his side. That large, capable body remained alert, his ears pitching forward in a perked motion, as Ryder gestured Arden forward. "He's all yours."

Arden dropped to her knees, extending a hand to the dog. Although she had no concern Murphy would harm her, she wanted to give him the courtesy of smelling her before moving straight in for a pat. They'd met before and while dogs inherently reveled in touch and the sense of security it provided, she deeply believed every creature deserved a chance to accept and acknowledge touch. Affection. Companionship.

It was an attitude that had served her well with the varied animals they had on the ranch, honed through years of observation. But it was life that had reinforced the determined notion sharing her world with other creatures, both human and non, was a gift.

Murphy responded quickly, his tail thumping as he gave her hand a quick sniff.

"Go ahead," Ryder encouraged and the dog didn't wait. He moved in, his big head bumping up against Arden's palm.

"There you are, beautiful boy." She ruffled the hair at his neck, using both hands to massage the thick, solid muscle before shifting toward the softer hair on his head and ears. "What a good boy you are."

Murphy bore up under the attention, admirably holding himself upright for nearly a minute before falling to his side and presenting his belly for the ultimate in trust and happiness. Tail wagging all the while, he lay in that position as Arden scratched the pale fur of his belly, murmuring words of praise and encouragement.

"The poor sucker never had a chance." Ryder crouched low beside her, adding a pat to Murphy's hindquarters.

"He's beautiful."

"That he is." Ryder's gaze skipped around the stable before landing back on hers. "For a place full of animals, I haven't seen any dogs."

"No." Arden affirmed, even as a small shot of remorse stuck under her breastbone. "We had a Dalmatian and a Weimaraner for the longest time. Lucy and Ethel. They were the best of friends and the very best dogs."

"How long have they been gone?"

"Five years. And I want to get another one—" she broke off with a broad smile "—actually, I'd like about five. But every time I think about it, something holds me back."

"There are a lot of dogs that need rescuing."

"I know."

And she did know. Hadn't she had that conversation with herself repeatedly? And hadn't she already masterminded several pet adoptions for the students at her yoga studio. She had no issue insisting others should move on and embrace the beauty of sharing their life with a pet.

Yet she'd held back.

The loss of Lucy and Ethel had been a part of nature. The natural course of loving and caring for a pet throughout his or her life. She'd known their lifespans would never match hers and had always been prepared for that fact. If nothing else, growing up on a farm ensured she well and truly understood that reality.

And yet—

Her relationship with Dan had ended—exploded? incinerated?—and then six months later she'd lost Lucy. A few months after that, Ethel had followed.

She had heard Hoyt and Reese talking about getting a pet. That after the baby came and they settled into their new home Hoyt was building on Reynolds land, they'd add a four-legged family member as well. It made her happy to imagine. Her niece or nephew should grow up with a pet, the two running wild and free over the land.

And somehow, that small bit of distance—Hoyt's family dog—made it all seem okay. She'd love it and spoil it but she could keep her own heart at a measured distance.

"You don't seem convinced."

Arden keyed back into Ryder's comments, her brother's imagined furry addition fading away. "I am convinced. There are so many pets that need to be rescued."

"But not by you?"

"Not right now." Arden gave Murphy one last pat before standing up.

Ryder's mouth opened before pressing closed once more and he stood with her. Murphy's tail slowed from a delirious wag to a gentle thump but he stayed on his side where he was, his gaze shifting between the two of them. Although she'd never ascribed to the idea that animals processed the world just like humans, Arden did give them credit for more base intelligence than was generally accepted.

Just because that intelligence was steeped in instinct

and nonverbal knowledge didn't mean it lacked understanding. It was moments like this, with those gentle
brown eyes staring up at her that reinforced her beliefs.

It was also that deep trust and affection Murphy held
for the agent that went a long way toward calming Arden's
suspicions. Which meant she'd give him one more chance.

"Okay, Agent Durant. Let's try this once more. What
do you want with my family?"

The face of his phone lit up with a steady stream of
text messages, alerts and appointment notices, but Rick
Statler ignored them all. He'd spent the better part of
the new year focused on shoring up his latest partnership and the constant barrage of work messages would
have to wait.

His extracurricular *investments* needed to take priority just a bit longer.

Besides, the field offices were humming like clock-
work. He'd put some of his best team members in place
and they hadn't disappointed. Beyond staying on top
of reports and authorizing a few end-of-year budget re-
quests and a few more to start the year, all was running
smoothly.

It had helped that he'd moved Noah Ross. A larger
field office and a promotion had been the easy part.
Getting the man's steady eye off Midnight Pass hadn't
proven as easy as he'd hoped. Word had trickled back
Ross hadn't quite let go of his old gig, keeping an eye
on "The Pass," as he referred to it in a few emails Rick
had intercepted.

That steady attention had been the only sticky spot in
his plans and it had forced him to bide a bit more time
than he'd originally anticipated.

Rick snagged the report he'd left on top of the stack and considered how much work he could toss at Ross. Dallas was a huge market and there was more than enough work. He needed something big enough to finally get good old Noah well and fully distracted from his old job. Something that would take up every waking moment the man possessed. He'd vaguely paid attention in the last team meeting on an Eastern European mob organization that was gaining ground in Dallas. Maybe he could shove Ross at that one.

In the meantime, he needed to put the next step in play in Midnight Pass. Shifting his gaze to the report, Rick read through the quick and easy style of Ryder Durant.

The agent had been in Midnight Pass about six months now and was making a name for himself with the locals. Word had floated back that the local PD liked working with him and, while not entirely necessary, Rick knew it might help grease the wheels a bit. People looked a bit slower in the direction of those they liked.

It had been his strategy for over a decade now and it had served him well.

Rick was the guy *everyone* liked. He chipped in to help out, always had a kind word for everyone and was known to buy a round of beers after department softball games. Rick Statler was a "hell-of-a-good guy" and he'd ridden the congenial smile and big blue eyes all the way to the bank. Why take a middling score when you could have the whole enchilada? Another delicious part of Texas that had grown on him after he transferred down from Boston so many years ago.

He'd been small-time in Boston, the local cops tapping the town pretty well. He'd turned a blind eye toward a few scores—kept both wide-open on others when it helped build his reputation—and had ultimately left the cold and the snow and the baked beans when the brass gave him the Bureau lead opportunity based out of El Paso.

The work down in Texas was different from what he'd honed in Boston. Less bare knuckles and more snake in the grass, biding its time to strike. The land was so spread out and the jurisdictions so vast, he'd found better ways to ply his trade, all while staying firmly off the radar.

The patience had paid off.

He'd made slow and steady contact with one of the lead cartels down in Colombia, finally winning the trust of its current head. A head who came to power after destroying his cousin, the former cartel lead, with several tips provided by Rick.

It had been a fruitful partnership so far. More than fruitful, Rick acknowledged, as he cross-referenced a few stakeout details currently planned for the coming week. In exchange for federally sourced intel and a blind eye to a few weak points at the border, Rick would receive an admirably fair cut of a massive cocaine shipment. All he had to do was divert his team toward a small score a hundred miles away and the cartel would cross the border with ease.

It was like a massive chessboard, only he was the only player. Which suited him just fine, he thought, as he tapped in the location of the week's small takedown.

The op would also give him some time to visit with his new honey. Although he was never long without female companionship, he'd been surprised to find himself falling for a woman he'd met in Midnight Pass. Quietly ambitious and seriously built, she had all the qualities he looked for in a woman.

And she liked sex.

He'd already begun thinking of ways he could keep her around, which, truth be told, had spooked him a bit. But he liked her. Enjoyed her company.

And wasn't that a kick in the ass?

He'd spent his life as a confirmed bachelor, more than happy with a series of one-night stands. Yet here he was, ready to settle down.

Would that be a bad thing?

Catching the direction of his thoughts, he tamped down on them and focused on the work. He wasn't ready to settle yet and he needed that shipment to come in free and clear. He had already mentally added the tally on that one to his Caymans account and there was no time to get sloppy.

After issuing a series of emails, shifting his team from existing missions to the new "lead" he'd received, Rick sat back and surveyed his dark, gray, government-issued office. The furniture was metallic and spotted with rust at the base of the legs and the chair creaked every time he moved. It should bother him, yet somehow he'd learned how to ignore it. Rust and the patina of age were a small price to pay for what awaited him.

When he took his early retirement package—and by his calculation that would come due at the end of the year—he'd put all that dull, gloomy metal far behind him. Let some other sap sit his ass in the creaky chair and pretend he was some sort of do-gooder. Rick knew the truth.

Good was for the weak.

The world belonged to the precious few who had the smarts and the insight to control it.

* * *

He should have been surprised. Realistically, Ryder understood that. Arden Reynolds was a yoga instructor, for Pete's sake. A fair profession, of course, but not one known for subterfuge and detective work.

Yet she had a sharp eye and a wicked street sense that continued to catch him off guard.

"I don't want anything with your family. I want access to your land. That's what I've been talking with Belle about and it's why I came out here tonight."

"Bull," Arden shot back.

"Truth. There's a difference."

"Then I'm out." Arden stood after giving Murphy one last pat. "There's no reason for you to come back to the house. You can see yourself to your truck."

The pull to tell her what he was about grew taut, even as his duty to the Bureau held him back.

The truth of it all was that Ryder *was* concerned there was a bad actor inside his team. It wasn't anything more than gut, and God knew he'd been wrong before, but something wasn't right. He'd been part of three drug busts since taking the job in The Pass and all of them had been small potatoes. Yet month after month, intel came in that more and more drugs were getting over the border.

Where was it all coming from? And how was it getting in? He knew the cartels were well trained in making the trek over the border, but the sheer amount of drugs moving into circulation was a surprise. The cartels were powerful but other influences had risen over the past decade, too. The Russian mob had made a heavy mark in nearly every major city in the country. Several other Eastern European and Asian gangs had carved out their markets as well.

Were several of them involved? And far, far worse, was there a leak in the FBI allowing them in?

That's why he needed this job. The Reynolds ranch offered a prime opportunity to figure it out.

"I won't put you in danger," he finally said.

"I'm not worried about that."

"Then why the pushback?"

"Because I don't like subterfuge and I really don't like liars."

"I'm not a liar."

Those pretty cornflower blue eyes raked over him. "You look like one to me."

The lack of warmth or even the tiniest bit of challenge in her gaze caught Ryder up short.

Look like one?

"What do liars look like then?"

"Pretty boys with cocky attitudes."

He had just as many street smarts as Arden Reynolds, and in that moment, Ryder would have bet quite a bit of money that someone had hurt her.

Badly.

And it looked like they'd both showed a few of their cards since walking into the stables.

Which only left one question.

Which one of them was going to show their hand first?

Chapter 3

"Breathe in."

Arden lifted her arms, extending them in front and behind her body as her feet shifted into position on her mat. Her students followed suit, their collective inhale of breath like a wave through the room.

"And move into Warrior One pose," she intoned.

This was one of her more advanced classes and as her gaze drifted around the room, she saw that everyone had easily assumed the pose, each form well-balanced and correctly positioned.

Which was too bad because it meant she had nowhere to focus but inside her own head. Which, she thought with no small measure of disgust, had been wretched company for the past four days.

"And exhale." She offered up the next pose, shifting into the position as her class followed suit.

Four days.

Four endless days since that damnable discussion in the barn.

One day, she'd give herself. Every woman was allowed a day of brooding when a good-looking man with a cocky swagger and a very fine ass walked into one's well-ordered life.

By day two it was old.

Day three had passed old and moved straight on to rank. And by today? She'd have kicked her own behind if she could have managed that anatomical feat.

Years of yoga had made her limber, but her skills didn't extend to defying the laws of physics.

Which was a damn shame because she was sick of her own company.

Her brothers had questioned her extensively when she'd come back in from the barn visit with Ryder. All were convinced that going along with the agent's plan was a bad idea.

Yet…

Try as she might, she couldn't say it was an altogether bad idea. Ill-advised, perhaps, but not out-and-out bad.

Ace was willing to push back on the whole thing on principle. His immediate default as the oldest was to protect, but that caution bordered on maddening at times.

Hoyt was so focused on Reese and the baby—as he should be—that there wasn't going to be any rational thought out of him for some time.

And Tate was skeptical because of what he and Belle had gone through the prior spring.

Her brothers' reasons were all fair ones. Sound. Rock-solid. And incapable of blazing a path to finally removing the stench that regularly made its way along their land.

They'd talked about it, over and over, year after year.

Well before Tate found the body that kicked off the investigation into Russ Grantham, they'd all known their land hid problems at the border. The craggy passages there were simply too tempting—and too easy to traverse. And no matter how hard they'd worked, short of putting up surveillance along thousands of acres of fence, there was simply no way to keep up with it all.

Yes, they'd put cameras on the weakest points, but those weren't the *only* points.

And that was the whole problem.

She still didn't care for Agent Durant's approach, but she was *interested* in a plan that might finally accomplish what her family had spent time and money trying to solve.

Arden led her students through several more poses, slowly increasing the time spent in position, pleased to see how easily each person held their form and built their own individual strength. It was one of the things she loved most about yoga. There was always something new to accomplish, even as all that had come before prepared you for the challenge.

Growth was personal and individual and you were judged by no one.

Which was a far cry from single life in a small town.

At that thought, Arden nearly bobbled her Tree pose, her "branches" definitely swaying under the assault of that image.

She hadn't spent much time thinking or worrying about her lack of a love life. Not since Dan had left and her world had cratered. So why was she thinking about it now?

One more thing to lay at the feet of Agent Ryder Durant and his cute, furry sidekick?

Or something else?

She had gotten over Dan a long time ago. She'd given up mooning and anger and that underlying sadness that spoke of regret. In the end, she'd come out the other side and had seen their breakup for the disguised blessing that it was. And for a long time, it had been enough.

More than enough, actually.

Until recently. When love had arrived at Reynolds Station with all the finesse of a spring tornado. And packing the same powerful punch.

All three of her brothers had settled down over the past year, one falling faster than the next, like big, strapping, cowboy dominoes. She was happy—genuinely—for each of them. Tate, Ace and Hoyt were wonderful men and they'd met equally wonderful women. Women who had become instant sisters.

But life had changed.

Love was in the air.

Great, huge, soaking waves of it, filling her home and seeming to spill from the windows. It was wonderful and there was much to celebrate. But for the first time in a long time, she had to admit to feeling left out.

Forgotten.

And maybe not needed any longer.

Although he was a man who appreciated exercise in all its forms, there was something about yoga that Ryder had never gotten a taste for. He tamped down on the shiver that raced his spine as he remembered a flexibility class he'd been required to take his first year on the K-9 team out of Fort Worth.

The idea had been to match their three-times-a-week strength training sessions with two weekly flexibility classes to round out muscle tone, physical balance and overall mental agility.

All Ryder had felt like was an idiot. A raging idiot who couldn't hold even the simplest pose to save his life.

He couldn't even touch his toes. A fact that rankled, even as he was able to easily increase his bench press totals and expand his four-times-a-week running routine.

So why in the ever-loving hell couldn't he touch his damn toes? Still?

Yoga was so not for him. Only today it had to be for him because he needed to talk to Arden Reynolds. And if his debacle of a conversation in her barn was any indication, he needed to move their next discussion onto more neutral territory.

Visiting her studio wasn't exactly neutral, he admitted to himself, but it also didn't have her three strapping brothers a backyard away.

Which would help.

It *had* to help.

Because he was getting desperate.

No matter how hard they worked, his office staff kept chasing their tails, never getting any closer to a big score. A fact very clearly reinforced this past week. They needed the Reynolds family. Badly.

The tip his office had gotten a few days prior had proven fruitful, yet still empty somehow. A full-on team had descended on a warehouse just outside the El Paso city limits, ready to take down a major player. It may have been put together quickly due to the time constraints— they'd been told that the perp and product were moving out fast—but it was still a sound op. One they'd worked on and prepared for, down to every detail, yet in the end it had given them squat when it came to fresh leads.

Or supply.

A duffel bag of heroin was their whopping score from the night's op. While it still took junk off the street, it also felt hollow.

Like a booby prize for him and the team.

Where was the big score? The one that indicated they'd actually cut off a real node on the ever-encroaching drug vine instead of a freaking gym bag?

And why did their intel keep coming up short?

He'd done some intel work of his own, researching each of his fellow teammates. Every person he'd looked at, from background to family to prior jobs, was clean. And he'd dug deep. He'd learned early to keep a dossier on his fellow officers and while it didn't exactly smack of teamwork, it worked for him and that was all that mattered.

He kept his eyes open and his nose clean. And he'd be damned if he was going to risk his reputation or his life on someone who wasn't.

That was why he loved working with Murphy so much. His partner was easy to read, always ready to work—and the only payoff the canine wanted was something containing beef at the end of a long day.

He was more than happy to oblige his sweet little carnivore.

Their partnership worked. And if it said something about Ryder's personality that he trusted dogs over people, again, he could live with that.

At least he'd be alive.

The studio had a quiet, soothing vibe when he stepped through the door. The winter weather showed its decidedly Texas roots as afternoon heat followed him into the entryway of the much cooler studio. An efficient check-in station took up the majority of the room, the chest-high counter containing a sign-in sheet for Arden's next class, a few pamphlets about well-being and a small notice, taped to the top, about fees for returned checks. A computer hummed at the desk with a screensaver that read Midnight Relaxation.

Definitely her turf.

Again.

So much for his careful strategy about finding neutral ground.

He was definitely not in his element. Especially when several women, dressed in a variety of tight workout clothes, came strolling out of the studio, all talking in animated tones. A few gave him the once-over, clearly curious about the guy in jeans and a T-shirt, standing in the lobby.

By the time the last woman left—number fourteen by his count—Ryder had nearly had enough of the calming music piping through the lobby and was about to pull back the curtain of the studio when Arden stepped through.

And wow, was she a sight.

Her rich red hair was pulled into a high ponytail and she wore the same type of tight-fitting outfit as her students. Purple-and-gray-printed material swirled over her legs, matched by a purple tank that both showed off her sculpted body and also revealed the thin sheen of sweat that dewed over her skin.

"Oh. Hi." Her eyes widened briefly before her pale eyebrows dropped into confused slashes. "What are you doing here?"

"Taking a class?"

She shot a pointed look toward the door. "You're an hour too late."

"I figured I'd sign up for the next one."

"You want to practice yoga?"

"Just a class. I figured I'd start easy. Same time tomorrow? I'll join that one."

"These were my most advanced students." Her gaze roamed over his chest briefly before she seemed to catch herself, her bright blue gaze snapping back to his. "You practice regularly?"

"Practice what?"

"Yoga."

"I've done class a few times."

She shook her head, barely veiling a light sigh. "It's called yoga practice. You don't 'do' class. I guide you through it."

"People pay you for this, right?"

"Yes."

"And you run the show?"

"I don't run anything. I—"

"Why don't we meet in the middle. You teach the practice, okay?"

He had no idea why this was so important to him—to win that small point—but for some reason it did matter. Like getting her to acquiesce to *something* was necessary in their battle of wills.

"Yes, I guess I do," she finally said, even as her tone suggested there was minimal agreement to his point.

"Good. I'll come tomorrow."

"I need to suggest you start a bit slower. I do beginners sessions three times a week."

"I have done yoga before. Besides, I'm fit. I think I can handle tomorrow's class."

"Show me your Warrior Two."

Ryder knew when he was caught and decided to focus on the real reason he was here. "How about if I show you tomorrow and take you to lunch now instead?"

"I'm not—" She broke off, a slim line between her eyes scrunching into a deep little furrow. "I mean, I don't need lunch."

"Have you eaten yet?"

"No."

"It's after one."

"So?" That lone syllable wasn't quite hostile but matched the continued lack of warmth in her tone and demeanor.

Oddly ready to spar with her after thinking about her for four days—and realizing that he was rather hungry—he kept after it. "So come join me for lunch."

She looked about to argue once more when a loud noise rose up from the general vicinity of her stomach. That furrow between her eyes smoothed out as a broad smile spread across her face. "Caught."

That split second of humor captivated him. For all her attempts to block him up to now, her smile was proof she wasn't an automaton, unable to see the situation for what it was. He found it even more attractive than the long, lush hair or firm body.

She was a woman who smiled.

Or who could smile, wide and guileless, when the right moment came along.

"Good," he added, that smile still drawing him in. "Now I can also make amends for the other evening."

"Amends?" She slipped behind the counter to grab a set of keys from the top desk drawer.

"Yep."

"For what?"

"I'll tell you after we order. And—" he neatly snatched the keys from her hand, pointing toward the curtain that covered the entryway to the studio "—please tell me you don't leave the keys out here when you're locked in there in a variety of torture poses."

"It's a small town."

"And you own a business and you leave the front desk unoccupied for stretches of time. Calm my panic and at least tell me you lock up the money?"

"I do."

Ryder jangled the keys as he finished locking up behind them. "With a key to the safe that *isn't* on this key ring."

When she remained silent, he shook his head, a wholly unnecessary shot of anger settling in his gut. "What the hell, Arden? You're a smart woman. Or I thought you were."

"You're giving me a lecture, Agent Durant?"

"Yes."

"I'm a grown woman."

"Exactly. You're a grown ass woman. You should know better."

When she only harrumphed her answer, Ryder handed over the keys. "Please correct that."

"This is a small town."

"A small town with an underlying crime problem. Don't make yourself a target."

She considered him for several beats before turning on her heel and heading for Maisey's Café. The restaurant was a few doors down from her studio and the swirl of air-conditioned cool welcomed them into the cozy restaurant. He'd discovered Maisey's cooking about a week after moving to Midnight Pass and took advantage of the woman's skills, either via carryout or for a quiet dinner, several times a week.

A fact he couldn't hide when Maisey herself called out from behind the counter. "Hey, Ryder. What can I get ya, good-lookin'?"

"A table for two."

Maisey stilled at that, her gaze finally registering Ryder's guest. "Well hey there, Arden."

"Hi, Maisey."

"Aren't you a sight. I haven't seen you in way too long." Maisey clucked and fussed as she set down menus and silverware. "I'm glad to see the wind's changed up a bit."

"You think?" Arden smiled as she slid into her seat.

"I hope." Maisey winked before heading off.

Despite the casual talk of the weather and the seeming pleasantries, Ryder knew small towns well enough to know far more was being said. And for some strange reason, it bothered him that Arden had brushed things off so easily.

There you go again, Durant. You're so pathetic even your dog would give you the side-eye right now.

"Now. What's this about amends?" Arden dived right in.

"I was heavy-handed the other night. In your barn."

"Unlike today?"

"It was nothing like today. That was at your home."

"And today's at my place of business." She reached for the glass of water one of the busboys had dropped off. "Keep going."

"I'd like to talk to you and make my case. Lunch is the least I can do."

"As far as I'm concerned, you made your case the other night. If my brothers were here, they'd say the same."

"None of you have given me an answer yet. Does that mean you've all thought about what I said."

She ran the tip of her finger over a wet spot from the base of the glass. "We've had an unspoken truce to ignore it for the time being."

Not quite what he was hoping for, but not an out-and-out no, either.

"But if I had to bet on my brothers," Arden continued, "when we do get back together to discuss it, I'm guessing it's going to be a no."

"They said that?"

"Let's say I've had a lifetime of practice reading Reynolds testosterone. I'm pretty confident in my assessment."

Ryder chewed on her point a moment. While it wasn't a surprise, he had to admit that he'd figured her and her family for a bit more decisiveness. The fact that they'd lingered over an answer for four days had been a surprise.

The reality that they'd still not discussed it was the revelation.

Granted, he'd been too busy with the fruitless op in El Paso to run them down on it, but it didn't change the fact that the entire Reynolds family had gone radio silent.

"I'm afraid I don't have much time to wait around for an answer."

"I suppose that's true. For you." Arden folded her menu before catching Maisey's eye. "But I also don't see the need to rush things."

Ryder held back, giving his own order and requesting a refill on his iced tea. It was only when Maisey was once again out of earshot that he leaned forward, unwilling to give up. "You don't see a need? There are nearly forty deaths from drug overdoses every day in this country. I'd say there's a huge need to make a decision."

He took some small, grim satisfaction in the dimming of her gaze. "You think I'm oblivious to the stakes?"

"I think you're complacent. There's a difference."

It was true that you got more flies with sugar than vinegar—and insulting someone you needed help from was a big heaping helping of vinegar—but he couldn't hold back. He and his team had moved well past desperate times and desperate measures and had gone straight to the nuclear option.

He was all out of time. Just like Pete had been all those years ago.

"Maybe I am. Or have been." Arden made a fuss of depositing her menu back into the small metal holder at the inside edge of their booth. Her gaze remained steadfast on that small task, but her words suggested a different story. "But it isn't for lack of caring or a desire to stall."

"Then what's it about?"

She finally lifted her gaze from the menu, and what he saw there didn't smack of complacence. Or lack of concern.

It spoke of quite the opposite.

"The protection of my family, Agent Durant. That's what it's about. What it's only about."

Arden didn't want to be moved. Didn't want to feel anything other than a ready skepticism of Agent Ryder Durant. Yet try as she might, she couldn't fully shut down her emotions around him.

Was it because he was so attractive?

She hadn't considered herself so shallow, but she also couldn't deny the awareness and tension that filled her body, tightening it in equal measure, each time she was in his company. The man was appealing, for both the physicality of his long, lean body, the breadth of his shoulders and the hard lines of his face.

Lines she'd almost call craggy and harsh if it weren't for the melted chocolate gaze that pulled her despite herself.

Or perhaps in spite of herself.

She hadn't revised her opinion on his so-called request. He wanted access to her land to do *something*—of that she was still positive. The real question was why she was willing to entertain the notion.

A nice ass and melty eyes wasn't a reason to put her family in danger. Even a case of the hots for a man, no matter how long it had been, wasn't at play here, either.

Something in his earnestness tugged at her. Drew her in and pulled at something deep inside she'd believed long buried. Or forgotten.

Or simply dead.

How long had it been since she felt fierce need to *do* something? To make a change that was permanent and lasting and that actually helped others?

To a person, her father's disgrace in the ranching business had closed her and her brothers off from others. Her subsequent relationship with Dan had only reinforced the desire to close in and hunker down. And then losing the baby…

She shut that one down fast, refusing to bring the baby into this. Refusing to give any bit of room for her heart to open up and unfurl. Fully refusing to allow that razor-sharp ache any opportunity to slide in and slice her to ribbons once more.

The past was past and there was no way she was bringing it into her present. Nor would she allow it to color her decision when it came to the agent's request.

"I've already told you, I can promise you protection."

"A promise?" She leaned forward, deliberately slowing her words as she allowed her gaze to penetrate his. "No guarantees?"

"I'm not selling car wax here, Arden." Ryder sat back against his booth seat, his gaze never breaking. "And we both know anyone who offers a guarantee against life isn't telling the truth."

"That doesn't mean people don't try."

"I'm not people."

"Then what are you?"

"I'm a federal agent. And I'm bound and determined to protect as many people as I can from an encroaching evil that refuses to stand still."

"You think you can stop it on your own?"

"No."

"Then why this idea? Why now? And why is it only you pressing the point? You've spoken to us but your manager hasn't. The head of your field office. I don't know much, but I know you're not the end of the line, Agent Durant."

"Ryder."

His name came out on a harsh snap and for the first time since that moment in the barn when he'd had what she believed was an unintentional slip, she saw his composure vanish.

You can't miss what you aren't told.

"Fine. Ryder."

"That's better."

"I'm willing to help you. I'm willing to go to the mat and press my family and even run the risk that we'll all put ourselves on the front line of danger. Because you're wrong. I *do* care about those other people. I care about them and their families."

And she did. "My sister-in-law lives with the repercussions of drug addiction every day."

"Reese?"

"Reese. Her mother, too. The lingering pain of their loss when Reese's brother Jamie died of a drug overdose. I've seen it firsthand."

"So you *will* help?"

"On one condition."

His mouth opened slightly before snapping shut once more, his lips compressing into a firm line. As if outside of herself, Arden saw the moment with stark clarity.

He knew what she was going to ask. She knew it with the same clarity as when a storm was coming in or when a mare was about to foal.

With nothing to lose, she leaned forward.

Because she also knew he was desperate enough not to deny her what she asked.

"I want to know the truth of who you're really after. And what's really behind this operation you're so hellbent to run."

Chapter 4

"You want answers?"

"I do." Arden said.

"Then I want a few of my own first."

Although she didn't say anything, anticipation lit her blue eyes. It surprised him how that struck somewhere low in his gut. Like he was enjoying getting a reaction—any reaction—from her.

"You don't like me very much, and I'd like to know why."

That small light winked out, fading away as if it had never been. "I have nothing against you."

"I'd say you do. You have since the first time we met." Ryder tilted his head toward the wide-open window beside them. "Right out there on Main Street."

He remembered the moment well. It had been a pretty fall day and he'd tied Murphy up outside the coffee shop to bask in the sun for a few minutes while he ran in to snag a quick cup. The night before, he'd run his first op since coming to Midnight Pass and was pretty much subsisting on fumes. He'd come back out to find Arden, expectantly waiting for him, full of barely veiled insult and clear irritation that he'd left his dog outside.

"I wasn't aware that Murphy was a working dog that day. I may have been a bit terse."

"And the other night? At your place?"

"I—" She stopped, clearly considering her words. He was surprised to find that he had the patience to wait for whatever it was she had to say. "I don't appreciate cocky arrogance."

"You live on a ranch full of testosterone-fueled cowboys. And in a town full of the same. Surely you come up against a bit of cocky banter now and again?"

"That's an excuse for it?"

"It's a fact. I'd have thought you'd be used to it by now."

"It doesn't mean I have to like it." Her tone was prim and her already strong, fit posture stiffened a few more degrees north.

Ryder was good at his job because he knew how to read people. It was also what made him a good K-9 handler. He paid attention and he read situations before reacting. And every instinct he possessed read this one as arising from something that had specifically happened to her.

With someone who had hurt her.

Someone, Ryder suspected, who had been cocky and arrogant and likely unkind to her.

It was that knowledge that had him softening a bit, tempering his tone. "Just so long as we're clear about something."

"What's that?"

"I take care of my own. I didn't come to you and your family because I'm some jackass federal cowboy who wants to shoot first and ask questions later. I'm good at my job. And I'm thorough."

"And you think that's enough?"

He heard the question, but more, he saw the subtle relaxation of her shoulders. She still looked stiff as a board but not quite so fragile, like she'd break in a good strong wind. "I'm actually damn good at my job. And if I've pulled you into this, it's as good as a promise. Better, even. It's my word."

"Alright." She nodded. "Since I do live with a bunch of testosterone-fueled cowboys, I get what you're saying. A man's word is his bond and all that."

"And a woman's isn't?"

Although he'd willingly admit to copping to gender roles that may now be a bit dated, from holding the door for a woman to watching his language in mixed company, he'd never bought into the idea that honor and valor were the sole purview of men.

"I can't speak for others—" Arden's chin went up, defiance layered through the gesture "—but mine's rock-solid."

"Good. Then believe me when I tell you, I will share what I can. I won't be deliberately misleading, but under no circumstances can I promise you the lowdown on every single detail of my work. Do you think you can accept that?"

Could she accept it? Arden asked herself. Did she have a choice?

Even as a sharp retort sprang to her lips, Arden pulled

it back. Ryder had been straight with her. Direct and fair, just the way she liked it.

He'd also pegged her life, far more accurately than she'd have expected. She *did* live in testosterone city, between her brothers and the ranch hands of Reynolds Station and every salesperson she dealt with from distribution to husbandry. Her brothers had always been wildly supportive of her, but they were still stubborn and bullheaded and often full of themselves when the moment warranted.

It was fun to see how love had taken them all down a peg, channeling that self-assurance into something more focused on a mutually successful relationship.

But Ryder was still spot-on. She had *a lot* of testosterone in her life. But she knew how to deal with it, she thought as a smile flickered at her lips. "What's that smile for?" A small one hovered on Ryder Durant's very impressive lips and Arden gave herself the tiniest moment to appreciate it.

"Just thinking about some misplaced male attitude, that's all."

"Oh?"

She waved it off. "It's nothing."

"Try me."

"About a year or so ago, we had a few salesmen come to the ranch, trying to foist off some low-quality feed products while also suggesting we needed to change our vaccination products. We take all of that seriously and don't make changes lightly."

"You give 'em hell for their presumption?"

"I simply suggested that I'd take a stronger interest in their product if they could identify a few body parts on my stock. A cow's stomach, to be exact."

"Let me guess. Neither of them knew jack about the reticulum, the rumen, the omasum or the abomasum?"

"You know that?"

"I'm a font of trivial knowledge."

The modest brush-off wasn't what she expected. Yet another proof point toward the idea that Ryder Durant wasn't quite the man he appeared on the surface. "I didn't realize veterinary knowledge was a requirement for the FBI."

"It's not. But it is worthwhile learning when you're prepping to pose as a ranch hand for an undefined period of time."

"But we haven't said yes yet."

"Can't blame a guy for the power of positive thinking."

His smile was broad, and yes, cocky. But it also came from a point of knowledge and she couldn't quite fault him for that.

"I guess not," she admitted. "But this is a situation that's not all that positive to start with."

"No, it's not."

Just like that, their conversation came crashing back down to earth. Arden was almost sorry to see the lighter banter fade, but she also wasn't ready to give up the quest for answers. "I answered your questions. What about mine?"

"I promised you answers and I'll stand by that, but can we talk about them somewhere else?"

He was right. This wasn't fodder for a public conversation. "I guess so. Where?"

"I need to go pick up Murphy. He's had a morning of fun at puppy day care and I need to get him. Why don't you come with me and we'll finish this up."

Intrigued by the idea of puppy day care and determined to still get answers to her questions, she nodded. And in moments found herself in Ryder's SUV, headed out of town. "Where are we going?"

"There's a new training farm about five miles outside of downtown. I've been trying to support their work and as part of that I take Murphy out there a few times a week."

"I think my sister-in-law Veronica mentioned something about that. Is this Darren Gabriel's farm?"

"Yeah. His daughter, Brennan, came back to town about six months ago and is trying to make a go of it. Her second litter is nearly ready to arrive and the first is showing promise."

"What will happen to the ones who don't show promise?"

"They'll make great pets for someone."

"Oh."

Ryder gave her a side-eye from the driver's seat. "She's a respectable breeder, Arden. Not every dog makes it into K-9 but Brennan's practices are sound and she's wild about those dogs."

"I know."

"You sure?"

She hadn't met Brennan Gabriel and had absolutely no reason to doubt the woman's commitment to her dogs. But she'd also seen more than her fair share of TV news stories about dogs bred in poor conditions and those images had lingered.

None of that made it any less startling to realize how quickly Ryder had read her anxiety. "Yes, I'm sure."

"Who knows." He shot one more glance at her before

fully focusing on the road. "You might just fall in love with one of them and take a puppy home."

"Today?" She swallowed back the squeak that tightened her voice. "I'm not getting a puppy today." *Or any day*, she added in her mind to mentally settle the issue.

"Maybe this visit'll plant a seed."

"I don't need puppy seeds. Or any other seeds," she added for good measure, struggling against the mix of longing and panic that seemed to be swatting at each other for dominance smack in the center of her chest.

But neither were a match for the raw skepticism that rushed in when she finally remembered their conversation in the barn. "Is this some grand plot to foist a dog off on me?"

"No."

"Because you seemed far too interested in this topic the other night and now you're bugging me again."

"I'm not bugging you. I need to pick up my dog. There are some cute, cuddly puppies to spoil as part of the trip. End of story."

It wasn't the end of the story. Someway, somehow, Arden knew that. Because no matter how he played a situation, from thinly veiled humor to self-assured arrogance to knowing puppy pusher, Ryder Durant wasn't the man he appeared on the surface at all.

And Arden wasn't quite sure what she was going to do about that.

He really did need to pick up his dog.

Ryder kept reminding himself of that fact as he drove through the entry to Gabriel Downs. The farm was small by ranch standards in Midnight Pass, but Darren Gabriel had a nice piece of property and ran a solid, working farm.

And his daughter had inherited the same work ethic and was building a strong, solid breeding business.

He didn't know Brennan's full story, just that she'd been up north somewhere for the better part of a decade before heading back home to build her business. She clearly loved animals and fawned over Murphy each time they visited. And Ryder appreciated that he had a place to bring Murph to work out his energy and keep him sharp.

And a pack of puppies was sure to do both.

A fact that was abundantly clear as he pulled around the back side of the ranch house to find Murphy being chased by three Belgian Malinois puppies, the tips of their pointy ears waving in the breeze as they yipped and barked after his gentle giant of a Lab.

He heard a sharp intake of breath from Arden's direction but diligently kept his gaze forward as he pulled into a small wedge of macadam off the main driveway. It would do her good to see the dogs and maybe rethink the lack of one in her life. Which, he well knew, was none of his damn business. He shouldn't care one way or the other if the woman had a dog. Or a cat. Or a freaking guinea pig if the mood struck her.

It. Wasn't. His. Business.

You're here to pick up Murphy, he reminded himself, even as he knew the irresistible lure of a small bundle of fur.

Brennan waved from where she stood inside a training pen with the other three dogs from the litter not currently chasing after Murphy. One was curled up against the fence asleep, its fur lifting slightly in the breeze. The other two were staring up soulfully at Brennan as she walked them through a training exercise, using treats from a small pouch at her waist.

Ryder swung out of his seat and was nearly around the SUV before Arden slipped out. He didn't miss the move for what it was—an attempt to keep them on a level playing field—and he gave her the moment.

And then gave himself a moment as he took in the glorious sweep of hair that spilled from her ponytail, glinting a goldish-red in the early afternoon sunlight. He'd never considered himself particularly fanciful, but there was something about the color of her hair that had him intrigued.

Captivated.

And itching to run his fingers through those long strands.

"Hey, Ryder!" Brennan lifted a hand and waved in their direction. Her shift in focus was enough to pull her young charges' attention away, and in moments, the two puppies at her feet were racing toward Arden. She was crouched down in an instant, petting their furry bodies through the fence, cooing over each of them.

The three chasing Murphy sensed a change in the air and veered toward their siblings, who even now were standing on their back paws, vying for affection and attention from their new visitor.

Amused, Ryder stood to watch it all. Did the woman not know what spell she wove over the animals? He'd seen it with Murphy and now he saw it again with the pups. They couldn't get enough of her and, by the obvious affection and excitement in her voice, the feeling was mutual.

Brennan headed their way and the move was enough to have the last sleeping member of the litter rouse himself from the fence. Although stumbling with sleep, he picked up speed, tumbling into his siblings by the time he reached the new humans who'd invaded his lawn.

"Whoa there, Newman." Brennan dropped down to rub his fur before standing back up and shifting her focus to Ryder and Arden. "Welcome to Puppy Kindergarten. Or, pending the moment, Puppy Bedlam."

"Isn't that the very definition of kindergarten?" Arden asked with a smile before standing and extending a hand to Brennan. In moments, the two women had introduced themselves and were chatting like old friends.

Ryder stood back and watched, Murphy sitting silently by his side.

"You own the yoga studio in town?" Ryder heard Brennan ask. "Midnight Relaxation?"

"That's mine."

"I've been wanting to get in for a practice."

Arden shot him a triumphant smile over her shoulder at Brennan's use of the word practice before turning back to her new friend. "First week is on me. Come on in when you can."

"I'll do that." Brennan smiled, her head nodding as she patted the heads of the mob of puppies jumping at her legs. It was only when she took a large step back, her hand hovering over her bag of treats, that the entire pack stilled.

One by one, they lined up, planting their little puppy butts on the ground even as their tails continued to wiggle. Ryder took in the small, fawn-colored backs, each mottled with different mappings of darker fur beneath and smiled in spite of himself. They looked innocent now, but in a matter of months, each would be a full-grown Malinois, defined by their imposing demeanor and smart, keen gaze.

For now, though, they were a wriggling mass of energetic youth, ready to be molded and shaped into top-notch working dogs.

With specific focus on each pup, Brennan worked her way down the line, requesting various responses from each and rewarding their participation with a small treat.

"That's amazing." Arden whispered, leaning slightly into him. "They're still so young and she's got them all following along."

"Her reputation is excellent but I hadn't seen her with pups this young."

Caught up in the display, Arden shifted another step closer, craning her neck to watch each little body respond to Brennan's command. Just then, one of the soft, restless breezes Texas was known for kicked up, shifting the air so that he caught a full breath of Arden.

She was light and air and somehow full of sunshine. Like that fresh scent that suffused wash on a line, heated from a day in the sun. It seemed like it should be a mismatch, especially as all their conversations to date had been tinged with rather dark subject matter. But there it was all the same.

The sad fragility he'd sensed earlier had vanished, in its place a woman who was young, vibrant and full of life.

Suddenly overcome by the urge to touch her, Ryder shifted his focus back to the puppies and off that sparking desire. It was a complication he didn't need, especially if things worked out on her ranch.

And if they didn't?

He still didn't need a messy attraction diverting him from his work. Or so he'd keep telling himself.

Resolved, he let out a low whistle and took a few steps closer to the furry row of charges. "I knew you were good, Brennan, but they're really coming along."

"They're bright and eager."

Ryder nearly had the words out when Arden stepped forward. "Even Newman?"

The sleeping pup had required some extra attention during the training exercises and Ryder hadn't missed that he'd needed some additional prompts from Brennan.

For her part, Brennan seemed unconcerned. "He's coming along slower. It may just be a function of his age and his own development. They're all still quite young. I'll know more in a few weeks."

Arden nodded, her gaze thoughtful. "My brother and his wife have been thinking about getting a dog. If things don't work out, will you let me know?"

"Of course. A week of yoga and a possible placement if things don't work out for this little guy." Brennan's smile widened as she dropped to her knees to pull Newman onto her lap. "You two should come by more often."

Arden's gaze never left the puppy and Ryder didn't miss the clear longing stamped in her blue eyes. "I'd like that."

With Murphy collected, Ryder shot a wave to Brennan. "Thanks for keeping the big guy for a few hours. He'll sleep well tonight."

"Anytime. He's good for them." Brennan lifted Newman and pressed a quick kiss to his head before setting him back down on the ground and standing. "I like to think he sets a good example."

They had turned and headed for the car before Arden ran back to the training area. Dropping down, she petted

Newman through the fence. Her voice was quiet, the tone low, but Ryder didn't miss her words. "You sweet baby."

Although he didn't count himself as a particularly patient man, he did believe the golden rule of comedy extended to most everything else in life. Timing *was* everything. It was why he waited until they were nearly back to town before he put voice to his thoughts.

"Newman change your mind on a new dog?"

"He's adorable. Which is why he'll be perfect for Hoyt and Reese if he doesn't make the cut as a working dog."

"You'd foist all that puppy energy off on a couple with a new baby?"

Arden shrugged lightly but there was the tiniest hint of doubt edging her voice. "They can grow up together. Newman and the baby."

"Or Reese'll have your head, more like it."

"My sister-in-law teaches high school. Nothing ruffles her."

Murphy gave a light sigh as he settled down in the back seat, his afternoon of setting a good example now behind him. Ryder reached back and gave him a light pat on the head, the gentle way Murphy pressed his skull into Ryder's palm one of their oldest moves.

Trust.

Affection.

Companionship.

He and Murphy had it all.

Which was the only reason Ryder gave himself for continuing to push the issue. "I saw your doe eyes there at the end. You want Newman for yourself."

"I want him to have a good home. Reynolds Station will provide him that in the event he doesn't take to training."

"He won't."

Arden's mouth dropped, her eyes going wide. "That's a terrible thing to say!"

"I know dogs and so does Brennan. She was being kind back there. That little guy doesn't have what it takes to make it in a K-9 program."

"You act like he's hopeless."

"Hardly. He's a fine dog and he'll make a fine pet for someone. He'll train to be a good dog but he doesn't have what it takes to be a working animal."

When she said nothing, just crossed her arms to stare through the windshield, Ryder decided to go for broke. She already thought he was a cocky bastard.

Might as well make the most of it.

"He liked you. There at the end. He looked at you like you were his sun, moon and stars. You should take him for yourself."

"I don't—"

He didn't give her the chance to get the head of steam going. "I know, I know. You don't want a dog or the seeds of one, whatever the hell those are. But I know different."

"Oh, you do?" Ryder didn't miss the dripping disdain as he pulled up along the sidewalk in front of her studio. Which only made him push harder.

"You are Shakespeare's dream."

Her hand was already on the door before she turned to him, her eyes blazing blue fire. "What does that even mean?"

"You protest far too much."

As arguments went, it wasn't his finest, but it made his point. And it had the desired effect of pissing her off, which was just fun all by itself.

"Quoting Shakespeare now? That on top of your vast

knowledge of animal husbandry and your deep-rooted need to foster out puppies. What could you possibly come up with next?"

"Go out with me and you can find out."

Just like his slip in the barn the other night, the response came out without his brain even remotely checking his mouth. Which didn't bother him nearly as much as it should.

"I'm not going out with you."

"Why not? You spent the afternoon with me. We even had a meal. Let's make it two."

"I don't need dinner with you."

"But you want it."

She tilted her head at that, her hand slipping from the door handle as she turned to fully face him. "What's your angle here?"

"I don't have an angle."

"Everyone has one. It's just a matter of finding it. I already know you want on my ranch. Buttering me up or irritating me beyond reason aren't the pathways to get there."

"I don't want a date with you to get on your ranch."

"Why do you want one then?"

First the puppy pushing. Then the date request.

Might as well make it a trifecta.

That was his last rational thought as his hand snaked out, settling on her back to pull her close. His mouth followed with nearly the same speed and he fastened his lips on hers, pleased when the surprised O of her open mouth only served to fuse them more tightly together.

Under normal circumstances, he had considerably more finesse when he kissed a woman. But just like the request for a date, impulse had overridden common sense and now that he was in the kiss, he might as well enjoy it.

A state she'd clearly reached before him when her hands moved up to his shoulders and a light moan echoed from the back of her throat.

Ryder deepened the kiss, his tongue sweeping through that O and settling against hers. The overwhelming urge to brand her rose up in him, a wild and primitive need that was as shocking as it was necessary. The scents that had assailed him earlier—springtime and sunshine— seemed richer somehow.

Deeper.

And even more heady, if that were possible.

Her hands tightened on the neck of his shirt, the heat of her fingertips branding his skin, even as the heat of her mouth left him burning from the inside out.

What was this madness?

Before he could consider the question further, her lips stilled and she pulled back, dark satisfaction deep in her eyes.

Triumph.

Ryder figured something similar rested in his gaze and, despite the sexual tension now tightening his body, he could only smile in response. "How do you like me now?"

"You're growing on me, Agent Durant." She let that comment hang there, a few beats too long, before she delivered her parting shot. "Sort of like a fungus."

"So you'll go out with me? Friday night?"

"Yes." Arden pushed out of the car and slammed the door in her wake. The quick departure was the only indication she might be a bit more affected by their kiss than that moment of triumph had let on.

Instead of calling her on it, he gave himself the sweet luxury of another moment so he could watch the way that vibrant print of material moved snugly over her hips.

And savored the taste of her on his lips.

Yet even in his semihazed state, he was unwilling to leave her with the last word. With a quick roll of the window, Ryder hollered at her back. "I'll pick you up at seven!"

The wave above her head was all he got as she bent forward to unlock her studio door.

It wasn't much, but it was a start.

He'd take it.

Chapter 5

It took her three days, but Arden finally worked up the courage to talk to Reese about the puppy. Which was silly since she and Reese could talk about anything. Except, apparently, a twenty-pound ball of fur who had spent more than a few minutes rumbling and pouncing around in Arden's mind these past few days.

Of course, those mental moments of frolicking puppy antics were a relief since it meant she didn't have to think about Ryder Durant. Or the tempting way he kissed. Or the even more tempting prospect of their upcoming date. Or even his odd, tempting insistence she adopt the puppy herself.

Temptation.

That's all any of this was.

And unlike Eve in the Garden, she was well able to ignore snakes. Especially now that she had a label for it.

It was just some good, old-fashioned, since-the-dawn-of-time-capital-T Temptation.

Especially apropos since the man could kiss like the very devil. A fact she kept reminding herself as she tried to watch his poses during practice a few days ago with nothing more than a teacher's eye.

But heaven help her, the man's Warrior One had a decidedly sexy edge to it.

Just like everything else about him.

Which got her thoughts all fixated once more on that hot, steamy kiss. A kiss that reluctantly faded at her sister-in-law's voice.

"Would you like some peach tea?" Reese asked from the counter as she rubbed big circles over her even bigger belly.

While Arden was anxious to meet the baby, Reese's due date was still about two weeks away and Arden wasn't sure how the baby would stay put that long.

"Let me get the tea. You sit down."

"I'm not ready to sit." Reese said, her voice matter-of-fact. "I sat all day at school and then my husband insists I sit the moment he sees me. I'm jailbroke for the next half hour until he gets in from taking care of the horses and I'm taking my bit of freedom."

"There's little that moves Hoyt once he sets his mind to something."

"Tell me about it." A mischievous smile hovered over Reese's lips before vanishing. "It's one of the things I love most about him, but he is predictable."

Reese shifted, pressing a hand on the lower part of her belly. "And I can officially confirm that his child is as immovable as his or her father. Apparently the lower right quadrant of my uterus is a perfect hammock."

"The baby isn't moving?"

"Moving arms and legs, yes." She handed over one of the glasses before moving back to the kitchen counter to lean against it. "But the baby's dug in with its cute little butt and hasn't shifted all day."

"Oh."

At the image of a small baby behind, Arden remembered the row of small, wiggly puppy butts lined up for their training treats.

"Now that's a smile."

"A little memory is all."

"Of?" Reese rubbed her lower back before lifting her hand in a waving motion. "Wait! Is it about super sexy Agent Durant?"

"What? No." Arden knew she'd responded too quickly and in a register only heard by dogs, but was it that obvious? Was it written all over her face that she'd kissed Ryder?

When Reese only frowned and dropped her hand to once again rub her lower back, the concern faded.

"Well that's a disappointment. Esteban Diaz's mother was in for a parent teacher conference at lunchtime to discuss his scholarship for the fall. She mentioned seeing you both earlier this week and well—" Reese broke off, her cheeks going a soft pink. "I'd hoped there was something to get excited about there."

"I was out with Agent Durant. We had lunch and then he took me out to the Gabriel farm. His K-9 dog spends time out there."

"You had lunch together?"

Not only hadn't Arden mentioned the puppy to Reese, but she'd also avoided the outstanding topic of whether they would allow an FBI presence on their land. She normally had no problem addressing issues that needed handling, but there was something different about this and she was still working up the right approach. Because after lunch with Ryder, she was more and more convinced they needed his help.

And they needed to give him theirs.

"He came to see me at the studio to plead his case once more to set up shop here on the property."

"Hoyt's still frustrated about all that." Reese's hazel eyes sobered, the excitement at the idea of Arden's date fading. "I'm not getting anywhere with him on it, but he knows I don't agree."

"You don't?"

"Not at all. We have a chance to get this blight handled and done with once and for all. I'm all for it." Reese took a sip of her drink before catching Arden's eye. "Don't you want that, too?"

"I do. And I agree with you. But there is a concern. Aren't we sort of inviting trouble?"

"We have trouble. And there hasn't been an invitation issued."

While she had never doubted Reese's innate strength and common sense, Arden was surprised by the level of conviction. It was humbling, to be sure, and rather inspiring.

"You're about to give birth. Aren't you worried?"

The hand that had rubbed soothing circles over her belly and back moved back to her stomach, settling flat over that large mound in a protective gesture. "Right now? I'm keeping the baby safe. What happens once he or she arrives? When they're running free here on the property. That's what really scares me. That there is so much happening so close by." Reese stopped, tears filling her eyes. "What happens then when I'm not close?"

Arden was up in a flash, pulling her sister-in-law into her arms. "It's going to be okay. We're all here. And we're all going to be keeping watch on the baby."

"I know. I do know." Reese sniffed. "But my parents kept an eye on my brother and in the end that didn't help."

She hadn't known Jamie Grantham beyond general recognition in town. He'd been several years ahead of her in school and they'd never run in the same circles. But she'd understood about his problems. Arden could still remember the quiet conversation she'd had with her mother in this very kitchen the evening she'd found her crying.

"What's the matter, Mom?" Arden wasn't used to seeing her mother cry beyond the occasional sappy movie and she moved in close, laying a hand on slim shoulders. "What's wrong?"

"It's nothing, baby."

The blue eyes so like her own were watery and red rimmed and Arden pressed. She was thirteen, after all. She was old enough to hear whatever it was that had her mother so upset. She poured a cup of coffee from the pot that was perpetually on over at the stove, quickly mixing in the flavored creamer her mother loved. Settling the mug onto the table, she pressed for whatever it was that had made her mother sad. "Come on. You can tell me."

"I'm just sad, sweetie. And thinking of my own children this evening and all the good things I want for all of you. The happy futures I want for each of you." Her mother took a sip of the coffee, her eyes closing briefly, whether to savor the hazelnut flavor or to gather her strength, Arden didn't know.

"What's wrong?"

"Jamie Grantham is sick again."

There were whispers all over school about Jamie Grantham. Just the other day, one of the other kids in her gym class poked at his sister, Reese, for it. They were all lined up for volleyball, the seventh graders on one team and the eighth graders on the other, and someone had called her brother a junkie. She'd been so curious about the word she'd come home and asked Hoyt about it.

Which had done nothing more than get his green eyes narrowed, his brows furrowing in his usual Hoyt seriousness. "Who told you that word?" he'd asked, all mad.

"Someone said it at school."

"To you?"

"No. To Reese."

"Grantham? The police lieutenant's daughter?"

At her agreement Hoyt had reluctantly told her what it all meant and that people were using unkind terms to talk about a condition that needed attention, not scorn or schoolyard jokes.

"He uses drugs," Arden finally said to her mother.

Her mom looked up from her coffee and blinked. "You know that?"

"Yeah. A lot of people know it." Arden shrugged. "They talk about it. And sometimes they even tease his sister about it."

"He's sick. And he needs help."

"Sick? From something he chooses to do?"

Her mother patted the seat next to her, inviting her to sit. "That's the whole problem, sweetie. Drugs create addiction. They're not harmless and they take away a person's ability to choose."

That long-ago conversation had faded into the mists

of memory, the reality of what Reese had lived through and still lived *with* staring Arden in the face. "It never really goes away, does it?"

"The pain? Or the anger?" Reese's hand remained protectively over her belly. "No. It doesn't go away but I have learned to channel it. With my students it takes the form of real, honest talk. And for my child…" Her sister-in-law let out a small laugh. "Well, let's just say I have a fiercely protective streak and about three thousand conversations I've already had in my mind, practicing for whatever moment may come up."

"And Hoyt's still putting up a block to the FBI with all that coming at him?"

"Maybe we just need to pool our resources." Reese took a sip of her tea. "Tonight. At dinner. You ready?"

While she'd been ready to endorse Ryder Durant's presence on their land, something had shifted in their conversation and that whispered memory of her mother.

She needed to do this. *They* needed to do this. "Yes."

"Good."

Reese took another sip of her iced tea before adding, "So back to you and Agent Durant and your trip to the Gabriel Farm. Brennan Gabriel's breeding dogs now. She trains them, too, right?"

"You don't miss a beat."

"May I remind you I work with teenagers." Reese tapped her forehead. "If you don't keep up with basically everything, they'll run right over you."

"That's what I wanted to talk to you about. The puppies."

"First things first. What were you doing at lunch with Agent Sexy? And then how'd you end up at a dog breeder's?"

"He's not. I mean—" Of its own accord, heat crept

up her neck and on into her cheeks in a flash. The curse of the redhead, her mother had always told her. "He's not Agent Sexy."

"He so is, but we'll just park that one for a minute. What does any of this have to do with me?"

"I want you to adopt one of Brennan's puppies." The directive rushed out, more of that infernal heat creeping up her cheeks. Heat and, Arden realized, something that felt a lot like jealousy. And fear.

That Reese would say no.

That sweet little Newman would go to someone else.

And that she had somehow opened a can of worms by agreeing to have dinner with Ryder. Only not in that order. Or maybe in that exact order.

Who knew anymore?

"Okay. Keeping up with teenagers aside, I realize I have a raging case of pregnancy brain, but how did we get from puppies to hot lunch dates to me getting a dog?"

"You didn't. I did."

"Why would I do that? I don't need a dog."

"Sure you do. The baby will have a playmate."

"One who isn't housebroken, is still teething and, if my mental calculations of most working dogs I've ever seen, will reach roughly one hundred pounds in the next six months."

"No more than about sixty. Maybe sixty-five. I checked."

Reese's hazel eyes widened to silver dollars before narrowing, a glint of knowing in them. Pregnancy brain had given way to the same clairvoyance she used on her teens and Arden knew the jig was up.

"What is this really about?"

"A puppy. You and Hoyt have talked about getting one and I have the perfect one for you."

"Nope. Not buying it. Try again."

"He's really cute. His name is Newman and he's part of Brennan's litter who likely won't make the K-9 cut."

Reese shook her head before finally taking a seat at the table. "You can keep laying that one down all you want but I'm still not picking it up. Tell me what's going on with Ryder."

"There's nothing to tell."

"I think there's a lot to tell. But for reasons that make no sense, you've decided forcing a puppy on a nine months pregnant woman is fair."

"Eight and a half months," Arden whispered.

"It feels like twenty," Reese muttered before her gaze sobered. "Ards. Come on."

"I have a date with him. Tomorrow night."

Arden didn't miss the shot of triumph that filled Reese's hazel gaze. One she didn't even bother to hide. "Now we're getting somewhere."

"We're not getting anywhere. And I really should cancel it."

"Why?"

"Because—" Arden blew out a breath she wasn't conscious of even holding. "Because he's cocky and arrogant and a pain in my ass and—" she paused "—unsuitable. Completely and absolutely unsuitable."

"I'm not sure I'd give you cocky. He's arrogant, but what cop isn't? And he's confident, but to be honest, I sort of want that in the people I trust to go after the bad guys."

"I suppose."

"And I haven't observed him to be a pain in the butt."

"He is in mine."

Reese smiled again, her white teeth flashing. "That's the best sort of pain. When it's all directed just at you."

Arden's gaze deliberately dropped to Reese's stomach before traveling back to her sister-in-law's amused face. "That's just more pregnancy brain talking."

"No, that's sex-starved pregnant woman talking. But this conversation isn't about me so don't try to change it."

"We have a date, Reese. Tomorrow night."

"A normal Friday evening activity for two single adults."

"He wants something from us." *And from me.* And why was that thought so heady and so confusing, all at once?

"So?"

"What if the two get mixed up?"

"I don't see the problem so think up another one."

"He's not for me."

"It's a date, Arden. Nothing more."

A date. One evening of her life. She could *do* this. And, more to the point, she wanted to do this.

So why was she convinced something as simple as a date meant so much more?

Ryder wasn't sure if he should be amused or irritated at Arden's directive that she'd meet him at the restaurant. But since his mother had drummed gentlemanly behavior in him since roughly, oh, *ever*, and he had three sisters he perpetually watched out for, he did understand the sentiment. It was safer for a woman to arrive herself on a first date.

Even as he couldn't help but wonder why he made her so skittish.

He didn't like the knowledge or the very obvious indication that she felt that way. The same brotherly instinct that wanted his sisters in happy and healthy relationships insistently pressed for the very same for Arden Reynolds.

And damn it, he was a good guy.

Which meant he needed to reinforce that point on this evening's date.

Somewhere, somehow, he liked her. And he'd had enough damn time to think about her, their Monday lunch date feeling like it happened an eon ago. He'd even done her class—no, practice—like he'd planned, suffering through one endless pose after another, half convinced he was going to land on his ass at any moment. It was only the abject fear of face planting all over her polished-to-a-high-gloss wood floors that kept him focused, his mind decidedly not on her attractive shape.

Nor had he gone back for a repeat performance, no matter how tempting the woman looked in peach-colored, formfitting workout clothes.

Did she even own anything else?

Despite that thought keeping him steady company for the better part of a week, he'd stayed away, giving them both some space instead. Which only left him to wonder why he couldn't stop thinking about her.

Sure, he thought about his future. And somewhere in that hazy distance, he pictured settling down and having a family. For reasons that made little sense, the haze had begun to clear these past few days and he kept getting glimpses of what a future looked like.

With Arden.

Which was as irritating as it was inconvenient. He was on the verge of running the biggest—and most dangerous—op of his career. He didn't need any distractions, no matter how attractive. Or interesting. Or wildly intriguing.

Before he could dwell too long on the implications of it all, she walked into the restaurant. Her hair fell around her shoulders in soft waves, that glorious red as striking beneath indoor lighting as it was with the sun glinting off the lush strands. Another vibrant swirl of color wrapped around her body, only instead of yoga clothes it was a long-sleeved dress in shades of indigo and gold hugging her frame.

She was gorgeous.

And for the briefest of moments, he forgot his name, the lone thought left in his mind was that yes, she did own more than yoga outfits.

Standing, he waved her over, leaning in to press a soft kiss to her cheek as she walked up. "Hello."

"Hi."

That same skittishness he'd observed—like a colt struggling to stand—was still there, but something more powerful hovered over top.

Confidence.

And that very real shot of warmth in her eyes that recognized he appreciated what he saw when he looked at her.

That small moment of triumph went a long way toward calming his nerves and he stepped aside to pull out her seat. "I'm glad you could join me."

"Thank you." Arden looked around. "I've heard wonderful things about this place."

"I haven't been here before but a colleague suggested it."

Although he hadn't been in The Pass long, he'd quickly come to realize that while the town wasn't backward, its focus wasn't on restaurants and shops. They did aim for some culture but it came in the musical and arts variety.

A small collection of musicians had a chorale group that placed signs up around town for regular performances. There was also a drama program that seemed to trade off with the school for monthly performances at the Midnight Pass town hall. And over the holidays several local artists had their work displayed in the lobby of the town hall, gallery style.

Beyond that, if you wanted something more, you had to head outside the city limits.

The steak restaurant about twenty minutes outside of The Pass had all the necessary ambience for a date. Dark paneled walls that matched a darkened, softly lit interior. Subtle strains of music piped in just loud enough to add to the environment without overpowering it. And, based on the waitress heading their way, large, heavy, leather-bound menus that would hold the key to any number of savory delights.

Arden accepted the menu before quietly looking around. "My brothers have been here and raved about it."

"It's not odd?" Ryder realized. "Owning a cattle ranch and then coming to sample the product."

"No." She shook her head. "I know what we do isn't popular with everyone, but I am able to accept it."

"People don't like it?"

"Ranching?" Arden laid down her menu. "Many don't. And I can't say I blame them. Many of the world's environmental problems are exacerbated by what we do. It's why we're so focused on sustainable practices and herd management. We can't solve all of it, but we can be as responsible as possible for our product."

"I'm sure it's not cheap or easy."

"No. But it's right. And it's well worth it. Not only are

we doing the right thing but I think we have a far better product for it."

"I haven't been down here in the area that long but one of the first things I learned is that the Reynolds name is synonymous with quality."

"Thanks."

Her shoulders stiffened briefly—if he'd glanced down even momentarily to his menu he'd have missed it—and had no idea about the reason.

Ryder selected his steak and folded his menu. "How long have you made those changes? I'd imagine the work of sustainability is tied to technology."

"A lot of it is. A lot more of it is common sense. Herd size and management. Soil management and water usage. Even the management of animal waste is a key component of doing our part."

"You have people on staff for that?"

"We do. It's usually a few lucky A&M interns that are surprisingly excited to handle all manner of animal activities. You should see them on breeding day."

Ryder couldn't hold back the grin. "Sex sells. It always does."

She closed her menu, a thoughtful look clouding the blue of her eyes before she seemed to come to some decision. "Reynolds didn't always stand for quality. We had a rough go of it. After my father got sick."

"What happened to him?"

"Stress. Strain. The natural end to a life poorly lived." Arden shrugged. "There are likely any number of answers, but in the end, he'd been discovered engaging in bad ranching practices and the stress of it all didn't take too long to put him into cardiac arrest."

"I'm sorry."

She'd reached for her water glass after the confession of Andrew Reynolds's sins and her gaze was thoughtful as she took a sip. "I am, too. It took me a while to reach that place. For a long time I was a mixture of angry and resigned. But never really sad. It's only been the past year, as I've watched my brothers battle their own lingering ghosts of the past that I've been forced to admit I have a few of my own."

It was such a surprise to hear her share something so intimate that he was afraid to mar the mood in any way, but he was curious. "What did your father do?"

"Got in trouble with debt and believed the only way out was to handle it himself and go on the cheap in all our production. The really bad part of it all was that he put the animals at risk. I'll spare you the details at dinner but he began the practice of rendering, which can lead to all sorts of issues including mad cow."

"You never had that issue?"

"Thankfully, no. Ace figured it all out. When he finally confronted our father, the news had hit the industry and we had a very large hole to dig out of."

"Which makes it all that much more impressive that you make the ongoing investment in sustainable practices. To my earlier point, that can't be cheap or easy."

"No." She tapped a finger over her menu, tracing the name of the restaurant embossed in the thick leather. "It wasn't easy at all. But in the end, Ace, Tate, Hoyt and I all agreed. We'd do it right or we wouldn't do it at all. There are two other big ranches in The Pass owned by the Crown and the Vasquez families. Either would have happily purchased our land if we'd let them. And for a while it looked like a foregone conclusion one of them would because we were so far in debt to the bank."

"But you all hung on?"

"We did. We got creative and did as much as we could to change our image. My brothers traveled a lot of weekends to meet with reluctant suppliers, pleading their case, presenting all the changes we made and convincing them to take another chance on us. I went out and courted restaurants more directly, making deals with some of the smaller, trendier places in Dallas, Houston and Austin who wanted to sass up their menus or who had chefs trying to make a mark. We got a deal with an up-and-coming restaurant chain that helped put us over the hump."

"Who?"

"Emmanuel's."

"I know them. When I got the job here last summer, we had my promotion party at one of his places." Ryder remembered the steak he'd eaten that evening. "That was Reynolds beef?"

"Yes."

"Wow. Thank you. That's the best rib-eye I've ever eaten."

She smiled, a mix of pleasure and pride painting her face. "Emmanuel's chefs do get some credit. But I like to say they have a pretty great canvas."

"Hell yeah, they do. I've had dreams about that steak."

The smile dimmed but didn't fade. "You're an odd man."

The remark caught him up, as much for the comment as for the steady gleam in her blue gaze that was part speculation, part humor. And just like her restaurant sale had gotten Reynolds Station over the hump, he couldn't help but feel they'd gotten over one, too.

"Because I dream about steak?"

"Because you don't pull any punches. You say what

you think. You ask what you want to know. Most people work up to that sort of thing."

"I've never been particularly good at hiding my opinions. And I wouldn't have gotten very far in the Bureau without being curious."

"I suppose."

Ryder sensed a "but" in there only he wasn't sure why. "Do the questions bother you?"

"They should. I mean, I don't talk about my father."

"Why not?"

"Because it's private and, frankly, embarrassing."

He didn't think it was embarrassing at all. Arden and her brothers hadn't made the bad choices or tried to run the family business into the ground. And they'd made the good choices to pull themselves back up. Only he suspected she didn't want to hear that from him. "Yet you told me."

"I did."

"But you didn't want to."

"That's the problem." She leaned forward, color high on her cheekbones as an animated sort of wonder limned her face. "I didn't want to tell you but here I am, singing like a canary."

"May I say you have very cute feathers."

A bark of husky laughter escaped her lips before she clapped a hand over her mouth.

"What?" he finally asked when she showed no signs of stopping.

"That's your suave pickup line?"

Ryder felt the heat creeping up his neck and fought the urge to drag at his tie. What was it about this woman and her ability to keep him on his back foot?

More to the point, why was he enjoying it so much?

"Your dress is very colorful. It seemed like a good idea at the time."

"Why don't you come up with a better idea."

"Like what?"

"Why don't you order us some wine. We'll see if we can manage this date like two normal people."

"What does that even mean?"

"Well, since you seem to have no inhibitions without liquor and that sentiment has clearly rubbed off on me, maybe the wine will have the opposite effect and shut us both up."

Chapter 6

She didn't shut up. Not once. And because of it, Arden couldn't remember a more enjoyable evening. Ryder Durant was a charming dinner companion. Funny and gentlemanly and wickedly sharp.

And they talked about everything and anything.

Their discussion of the ranch had swiftly moved into his work at the Bureau and with Murphy, his sweet and often silly perspective on his three sisters and a rather spirited debate over superhero movies.

All of which made it harder and harder to dislike the agent. Or, more to the point, stand on her principle that he was too good-looking to be anything but a cocky, arrogant jerk.

Which he wasn't.

"That's a thoughtful look. I appreciate we nearly came to some hand-to-hand combat over who is the premiere superhero. And, based on my sisters' usual swooning I know Chris Evans inspires serious devotion, but he usually doesn't inspire a frown."

"Chris Evans inspires sonnets and seriously butt-kicking workout sessions and relatively the same level of joy as a new puppy. Chris has the edge on the puppy, though." When Ryder only waited expectantly for her reasons, she added, "The delicious side effect of happy hormones and a serious endorphin rush with no messes to clean up in the corner."

"Who can argue with that?"

Arden shrugged. "No one."

"So why the serious face?"

She'd already been more forthcoming than was comfortable. Did she keep on?

Why stop?

"I shouldn't like you."

"But you do."

"I do."

He settled back in his chair, his long fingers playing over the edge of the handle of his coffee cup. "Why shouldn't you like me?"

"You're too much. Too attractive. Too self-assured. Too—" She let out a sigh and reached for her own cup. "Too everything."

"That bothers you."

Where she might have expected a lighthearted joke or even a hint of annoyance, all she got was that continued, steady gaze.

"It should."

"Why?"

"I've been burned before. Pretty boys with too much belief in their own powers of persuasion and little care or concern for the chaos that blows back in their wake."

And there it was. The steady reality that she'd lived

with for nearly her entire adult life along with the shameful realization that she'd never really worked through it.

At all.

His dark eyes still thoughtful and serious, Ryder leaned forward. "I'm not sure physical aesthetics has anything to do with behaving like a decent human being, but let's for a moment assume it does."

"Good-looking people get away with an awful lot."

"Then by those standards you're running around town taking whatever you want and hurting anyone who stands in your way."

"A nice thing to say but—"

"It's the truth. But continue."

Arden wasn't sure why it was so important to her to make her point, but in that moment, it was. She'd lived with Dan's uncaring, casual behavior once things went sideways between them and knew damn well he'd believed himself above the normal consequences of behavior. Hell, he'd said as much on his way out the door.

I've got too much living to do to be tied down by a mistake.

Did you actually think this relationship was going somewhere?

When have I ever mentioned I wanted to be a father?

And it wasn't like she'd gotten pregnant on her own. Or that she hadn't been careful. But in the end, a mistake with her birth control pills—and sleepily taking the placebos by accident because of her early morning wake up calls to travel the state for Reynolds Station—had been the culprit.

A dumb, careless mistake. One she'd questioned at the time as subconscious subterfuge but which, in the clear light of time, had simply been an accident.

The memory of which faded as she realized Ryder still waited.

"This isn't about me."

"Well I'm making it about you."

"All I meant is that we live in a culture that idolizes beauty. Good-looking men use that to their advantage."

"And some people are just jerks, no matter their genetic advantage. You're creating a correlation when, in reality, you just got a rotten apple."

Before she could respond to that, Ryder added, "Maybe you'll tell me about that sometime. In the meantime, I meant what I said. Look in the mirror. You're gorgeous. You're good and decent and way too obsessed with puppies."

The steady head of steam building up over defending her opinions of good-looking men slammed into the brick wall of Ryder's odd logic.

Puppies?

"I'm not obsessed with puppies."

"Sure you are. First Brennan's brood. And now comparing them to Chris Evans. You've got puppies on the brain, woman."

"Why do we keep coming back to that?"

"Because one day you're going to thank me for it."

"For talking about puppies?"

"For convincing you that you wanted one all along."

Ryder knew he kept pressing his luck, but there was something about Arden Reynolds that kept him nagging at her. Persisting even when he knew he should just shut up and leave her alone.

Only he couldn't.

She pulled at him. He'd meant what he said. She was

gorgeous, in a way that was natural and easy and welcoming. She wasn't over-the-top with it, but had a simple, elegant beauty that made you happy to be in her presence. A willing subject enthralled in the presence of a benevolent queen.

And clearly he'd moved past attracted and straight on to sappy and stupid. Yet there it was anyway.

He was interested.

"Arden!"

The conversational hole he'd dug with his puppy comment faded away as they both turned in the direction of a happy voice.

"Shayne." Arden stood, extending her arms to the pretty blonde who'd moved up to their table.

Ryder was already on his feet to say hello when he caught sight of the man standing behind the blonde. "Rick?"

The man nodded. "Durant."

Introductions were quickly made all around as Ryder took in the uncomfortable set of his boss's shoulders. He hadn't worked with Rick Statler for long, but there was something about the man that hadn't set well with Ryder from the first. He liked him well enough and he had no reason to think less of the man. Statler had already been instrumental in Noah Ross's promotion to the bigger office up in Dallas and he'd taken a genuine interest in the work they were doing in The Pass.

So why did something about the man give him an instant sense of dislike? It was vague and unformed—and completely unfounded—but it persisted all the same. Ignoring that sneaking voice, Ryder extended a hand to invite them to sit down. "It looks like you're starting your evening but let's have one more round."

Shayne had already begun a steady stream of conversation with Arden, her voice light and full of verve as they talked of the yoga Shayne took at Midnight Relaxation and the latest poses she'd mastered.

"Small world, isn't it?" Statler started in, his gaze latching onto the bourbon their waitress dropped off.

"Sure is. But as far as nice date places go down in this part of the world, maybe it's not so rare after all."

"You seeing Arden Reynolds?" Rick's voice was low and quietly conversational, but Ryder didn't miss the questions.

Or the clear interest in gathering more intel.

"Her family farm was the site of some bad business last spring," Statler continued on, only reinforcing Ryder's mental point.

Intel.

"I know. Noah Ross's files were pretty clear on all that went down."

The slightest flicker flashed through Statler's gaze at Noah Ross's name, but it vanished as quickly as it came. Like a gambler who spots an ace in his hand. "How'd you come to meet her?"

Again, the question was voiced in casual tones, but the underlying question was clear.

What are you doing here?

"It was the damnedest thing. I met her on the street downtown. She was heading into the coffee shop and I was on my way out. Nearly bobbled my latte she caught me so hard."

Rick took a slug of his bourbon, his gaze settling on Shayne. "Sometimes you just know."

"Know what?"

"Chemistry. Attraction. Combustion." Rick shrugged his shoulders. "All of it if you're lucky."

Once again, Ryder wasn't sure where the distinct sense of menace came from but something struck him as off. While he didn't begrudge the man a relationship—and it was known to happen even while on the job—something about the way Statler kept an eye on Shayne was unsettling.

Like he was calculating how to keep her by his side.

For her part, Shayne Erickson looked as pretty as a postcard and kept shooting Rick intermittent smiles. Her hand drifted toward his several times, her fingers playing over Statler's, and it seemed she was as into the relationship as he was.

So why the wariness?

Despite the odd bent of his conversation with Arden during dinner, Ryder had observed people long enough to know that relationships were fraught with complications. And a partnership where one member of the relationship viewed the other as some sort of attractive property to be owned and trotted out for photo ops rarely went well.

Or ever, if Ryder really thought about it.

"So, Ryder, how do you like working down here in The Pass?" Shayne smoothly shifted the conversation, drawing them all into the discussion together as her fingers fully linked with Statler's. It was simple and easy and Ryder had to acknowledge Shayne and Statler looked like any other couple out on a Friday night.

Even if that subtle sense that something was off refused to stop knocking.

"It's been a great gig." Ryder kept his smile easy as his gaze drifted meaningfully to Arden. "The people are wonderful and it's a part of Texas I'm grateful to experience."

"Where are you from?"

"Fort Worth most recently. I moved around a bit growing up with my father in the military but settled in Austin for school and then on to Fort Worth for work after that."

"So what you're saying is you traded big cow country for more big cow country," Shayne smiled, and again, all Ryder saw was softness and warmth and a friendly, congenial air that held little pretense.

Rick's hand settled over Shayne's. "I think I see them waving us over for our table. We should be going."

Rick reached for his wallet but Ryder quickly waved it off. "It was my pleasure. It was good to see you both tonight. And, Shayne, great to meet you."

Although it was mildly out of protocol—it would have been fair to pick up their own tabs or Rick to take the bill as his superior—Ryder let the challenge stand.

And sensed he was going to need to use the suggestion of a group date as a future arrow in his quiver.

"Now I know why she's been so happy lately," Arden mused as they walked toward the car. "Floating, really."

"Shayne?"

"No, Ryder, my aunt Susie." Arden stopped to stare at him, her focused attention more than clear under the overhead lights of the restaurant parking lot. "Yes, Shayne."

"I'm not sure what she sees in him."

"Your boss?"

"Yes."

Arden's happy smile fell, her tone as serious as her frown. "What do you know?"

She moved in a bit closer and once again, Ryder realized how quickly he misstepped with her. What in the hell was wrong with him? He knew how to keep his counsel. Was damn good at it as a matter of fact. Yet a few hours in this woman's presence and he was spilling his guts.

"Nothing, Arden. I don't know a damn thing."

"That didn't sound like nothing. In fact, it sounded distinctly like something. Something bad."

Just like over their drink inside and, hell, every conversation he'd had with Rick Statler since meeting the man, Ryder felt that distinct sense of discomfort. Something oily and noxious, even if he had no solid reason for any of it.

Not one single shred of evidence that gave credence to the subtle layer of slime roiling in his gut. "Don't ladder your suspicions onto me."

"Excuse me?"

Despite the warm breeze wafting over them, hinting at the spring soon to come, Ryder felt the ice.

"You're so convinced I'm holding something back you're ready to leap at every damn word that comes out of my mouth."

She stepped back as if struck, her body going completely rigid even as wild waves of anger and electricity seemed to zap off her still form.

Damn, but he'd messed up again and said way more to her than he should have. His suspicions on his boss were just that. Suspicions. Unfounded ones at that. He could hardly go around sharing them with a civilian.

Hell, he couldn't even share them at work.

He was frustrated. And not at her—at himself. So of course, he went on the offensive.

"You spent half our damn dinner telling me how attractive men can't be trusted. I suggest the same and I'm hiding something?"

"I didn't—" She broke off, her hands balling into fists at her side. "This isn't the same. I'm talking about someone I know dating someone you know. If you have information that the man is a jerk I should tell her."

"Why?"

"Because it's the right thing to do."

"It's right to push your way into someone else's relationship. Someone who, by your own telling, is happy?"

"It is if he's a bad guy."

Frustration welled up and it was only his glance toward the sky for patience that gave him the glimpse of someone lurking at the restaurant doorway. For anyone looking, the man appeared to have stepped outside for a cigarette, but it was the incongruity of it all that had Ryder moving.

Without waiting a beat, he pulled Arden close against his chest, wrapping his arms around her in a move designed to still as much as present the image of a couple entwined.

Her heavy gasp of breath was nearly a hoarse moan of outrage before he managed to still her, his words low and urgent. "You need to play along with me. Now."

Whatever distance had lain between them as they'd argued over Shayne and Rick vanished as Arden sank into the kiss. The change in her body was immediate, tension leaving her frame as her arms wrapped around his neck.

But it was the equally low response against his lips that had him smiling in spite of himself.

"You owe me one hell of an explanation, Durant."

He might owe her an explanation but, good Lord, the man knew how to kiss. She'd thought so the other day when he'd laid that first one on her and had spent the past four days wondering if it could possibly have been as good as she'd remembered.

Newsflash: It was better.

Strong hands roamed over her spine, soft and tender even as they maintained firm pressure on her body. It was a revelation, actually, that combination of strength and gentleness. And potent to realize how enjoyable it was to be treated as an equal.

As someone who could engage in passion with as much strength and solid enjoyment as her partner.

His tongue matched the style of his hands, firm and determined, as their kiss grew deeper in the warm evening air. His body was hot against hers, the solid planes of muscle firm and unyielding and seemingly heated just for her.

As someone who worked hard on her fitness for the health benefits it gave both mind and body, she had to admit her focus on Ryder Durant's body was more basic.

Carnal.

And entirely feminine as she nearly sighed at the hard, masculine strength of him.

Each ripple of muscle, each sigh, each shift of his lips upon hers. All combined into a moment of complete perfection and the ultimate in escape.

And it was that very realization that had her coming back to earth.

"Ryder." She whispered against his lips, not quite ready to break their hold in the event he needed her in place a few moments longer.

"We're good."

He pressed one last lingering kiss before lifting his head. His dark eyes made their way back toward the restaurant and those same lips that had only moments before been rocking her world now straightened into a firm, thin line.

"What was it?"

"Nothing I want to discuss here."

"But you will discuss it?"

He shot one last glance toward the door before returning to meet her gaze. "Yes."

It wasn't much but she'd take it.

Rick tossed the cigarette into a small puddle and headed back for the restaurant.

And Shayne.

Of all the damn luck, meeting Ryder Durant here.

And worse luck, his subtle attempt to spy on the man had only given him a peep show to a parking lot make-out session.

What a waste of time.

He'd pushed to stay in, attempting to sweet-talk Shayne with flowers and sex, but she'd dug in this time, adamant about going out. Pressing him that he was working too hard and was too young to give up his opportunity to have a little fun.

And he'd bought it.

The woman made him oddly unfocused and he wasn't quite sure what to do about it. But hell and damn if he wasn't thinking about her more and more. If he didn't take her suggestions more and more to heart.

Besides, none of them were forbidden from having lives. He'd always kept his quiet and out of others' sight, but it wasn't suspicious to be seen out. Only now here he was, having cocktail hour and making small talk on a damn date with one of his direct reports.

A direct report whose devil-may-care grin couldn't hide the cop behind the dark gaze.

He'd sensed it in the man's keenly worded reports but it was different sitting opposite him, a casual drink in hand. And it was the very nature of that casual encounter that had Rick reconsidering everything.

Durant saw too much. And that made him far too much like Noah Ross for Rick's comfort. While he couldn't quite name the feeling, instinct had him struggling to take the man at face value.

Oh, Durant was respectful. His emails had always been buttoned-up and sharp. His reports brief and to the point. And Rick had no reason to think there was anything to worry about.

But now? After sitting across from him for a half hour outside of work, now he had something to think about.

That blended image in his mind, comparing Noah Ross to Ryder Durant wavered again. He'd moved Ross with the carrot of more work and a promotion, but in the end, it was nothing more than a diversion to keep him occupied.

Perhaps he could do the same here.

Even as he considered it, Rick knew the idea had merit. A big diversion would give him time and would help him gauge Durant's overall interest in Arden Reynolds.

And then he'd know if he had another sharp-eyed problem in his house that he needed to get rid of.

Ryder drove behind her all the way back into Midnight Pass, through the wide gates of Reynolds Station. In the cool light of their date she had no idea why she'd insisted on driving herself and meeting him there.

Something about independence and making a point.

But now after their date, Arden could only acknowledge that her actions had been somehow petty and small.

She never apologized for how she approached dating. A woman had every right to look out for herself, and letting others know where she was going and finding a way to transport herself was always acceptable. But she knew Ryder Durant. Had spent time in his company and further knew he came highly regarded by her sister-in-law.

Because of all those reasons, she knew that driving by herself hadn't been about safety at all. It had been about one-upmanship and games. And she had zero interest in either.

She pulled into her spot between the house and the stables and he pulled in behind her, cutting the lights. The house was quiet and she imagined everyone had already gone up to their respective rooms. When it had become evident they were all going to stay close to home, her brothers had added on to the house, building individual wings for each of them. It had ensured some privacy and an ability to have some sense of separateness, even as they were all together.

The approach had worked, even as her brothers settled down and married. Hoyt and Reese would be moving out into their own place once the baby had arrived and the construction had wrapped up, but so far Tate and Belle and Ace and Veronica seemed content with the arrangement.

And until that very moment, Arden had been as well.

It was only now, when faced with possible discovery, that she'd have preferred to be a bit farther from her family.

A woman liked a bit of distance, after all, when she owed a good man an apology.

She shut off the engine and nearly had her door open

when she felt a light tap on her window. Ryder stood there, quietly getting her attention before he opened the door.

And there it was again.

He was a gentleman. He might be direct in his approach but he was caring and considerate. Kind.

In the end, that meant far more to her than any show of strength ever could.

Once she'd cleared the driver's side door, he closed it with a gentle thud. Arden waited another heartbeat, captivated by the play of moonlight over his dark hair, before diving in.

"Thank you for seeing me home."

"Of course. I'd have done it regardless, but there are still things to be said."

"Yes." *By me.*

The acknowledgment struck swift and hard, an urgent reminder that she owed him an apology.

"Maybe we could talk in the barn. It's a bit more private than the kitchen."

"Nosy brothers?"

"Potentially." Arden gestured him toward the barn before heading that way. "More that I'd rather talk to you without interruption."

"Of course."

If he was curious about a late-night meeting mixed in and among the horses, he didn't show it, but rather, followed behind her to the large stable doors. Arden tapped in the electronic code and heard the lock gently snick open from inside the heavy wooden panel.

Soft lights played over the stalls, the horses already bedded down for the night. Several moved toward their stall doors, light whinnies muffled by the thick wood and fresh hay laid down throughout the large structure.

Still, Arden caught their curiosity at the late visit.

Reynolds Station might be a working ranch, and as a place of work, life moved on a schedule and a routine. It was rare for anyone to make their way into the stables this late at night. Even more rare for two people to come in for a casual conversation.

"I've been inconsiderate with you. Careless, even," Arden began, her gaze on the long row of stalls.

"I don't know about that."

"I have. And I'm sorry for it."

She knew she should turn around. She wasn't someone who hid from the things that were hard, yet in that moment, Arden struggled to turn and face Ryder. She'd provoked him. Deliberately and repeatedly. For no discernable reason other than some combative sense that flared up when she was in his presence.

And as a result of feelings she'd believed long since handled and managed.

Buried.

It was the very fact that she didn't want to turn around that finally had her moving. That and the determined snort that came from Tot's stall near the end of the row. Tate's horse had never been shy, and she'd sworn more than once the horse had the personality of a troublemaker. Rather like her brother.

But damn it if it didn't seem as if the horse was mocking her.

Equine shaming at its finest.

She might have spent more time questioning that line of thinking but she wasn't a coward and she'd been raised to give a fair and honest apology.

And side-eyeing her brother's horse wasn't getting it done.

Which was the only reason Ryder caught her off guard. Or so she'd convince herself later.

She turned on her heel to face him just as he moved up behind her. The edge of her shoulder hit Ryder's solid chest as she rotated away from Tot's mocking gaze, the move hard enough to have the man emitting a solid "oof" and clumsy enough to have her slipping off-balance, wobbling on one very high heel.

"Arden—"

Whatever else he was about to say washed away on a hard exhale as she tumbled over him, unable to right herself from her heel. He caught her—or tried to—and only ended up going down in a heap in front of one of the stall doors. She stumbled a few more feet and it was only the steady motion of his hands—and determined grip on her waist—that had her falling straight on top of him.

It might have taken all of three seconds but Arden could have sworn it felt like three hours.

And before she knew it, she lay on top of Ryder Durant on the floor of her barn. Splayed across his chest. Tucked intimately between his legs. Their faces barely inches from each other.

Before she could even think to scramble up and move, the overhead lights flashed on, flooding the barn with bright, fluorescent light.

And her brothers stood in a tidy row at the gaping entrance to the Reynolds stable, each one's face more interested than the next.

Chapter 7

Ryder was torn between self-preservation and the simple enjoyment of a few more moments with Arden Reynolds wrapped tight in his arms. In the end, he didn't need to make the choice himself because Arden scrambled off of him, part crab, part singed cat as she disengaged from their tangle of limbs.

"Problem with the kitchen?" Ace finally asked. "The table usually does just fine for a conversation."

"No." Arden moved right up to her brothers, her hands already making a beeline for her hips. "What are the three of you doing in here?"

"The notification went off on the barn. It goes straight to our phones," Tate pointed out, his tone reasonable even as Ryder saw the quick grin.

"I'm well aware of that fact." Arden finally said.

"And you didn't think we'd come investigate?" Tate added.

"I figured, since you know I know the code, you'd also know I had my reasons for being in the barn."

"What were those reasons? Exactly?" Hoyt asked.

"Since I'm staring down three stubborn, pigheaded brothers, I'll give you one guess."

If she'd meant the jab as insult, Ryder figured she'd be surely disappointed. Especially since her brothers seemed in high form, each one doing little to quell the smiles on their faces. On a resigned sigh, she flipped that pretty fall of red hair back over her shoulders. "Let's go to the kitchen then. I'm sure the horses weren't looking for a party at midnight."

"They'll survive." Tate's gaze went unerringly to his horse before flicking back and landing squarely on Ryder. "And Tot loves a party. But since the agent went to all the trouble of coming out here, we'll join you in the kitchen."

"Why?" Arden asked, suspicion layered deep in that lone word.

"We owe the man an answer."

He should have been satisfied. If the Reynolds family was going to say no to his request to use their property, they wouldn't need a parade to the kitchen to give him the news.

So why did it feel hollow?

Or maybe a more apt thought was why it felt emptier than he'd have expected. He'd been working out this plan for a while. Setting up on the edge of the Reynolds property should deliver the professional success he was looking for.

Yet something nagged at him anyway.

Was it Statler?

Once again, the odd image of the man coming out to

the front of the restaurant to grab a cigarette didn't sit well with Ryder. He didn't know his boss particularly well and they didn't socialize, but he hadn't pictured the fit Statler as a smoker. Add on that the move seemed designed to watch him and Arden as they left the restaurant and it left him even more uneasy now than when it had happened.

Vowing to reread all of the notes he'd made on Statler, Ryder moved up behind Arden, following the odd parade back out of the Reynolds barn. While he admired her Grecian goddess routine, head held high as she walked toward the ranch house like the queen of the manor, he nearly laughed when he caught sight of the bits of straw sticking up from her crown.

"Arden." When she didn't turn around, he added in a louder hiss. "Arden."

"What?"

"Come here."

She stilled, her brothers moving on ahead of her, but didn't come back to him. Which only added to the pleasure of his task as he moved up into her space and plucked out the offending pieces. "You may want to run a hand through your hair." He held up a long piece of straw. "Shake out anything else."

Her blue gaze filtered over him, assessing his face, his hair and then on to his shoulders. With another sigh, this one softer than the one in the barn, she brushed off his shoulders before adding, "Turn around."

"For what?"

"You've got more straw on you than me. We keep a clean barn but animals live here. And you landed smack in front of Marigold's stall. She loves to kick up a bit of dust by the door."

Just like earlier, when he allowed himself the pleasure of a simple moment with Arden in his arms, he gave himself up to the feeling of having her hands on him. Delicate yet efficient, her hands drifted over his shoulders and down on over his spine, brushing away bits of dirt and hay.

"There. You're presentable. Those clothes are still going to need the cleaners, but you won't track barn dirt into the kitchen."

"That's where we're going?"

"Looks like." With a last flick of her hair she headed for the exit. Ryder caught up with her just before she cleared the large, sliding barn door.

He wasn't sure why he felt the urge to say something, but as he stood there looking at her in the lights thrown off by the barn and the house, he couldn't hold back. "You don't owe your brothers an explanation for your evening."

"No, I don't."

"Then why the rush to get inside?"

"You've been waiting on a decision. I'd expect you'd be running for the kitchen door."

Ryder shoved his hands into his pockets to keep from touching her again. "I thought we were out here so I could give you an apology and fill you in on what went down after dinner."

The stiff back and regal air that had come upon her with the arrival of her brothers faded. "We'll save that for after. Let's hear them out, okay?"

"Sure."

She hesitated for the briefest of moments before pressing on. "I meant what I said before. I owe you an apology, too. I promise, you won't leave here before I give it."

* * *

The feel of Ryder Durant's hands on her—her waist, her shoulders, even the gentle brush over her head to remove that bit of straw—still lingered a short while later as they all assembled around the kitchen table. Her sisters-in-law were all up as well, seated with their husbands, one as wide-eyed as the next as they took in Ryder's still form.

The man hadn't moved.

Which was as impressive as it was scary. He'd taken a spot leaning against the edge of the counter next to the fridge and best Arden could tell, had barely taken a breath let alone shifted his position.

Was that what he'd be like on an op?

It amazed her how much power filled that still and steady stance. Almost as if the absence of needing to move showed just how calm and in control you actually were.

The stillness was also a contrast to all she'd observed of him so far. Where she'd seen amusement or gentleness or even that same steady cop focus she often saw in Belle, this was something else. And it proved the one thing she'd sensed but not yet observed.

Ryder Durant was a bad ass.

He worked in the highest echelons of a major government agency and, she thought with no small measure of awe, he clearly belonged there.

"Let's get down to business then." Ace spoke up, his focus on Ryder. "We heard you out more than a week ago and you've been more than fair with your patience on an answer."

Ryder nodded, his voice quiet when he spoke. "It's a big decision."

"It is. But Belle pointed out something to all of us I didn't consider at first." Ace glanced around the room, his gaze meeting each of his brothers, their wives and Arden in turn, before finally settling on Veronica. The silent encouragement that arced between them was as clear as their love for each other. "You wouldn't be asking if this wasn't important."

"That's right."

"Nor would you be asking if there was another way." Hoyt said.

Arden had had more than a few conversations with her oldest brother over the past week. His overriding concern for Hoyt and Reese and their new baby as well as the ranch had finally been put to rest by the reality of the situation.

Their land provided access to dealing with a problem. They could step up and be part of the solution or they could allow the problems to continue running rampant. A choice that could have far worse consequences in future if the situation was left to fester and spread.

Ryder moved then, shifting off the counter and standing tall. "I've been over it and over it, searching for a different solution. I know the concerns you have and I know my responsibilities here. Your family's protection is the priority."

"Thank you." Hoyt extended his hand to Ryder. "There is nothing more important to me."

Ryder accepted the gesture, that same stoic calm still in evidence. "Understood."

After a pause, Ace continued.

"We may understand the reasons why and the need for this, but it doesn't change the fact that we want to be kept in the loop. We need to understand the dangers."

"As I told you before, I'll share what I can within the bounds of what isn't confidential or classified."

"I'm afraid that's not enough." Ace held up a hand before anyone could get up a head of steam. "My family and I have no interest in interfering, but we can support your work. Tate, Hoyt, Arden and I know this land. We were raised here. Hoyt was Special Ops and understands the need for secrecy to maintain security and complete a mission. And Belle is one of the finest officers I've ever met. We're not ignorant and we can help you."

Ryder seemed to consider things for a moment and Arden became aware of holding her breath as she waited for his answer.

"I appreciate that. And to your point earlier about realizations, I've come to a few of my own." He stopped, his gaze traveling the room on the same path Ace's had followed. The only difference was when all that dark warmth finally settled on her, Arden felt the power of his conviction.

And the bottomless depths of his intention to keep them safe.

"I won't lie to you and I won't mislead you. But you have to trust my judgment on the matters I can't share."

Tate stepped forward, his hand running over the back of Belle's shoulders as he moved. "I nearly lost Belle because I couldn't see my way past trusting her. Because I couldn't accept that her training and her dedication to her job were as much a component of doing that job and staying safe. You have my agreement."

Just like Hoyt, Tate extended his hand to Ryder, his handshake as solid as his word.

Seemingly satisfied, Ace waited until Veronica, Reese and Belle asked any lingering questions, before they all agreed that they'd get some rest and look toward a formal briefing on Sunday afternoon, in time for Ryder to begin setting things in motion on Monday.

As abruptly as the family meeting began, it ended, each couple making their way from the room until Arden was left seated at the table and Ryder resumed his place back against the counter.

Ryder spoke first. "That's one solid bond."

"We're a family." The answer was so simple—so deeply felt—Arden had no other words for it.

"Yes, you are. And a close one. I always thought I had that with mine and I'd certainly call us close, but there's something unspoken between all of you that goes beyond the basics of family."

"My brothers and I were close growing up. You know, we did the usual bickering and Ace and I have an almost seven-year age difference so that's a gap, but something changed—" She broke off, the memory of that time after her father's betrayal sticking hard in her mind. "After."

"After your father."

"Yes."

As they'd sat through dinner, Arden had wondered why she'd shared so much. Their conversation about her father and his betrayal of the ranch and his heritage had sort of streamed out, like heavy spring rains rushing over a spillway. But now, with Ryder's comment about her and her brothers still looming large, Arden knew it was something more.

Andrew Reynolds had betrayed them.

His children.

She never talked about those dark days after her father's crimes had come to light. With anyone. Somewhere, somehow she'd always assumed it was the embarrassment of what he'd done that had sat at the core of her reticence to rehash those times.

But now she realized it was something so much more. And fathoms deeper. He hadn't simply betrayed them. He'd stolen the one thing that should never be broken between a parent and a child.

Unassailable trust.

Yet as she looked back on it, her father's actions had done one thing none of them could have ever expected. As if by unspoken agreement, she and her brothers had chosen the exact opposite way to live their lives and with each other.

Trust was the bedrock of their family relationship and all else flowed from there.

Belle, Reese and Veronica had only reinforced those bonds, the women who'd come into her brothers' lives seemingly perfect for their deep understanding and acknowledgment of what it was to be a member of the Reynolds family.

Ryder eyed her from where he stood across the kitchen. "I meant what I said earlier. I owe you an explanation for what happened before. At the restaurant."

With the sense memories still branded on her skin of the way he felt pressed against her in the parking lot, Arden couldn't resist poking at him a bit. "You mean when you laid that kiss on me."

"Yes."

She cocked her head, the motion slightly exaggerated to make her point. "You mean when you interrupted my concern for my friend and the possibility that she's dating a jerk."

"That's the one."

"Is she dating a jerk?"

"I'm not sure."

Just like the spark that started their argument in the parking lot, she saw the discomfort paint itself over his features. Ryder Durant might be a badass agent but the thinned lips and flat eyes weren't his usual MO. She'd observed a ready smile and that sexy glint in his eye far more often, and it was the lack of both that telegraphed his emotion so clearly.

"That bothers you."

"I should be able to trust, without question, anyone on my team. That goes double for my superiors."

"Yet you don't like Rick?"

"*Like* has nothing to do with it." Ryder scrubbed a hand over his face. "I don't trust him."

"Did something happen?"

"No. Which is the damn problem." He reached for a chair, dragging it away from the table and dropping into it. "We all know you don't go around accusing people of things without proof. That goes double in the Bureau. Men and women spend their lives working for their positions and it's not a light matter to accuse someone of wrongdoing."

"I've yet to hear you make an accusation."

"Doubt, even shadows of doubt, are tantamount to the same."

"Which takes me back to my question. Is Shayne in danger?"

"Hell if I know."

Arden was a fierce protector of others, and her belief in the support and power of the sisterhood was bone-deep. The thought of a woman even potentially linked to danger set off her protective vibes with whip-quick speed. So it was alarming to realize Ryder's lack of evidence—

coupled with Shayne's bubbly happiness at her new relationship—made it so much harder to know what to do.

How did you even broach that conversation? *Oh, Shayne. Do you think your FBI boyfriend is running the shady behind your back? Using you for cover? Engineering some sort of covert criminal activity?*

None of it played. And because it didn't, she was forced to fall back on that larger promise Ryder had made earlier.

I won't lie to you and I won't mislead you. But you have to trust my judgment on the matters I can't share.

"Can I ask you something?"

"Of course."

"You said before we should trust your judgment."

"I did."

"Would you give me the room to trust mine? If you feel there's any reason to pull her out of danger, would you give me the leeway to do that? To talk to her and warn her."

"Yes."

The lack of wavering or prevarication was swift and immediate, Ryder's commitment absolute.

"Okay." She nodded, taking it in and rearranging her expectations of how to act to protect another. And vowed to herself to keep an eye out. Shayne was a regular student and her presence in the studio would give Arden a chance to do her own assessment, keeping close watch.

In the meantime, she had to trust in the bigger picture. Ryder's ability to keep them safe. And, weird vibes or not, that the FBI hadn't hired a madman to oversee The Pass.

Ryder had always suspected an agent knew it was time to hang it up when they began to lose their edge. A slow descent into less effective ops, vaguer, more distracted thoughts and an overall sense that something was fading away.

Oh yes, he'd believed that. Believed it down to his marrow.

That was before Arden Reynolds came into his life.

And now?

Now he was beginning to wonder if losing one's edge had nothing to do with age or years in, but rather a wild, out of control sense that something bigger had come into your life.

She sat across the table, still as luminous and vivid as she'd been three hours before over dinner. That, even with the rather heavy dinner conversation, the weird encounter with Statler and the decision to allow him access to the ranch for his op.

The sheer determination in her pulled his deepest respect. The fierce devotion to her family had kept him in awe from the start. And her beauty continued to draw him in, clawing at him from the inside out with a mixture of attraction and desire and a sort of ready need that was frightening in its intensity.

He'd always considered himself a protector, but never before had he felt the description so keenly.

The Reynolds family clearly knew how to take care of their own. But there was no way he wouldn't add himself to their number and do everything in his power to protect them all.

Which made the situation with Statler that much more concerning.

Did he dare attempt an op the size of the one he envisioned for the Reynolds property and not let his boss know?

Did he have a choice?

"Those look like some heavy thoughts," Arden said.

"They are. I'd actually be more worried if I was preparing for an op and it didn't weigh heavy." He left off, even as he knew there was a "but" hanging in the air between them.

As if reading the sheer heft of his concerns, Arden added, "But this weighs heavier than most."

"It does. The stakes keep getting higher and higher. And the news stories don't know the half of it. The crime networks are like hydra. You cut off a head and three more seem to sprout in its place."

Arden stared at him a moment, her narrowed gaze seeming to size him up. "And you think you can do something about it? From our property?"

Normally he'd weigh just how much he'd share, but not now. Not with her. And once more, that sense he was losing his edge speared him clean through, even as he began to speak. "The Pass has too many easy access points."

"That is how we got our name."

"And it's as applicable now as it was at the town's founding. More so, since the natural formations provide as much protection in their physical characteristics as for the fact that technology can't traverse the land very well, either. Cell dead zones, no place for security cameras and all that natural protection. It's a smuggler's paradise."

"You said crime networks. You don't think this is the movement of drugs?"

"It's about movement and power, land grabs and turf wars. Those with the best routes risk less. And because of it, they'll protect their spots to the death."

"You think that's what's happening here?"

"I know it is. The drugs come up from South America but they're distributed across some serious networks. The cartels are powerful and may get the news coverage from the border, but so are the mob bosses they work with. Those networks are even stronger, more often than not."

"I always assumed they all kept to themselves. Did their own dirty business and tried to leave one another alone."

"Maybe in years past. Different factions own different towns. But it's bigger now. More vast. The hubs work out of major cities, well-to-do suburbs. Wherever they can traffic out to buyers."

"And buyers are everywhere."

Ryder sighed. "Yeah. My buddies over in federal probation and in the courts can give you stories that'll make your toes curl."

"Why are you telling me this?"

"Because you deserve to know. You need to know what we're dealing with. What you've said yes to. And what you stand a chance to help reduce, remove and ultimately punish."

Arden chose that moment to lean forward, her head tilted to the side as she tapped a finger to her lips. The deep blue of her dress shaded the vivid blue of her eyes several notches darker and he had the thought he could get lost there. Before another one, even more fleeting, wondered if he might find himself instead.

"And what do you deserve, Agent Durant?"

"The chance to do my job. To see that it's done."

"There aren't others who can do that?"

While their conversations had carried a rather large amount of sparring up to now, all argument had fled from her tone.

"They can't do it my way."

"The right way." It wasn't a question, but rather, fact.

"Yes."

"You're not shy about what you want or what you believe. But as I told you earlier, you're not leaving here without an apology."

Shy?

He'd lost *shy* more than a decade ago. You never forgot your first op gone bad and his had gone left, right and sideways before being so fouled up the nightmares *still* came calling every now and again.

His first partner, Pete, had been so excited to go undercover. To move up in the department and show his mettle, more than ready to take down a large cell operating in downtown Fort Worth. Only the job had taken him down at the knees. He'd gotten in over his head, unable to resist the drugs and the lifestyle. He'd paid for it with his life when the mob boss caught wind of his employer.

But first he'd paid for his mistake with a lot of spilled blood, the expected payment for his betrayal.

"Ryder?" Arden's use of his name—and the inherent question he heard beneath those two syllables—pulled him back from the nightmare.

"I'm sorry. You and your family have given me a lot to think about."

"Let me give you one more." She sat up straight, the regal arch of her back at odds with the humbling words. "I misjudged you. And I mistook something that clearly runs bone-deep inside of you for cocky showboating."

"And now?"

"I've changed my mind."

"Thank you."

Her spine was still rail-straight, but a small smile tilted the edge of her lips. "That still wasn't an apology."

"Why have you changed your mind?"

"I'm working up to that."

Her body was so stiff it looked as if she might shatter.

It was only when she finally spoke that Ryder changed his opinion.

She might look fragile but that was surface only.

"I owe you an apology because I lumped you in with someone else. Someone who hurt me and nearly broke me. I took all that surface charm and branded you with a label that wasn't simply unfair, but flat-out wrong."

"Then this time I really thank you. It takes a lot to admit that." He reached out and laid a hand on her forearm. "A lot more to say it."

"I just thought you should know."

From the beginning, he'd sensed a fierce protection in Arden Reynolds. For her family. For their ranch. Even for her students, as evidenced by her ready defense of Shayne earlier. That quality made it even starker to realize that the woman opposite him—for all her ready defense of others—was hanging on by some very thin threads of her own.

Because what he saw in her face and the stiffly still lines of her body wasn't protection.

It was self-preservation.

On a base level, he knew she wasn't prepared to tell him why and he'd give her leave of her privacy. But he would know her reasons.

And until then, he would prove in every way possible that whoever had hurt her had never been worthy of her in the first place.

Chapter 8

Arden rolled over and stared at the clock.

Again.

It was exactly six minutes after the last time she'd looked. Which meant that she'd now watched roughly four hours tick by. Endlessly.

What it also meant was that she'd finally outlasted the night, the first hints of hazy, dark blue lighting up her window.

She mentally cycled through their various horses' exercise schedule and decided to give Macaroni a chance to stretch her legs. She'd loved the idea of a pony named Macaroni—a throwback to childhood—and had loved the sweet bay from the moment she'd seen her at auction a few years before. Steady and sturdy, Macaroni had a personality to match. Stalwart. Strong. And always an equine friend in need.

And wow, did she need one this morning.

Friday night had been intense, the roiling feelings that had dogged her for the past few weeks even more so. She'd genuinely believed that she was far over Dan. That time in her life was firmly in the past, and with hard work and determination and a lot of self-care, she'd moved past it.

Only not nearly as far as she'd thought.

How was it that she'd so easily recalled those feelings of hurt and betrayal and, frankly, inner shock that her instincts had been so damn wrong?

And how bad did she feel that she'd painted Ryder Durant with the same brush?

While she had no idea if he'd turn out to be a jerk in the end, there was something about him that tugged at her and made her reconsider—maybe her instincts *weren't* all wrong. After all, if she assessed her past with fair and open eyes, she could remember the chinks in Dan's armor.

Although she hadn't allowed herself to think about them much in the years since—perhaps too busy blaming herself for what had happened—she had seen a less appealing side to him crop up from time to time. His odd frustrations when he didn't get his way on something as simple as the movie they'd picked for the evening or what they'd select as a dessert or a sharp comment to a waiter or waitress.

All little things she'd shrugged off at the time as small slips, but were they?

Or were they advance warning that Dan was an inherently selfish, self-centered individual. The moment she hadn't lived up to his expectations or to his plans for his future, he'd grown frustrated and discarded her as easily as other things in his life.

On a sigh Arden pushed out of bed, determined to take advantage of the early hour.

She'd been out of sorts and frustrated in the nearly thirty-six hours since her date ended with Ryder. She'd spent the day before channeling it into work around the house, a lunch date with Belle, Veronica and Reese and a double yoga practice that she'd believed would wear her out.

And had *still* lain awake all night tossing and turning. Enough.

She might have no idea what to do about Ryder Durant and this sly, persistent attraction, but she did know that a good man like him and one like Dan didn't belong in the same swirl of thought.

In less than fifteen minutes she was dressed in her jeans, T-shirt and boots, and was out in the barn, opening Macaroni's stall. "Hello, pretty girl."

Macaroni was already at the stall door to greet her, nuzzling her neck and filling Arden's senses with all that wonderful horse smell. Earthy and pure, it was a scent she associated with home. And freedom. And belonging.

Arden slipped the horse a few of the sugar cubes she'd nicked on the way out of the kitchen, pleased when they disappeared. After Macaroni had enjoyed her treat, Arden made quick work of getting her saddled and ready for their ride.

"You up for a good long ride this morning?"

Although she wasn't expecting an answer, the slight whinny confirmed she'd selected the perfect companion for her early morning jaunt across Reynolds Station. As they started out, the sky had continued to lighten, the early morning sun peeking through hazy clouds. The March air was crisp and she was glad she'd thrown on a jacket at the last minute. Although she had no doubt she'd be tying it around her waist by the end of the ride, she needed it now.

Settling into the saddle, she led Macaroni out of the paddock and toward the vast property that spread out in all directions. She could see lights on the in bunkhouse and knew the hands were stirring. Work was lighter on the weekend, but not nonexistent, and the crew on weekend duty would be up and out by seven.

The reality of a working ranch, she mused as she rode past, and knew her brothers would be out in the morning as well, checking on the stock, reviewing fence line and any other chores that needed attending to. She helped out where she could but had decided a long time ago that her skills were more suited to the business details than active management of the property. It didn't mean she wouldn't do her part by keeping her eyes open for areas that needed tending and handling the things that she could.

The cool air swirled around her, clearing the morning cobwebs and the last vestiges of a restless, nearly sleepless night. She was grateful for the exercise and the fresh air and the opportunity to get out of her head for a bit. She'd been spending way more time there than was comfortable and was sick to death of her own thoughts.

So instead of focusing on any of it, she rode, allowing Macaroni to set the pace and the direction. Although Reynolds Station covered several thousand acres, over the years they'd carved a series of paths and roads through the property. The management and movement of the herd had necessitated a system and the roads her grandfather had the foresight to install nearly fifty years before enabled them to map out the property and administer it in quadrants.

As she moved through the northwest section and worked her way south, she considered the endless vista. Her great-grandfather had settled the land. He'd found his calling and reformed his ways, becoming a well-respected rancher with some of the highest quality product in the state. His son had followed suit.

Generations later, it was her father who had fallen out of favor with the land, with their product and with the larger ranching community. And they'd almost fallen into ruin as a result.

Although she and her brothers had moved well past that, it was amazing how easy it was to remember those days. The fear and the very vivid reality that this all might go away.

For what?

A temporary financial fix? A soothing of ego? Or had it been something more?

She'd always believed her father had betrayed his legacy, but what if he'd never wanted it to begin with? It wasn't an excuse to desecrate it and the product they sold—nor was it an excuse to blindside and lie to his children—but until that moment, she'd never looked out over the property and seen it as anything other than beautiful. Vast and wonderful and *theirs*

But maybe it had never been that for her father.

And perhaps when he looked out over the land all he'd seen was a noose.

There was no way of knowing now. No opportunity to ask or to try to understand. And no way to give him even the tiniest benefit of explaining himself.

With a resigned sigh, she pressed her knees to Macaroni's side, gently signaling her to move. Her sweet companion had been content to munch a bit of breakfast as Arden stared out over the land, but also sensed Arden's desire to get on with it. With ease, Macaroni moved into a steady walk, gathering speed when Arden caught something on the far side of the field her horse had been grazing in.

It was a glint of morning sun, she told herself. A trick of the light.

What else could it be?

Even as she questioned herself, Arden shifted direction, Macaroni easily reading her movements and heading for the glimpse Arden had seen in the distance.

Once more, something flashed in the early morning sun. She had no idea what it was, but wasn't going to move on until she saw to it. The late winter rains had started a few weeks earlier with their impending promise of spring, and while it looked like it would be a beautiful day, the ground was still soft and the grass was high enough to wave in the early morning breeze.

That glint flashed once more as she moved closer, but it was the ever-growing shape she saw in the grass as she approached that had her putting pressure on Macaroni's saddle as she leaned forward.

The sun had found the wide oval shape of a belt buckle and continued to reflect off the highly polished metal. All while illuminating the outline of a large body, clad head to toe in denim.

A harsh cry filled Arden's throat as she recognized one of their ranch hands, Tris Bradshaw.

"Oh God." Arden dropped off of Macaroni's back, barely aware of her movements as she raced toward Tris.

And quickly stepped back as she took in the large gunshot wound in the dead center of his forehead.

Ryder caught the whispers around noon. He'd headed into town with Murphy to play a bit on the town square—the weekly pickup games of Frisbee something they'd both taken a shine to upon their arrival in The Pass—and it hadn't taken long for word to drift his way.

Trouble out at the Reynolds ranch early that morning.

Flashing sirens as several MPPD members hauled it out of town toward Reynolds Station.

A ranch hand's death.

Ryder kept his cool, trying to modulate his interest toward the gossip side of the equation instead of the professional one, asking as much as he could without seeming suspicious, but he needed to get out there. The case was outside his jurisdiction but based on the raw pulsing in his gut, he could give a damn about who owned what or whose authority took precedence.

He needed to get to Arden.

He'd already spent all day Saturday thinking about her and how Friday night had gone down between them. Had spent even more time thinking about how he'd ask her out again. But now? With a purported death?

That required no thought, only action.

Rounding up Murphy, Ryder was off the square and bumping over the two-lane road out to the Reynolds ranch in a matter of minutes. Murphy sat tall and straight in the back seat, seemingly unfazed by the interruption to their schedule. In the kinship they'd had since the dog had been a puppy, Ryder's partner was in work mode.

Alert.

Aware.

And ready for action.

"We're just going to make sure she's alright." Ryder caught the dog's eyes in the rearview mirror and would have sworn Murphy was as anxious as he.

But it was the complete absence of a wagging tail that truly gave his partner away.

One of their most keen forms of communication, Murphy's tail was the telegraph to his partner's moods, feelings and instincts. And the lack of any emotion only reinforced Ryder's concerns for what they would find at the end of the trip.

The ranch was in the far reaches of the town, Reynolds Station as well as the Crown and Vasquez ranches making a sort of large, oversize halo around Midnight Pass as all three pieces of property fanned away from the border. He'd seen aerial photos and could picture it all from memory.

And wondered how something terrible could befall the Reynolds family once again.

Yes, he wanted to stake out the ranch and set up his op and he well knew there'd be danger involved. But this? A death on the ranch?

Murder, more like, his thoughts corrected him.

Again.

What was going on? And what would it take to end this blight on the Reynolds family and their continuous troubles?

The property gates were open and Ryder saw one of the MPPD's cars parked at the entrance. He waved at the officer sitting in the front seat, slowing to talk to him through the open front window.

"Agent Durant. Good to see you."

Ryder cycled through the various police officers he'd

met before nodding in kind. "Officer Haines. Sorry about the bad business out here."

That momentary spark—and the acknowledgment of a greeting by name—went a long way, and Haines was already leaning out on an elbow.

Although the Midnight Pass Police Department was on the lean side, it wasn't small-town, nor did it match what typically passed for small-town law enforcement. He'd been impressed with their equipment and training and the fact that they kept several officers on duty. One more sign The Pass required more protection than its size would normally suggest.

"I heard some rumbling in town of trouble. I was hoping it wasn't true," Ryder added.

Haines shook his head. "Afraid the rumors are true. One of the Reynolds ranch hands was murdered last night."

While gossip moved through small towns—heck, medium and large ones, too—at lightning speed, Ryder had hoped on the entire drive over something might have been a bit off with the intel. An accident, maybe. Or even a heated fight gone accidentally bad.

But murder was on another level entirely.

Murphy's tail had been right all along.

"Hear you've been spotted out and about with Miss Arden. I won't keep you." Haines jerked a thumb toward the long driveway that led to the house. "She's the one who found him."

In less than a heartbeat, Ryder went from concerned and uneasy to wildly anxious to see her. Keeping his countenance as stoic as he could manage, he nodded his head and moved through the gates. Murphy's light whine from the back seat was only reinforcement for the upset.

"We'll get to her, boy," Ryder vowed. "Make sure she's alright."

As the house came into view he hoped like hell she was.

Arden stared at the mug of coffee that had gone cold, the dark brew fading in and out with the images of Tris she still held in her mind.

What had happened to him? And on a property as large and vast as theirs, how had she even found him?

The questions haunted her, chilling her deeply. Reese had wrapped a blanket around her shoulders earlier and Arden nestled into it, finding the thick material did little to warm the cold deep inside her bones.

Who would do this?

Belle had already issued orders to her team, all of them arriving after Arden had stumbled into the kitchen, numb and frightened and still questioning herself about if what she'd seen was true.

Only it was.

She'd heard Tate talking low on his mobile when Belle called him and then heard him giving directions to the various officers before taking them out on the property.

"Arden?" Reese's voice interrupted her thoughts. "Would you like some more coffee?"

She looked up, her sister-in-law's hazel gaze soft. Although she saw concern, Arden saw no pity. Instead, she did see a quiet sort of understanding that provided more warmth than the blanket. "I would, but only if you sit down with me."

She'd already seen Reese rubbing low along her back and knew the late stage of her sister-in-law's pregnancy had grown terribly uncomfortable. "Come on. Off your feet."

Reese sighed but did as requested after setting the coffeepot back on its warming plate. "You're as bad as Hoyt."

"Family curse."

With nothing more than an answering smile and an extended hand, Reese reached for her. Arden took the offered warmth and comfort as their hands linked over the table. "I just don't understand this. Who would do this to Tris?"

"I don't know." Reese shook her head. "He seemed well-liked. Hardworking."

"Tate had a few questions about him last year when—" Arden broke off, the memory of that time inexorably linked with Reese's father.

"When the body was discovered." Reese said firmly. "Go on. What sort of questions did they have?"

"Nothing concrete, but he was new at the time. He was friendly enough and did his work, but there was a distance that was a bit out of the ordinary. I don't know." Arden shrugged, searching for the right words to speak of the dead. "He was quiet and kept to himself, which isn't a crime, but at the time it just seemed like a bit more than that. Most guys warm up after a bit. Ease in, I guess."

"And since?" Reese probed.

"Since then I haven't given it any thought."

They were still for a moment, Reese's quiet strength a soothing balm for the roiling thoughts and grizzly images that still filled Arden's mind.

"It's not wrong to wonder about people, you know," Reese said. "To question what's beneath the surface."

Although Reese rarely minced words, it was clear

there was something more to her comment. "I suppose that's true, but what about someone's right to their own private thoughts?"

"When those private thoughts put others at risk." Reese's shoulders lifted in a small shrug. "I guess I'm not so sure."

"You mean your dad?"

"My dad. My brother. Even Loretta's vendetta against me last year. All I'm saying is that it's not wrong to question someone else's motives or wonder about them. Sometimes it's important to pay attention. Necessary, even."

Reese rarely dwelled on the past, and her happiness with Hoyt and their soon-to-be parenthood had suggested she'd dealt with the horrors of the previous year as best she could. But in that moment, Arden realized that they still left scars, even on someone as strong as Reese. The pain of losing her brother to drugs when they were still in school. The shock of her father's vengeful response to that tragedy. And even the strange stalking and pent-up venom that had come from Loretta, Jamie Grantham's high school girlfriend.

All had left their mark.

She believed Reese was stronger for all of it, but to assume her sister-in-law's warm and caring attitude and happiness in her marriage made those tragedies vanish somehow wasn't the correct assumption, either.

"I'm sorry." Arden whispered the words as she squeezed Reese's hand.

"For what?"

"For sometimes forgetting what you've been through." Arden stopped and shook her head. "Actually, *forget* isn't the right word. It's that I've assumed those things have faded so much they don't still have power."

"Thank you." Reese squeezed back. "But I can tell you their power has changed."

Intrigued, Arden considered that. "How?"

"Over the past year I've come to realize that our history remains as rocky or as calm as we want it to be. For my father and Loretta, it was all rocky terrain that grew impossible to navigate after a while."

"And for you?"

Reese smiled then and Arden saw joy and happiness and contentment.

And hope.

"For me, I'd like to think I could have walked the calm path no matter what, but I don't know. All I do know is that Hoyt came into my life and has given me everything I need to keep the past in proper perspective."

"Love?"

"Yes, but he's also given me support. Respect. Laughter. All facets of love I never understood were so key to keeping the way smooth and our gaze focused on the future."

"He's changed, you know."

"Hoyt?" Reese looked surprised at that and Arden was tickled to see she'd caught her unaware.

"You may not realize it, but you've given him the same. My mother always said Hoyt had still waters, but after she died and my father ruined the ranch those still waters nearly drowned him. I think his time in the military was the only thing that kept him going, but there was incredible stress and pressure there, too."

"He doesn't talk about that time much."

"I believe it. I've always gotten the sense he did his

service and has found some level of satisfaction there."
Arden considered the change in her brother—in all of her
brothers since they'd each found their mates for life—and
realized there was a common thread across all of them.

But Hoyt most of all.

"My brother wasn't a man who found much joy in
things and now he does. Because of you."

"Thank you for telling me that." Reese leaned in, her
gaze direct. "And what about you? Are you looking for
that same joy?"

"I'm not… I mean—" Arden sighed. "I'm not sure
that's my journey."

Belle would have argued the point and Veronica would
have analyzed with her scientific mind, but not Reese.
She simply projected that quiet air and determined focus
that likely made her an excellent high school teacher,
responsible each day for young, impressionable minds.
"Why not?"

"Whether rocky or calm, some pasts set us in motion
for our future."

"So the future is unchanging and immutable?"

"For some, yes."

Reese stared down at her large belly and laid a hand
over top. "You seem rather set on that."

"I am."

And she was.

Or had been until the past few weeks when Ryder had
stirred up all sort of thoughts in her head. Or worse, really. He'd churned up *feelings*. And needs. And desires
she'd believed long buried.

Feelings that…

The door burst open on a hard gust of early March

wind, slamming against the counter. Ryder Durant stood in the doorway, his dog at his side, his dark gaze wild.

A gaze that landed squarely on her. "You're okay."

Before she could say a word, he was across the kitchen and hauling her up into his arms.

Every rocky emotion that had battered and buffeted her for the past few weeks stilled, something calm building in her center.

He was here.

He had her wrapped tight against his chest.

And for the moment, that was enough.

Chapter 9

Ryder held her close, breathing deep now that he was with her. The driveway to the Reynolds house was a long one, but it had felt endless as he finished his conversation with Officer Haines and raced to find Arden.

The sheer relief at finding her, seated at the table with Reese, had tension and determination fading in equal measure at the reality that she was okay.

And forced the realization that she mattered more than he'd suspected or realized.

Images of her discovering a body filled his thoughts, even as he fought to calm his breathing and hide the depth of his fear. The possible danger from a killer still in the vicinity and the terror that would have dogged her all the way back to the house were as clear in his mind as the walls that stood around them.

None of it was acceptable.

And all of it was proof that, once again, someone was playing a dangerous game in Midnight Pass.

"Are you okay?" Ryder shifted to stare down at Arden.

"Yeah." She nodded, her red-rimmed eyes shifting toward Murphy as a small smile tinged her lips. "You two were like the cavalry charging in here."

"I—" His words fell short as Ryder sought to come up with something pithy.

All he got instead was a whoosh of air on his exhale and that continued, stark realization that she mattered.

"I'll just give you two a few minutes." Reese said on a light cough. Ryder saw the pregnant woman's struggle to stand and moved to help her, grateful for the distraction.

"Would you like me to call anyone?"

Reese's gaze was knowing as she patted him on the shoulder. "Everyone's where they need to be right now. Which is why I'm heading to the couch and the latest episode of my favorite medical drama."

Ryder glanced at her stomach before he could stop the move. "Are you sure that's a good idea?"

Reese's gentle smile only grew broader. "I'm made of sterner stuff. But, if it won't interfere with his working, I'd love to have Murphy for company."

Murphy heard his name and at Ryder's subtle gesture, followed Reese from the room, carefully paced beside her. "Don't let him hog the entire couch."

"Highly doubtful." The words came winging back over her shoulder. "The only one hogging anything right now is me."

"She's convinced she's a house right now," Arden said, moving to the fridge once Reese was out of earshot. "We can't seem to convince her otherwise."

"She looks beautiful." The words were as ephemeral

as the thought, and as they spilled out Ryder recognized something else in them.

The sheer awe and strangely pulsing need that had him wanting the same.

New life.

And the fresh hope it brought with it.

Arden poured glasses of water from a pitcher full of what smelled like cucumbers and handed him one. Oblivious to the direction of his thoughts, he took the glass with a quiet thanks and buried whatever odd emotion had suddenly taken over.

He was a cop, damn it. A good one. So that's where he'd focus. Where he *had* to focus.

"Tell me what happened."

Although she didn't cry, a lingering sheen of moisture still filled her eyes, turning her normally bright gaze a watery blue. "I didn't sleep well and was up early. I haven't ridden in a few days and I thought that would be a good way to clear my head. Get rid of my thoughts for a while."

Because of him.

Yes, it was presumptuous but he was as aware as she was of how they left things the last time they were together.

"I'm sorry our date ended on a negative note."

"You weren't expecting your boss. And… Well…" She let out a soft sigh. "You gave me something to think about. What you do. It's not a game."

"No."

"I knew that. Of course I knew it. But—" Arden ran the tip of her finger over the condensation of her glass. "It never occurred to me what you live with day in and day out. I see it with Belle, but I know her. And I have known her since she became a cop. You." She laughed lightly, the sound small and tough. "You're sort of like Venus, fully formed. It's something to think about."

"I'm sorry I dragged you into my suspicions about Rick."

Her eyes shot up from where she stared at the glass, going wide. "I won't share what you told me. Your concerns. None of it."

"It still wasn't fair to burden you with it."

"We made a pact. If Shayne is at risk, I want to know about it."

He reached for her, taking one of her hands in his. "I won't forget."

"Thank you." She squeezed his hand before squeezing her eyes into twin tight lines. "So. This morning."

Ryder said nothing, just kept her hand in his and allowed the story to spill out.

Arden wasn't sure how it happened, but in the retelling of her grisly discovery she found some peace. Ryder's quiet strength and the steady strokes of his thumb against the back of her hand gave her a tranquil and steady attitude she didn't know she possessed. Or could possess.

Her family had given her a warm place to land.

But Ryder gave her safety.

That endless sea of calm as he listened, asking minimal questions yet when he did ask, it was with a clarity that spoke of skill and understanding and a determination to find out who had done this terrible thing.

"Did Tris have any enemies?" Ryder asked. "Anyone he seemed on the outs with?"

"No. We were discussing it before. He was a quiet man and he kept to himself, but he wasn't hostile or difficult. Distant, but in a standoffish way, you know. Maybe it was shy. Maybe it was just his personality to watch from the sidelines." She shrugged, well aware whatever they thought didn't matter any longer. "Separate, but not threatening or violent. That's the best way I can describe him."

"There still may be something there. Or something the other ranch hands know that hasn't whispered back to the family yet."

"Our foreman knows those men. He'd have let one of us know if there are issues."

"And there are plenty who know how to hide things from the boss." Ryder kept his countenance as even as his words. "That's what an investigation will help turn up."

Was it possible there was something going on? Although she believed her brothers had a good handle on the day-to-day running of the ranch, especially when it came to their employees, Ryder did have a point. Quiet conflicts or dustups would likely have been kept from the boss.

The same way they kept their own counsel as a family and as ranch owners, sharing something when it was ready for others to know.

Sort of like Ryder's situation.

"I can see the wheels turning," Ryder said.

"It's just like you said. What people keep from the boss. That goes both ways."

"Did you remember something?"

"I'm thinking about your situation. How much does Statler know that you don't?"

Arden saw the moment her point registered, his mind whipping quickly from talk of Tris's murder to his work with the field office. "I suppose he keeps his own thoughts on a lot of things. I've gotten additional clearance with each promotion but he's still my superior. I'd be a fool to think there aren't things he knows that I don't. Information he has access to that I don't." He did smile then, even if it didn't reach his face. "The privileges of management."

"*Privilege* might be an overstatement, but it is something. And with that responsibility I assume there would be some additional ways he could hide things or manage the flow of information."

"If you were crafty enough, I guess anyone could. But yes, each step up the ladder comes with more ownership, more responsibility." He paused, before adding, "More trust."

"The necessary trade-off for shared responsibility and a large, matrixed organization."

"Yes."

"That's how you catch him." Arden stopped, surprised by how quickly she leaped to that conclusion, ready to convict the man after a brief meeting and on the basis of Ryder's gut instinct only. "Or how you prove he's doing nothing wrong."

"What are you aiming at?"

"Here. The ranch. Your plans for an op. You've wanted to set a trap for the bad guys. So set it. Only instead of focusing on what's trafficking back and forth across the border, you focus on the who."

"Arden. This is irrational talk. I'm not bringing that to your doorstep. I've put you all in a challenging position already. I'm not tossing internal Bureau suspicions on top of it."

"Why not? We've given you the perfect cover."

He stood, his chair scraping over the old wood floor.

"Not on your life. And it will be your damn life if Statler is even remotely shady. He's a federally trained law enforcement officer. He knows how to handle himself and he shoots to kill."

Something in that deadly thought sparked, lighting kindling she hadn't even known was there. "So do you."

"And what if I'm wrong?"

"Then you pivot and catch whomever is. We've already given you access to the land. You said yourself you want to fix the problem. So fix it."

"No. Just no."

"Then what's the point?"

The question was as effective as a gunshot and Ryder stilled his pacing across the kitchen. His expression was stark, devoid of any of the humor she normally saw there, and his eyes glittered like black diamonds. Hard. Unforgiving. "Excuse me?"

"You heard me. What's the point?" Arden got to her feet, unwilling to have this discussion on anything but even ground. "What's the point of any of it if you don't stop the damned problems that continue to blight Midnight Pass?"

"Don't tell me how to do my job, Arden."

"Then don't give me a reason to."

When he remained still, that hard, immovable, implacable wall, she tried a fresh approach. "We can't keep on like this, Ryder. My family and I. We've had enough."

As the words spilled out, Arden knew them with the deepest certainty. This wasn't a new tack to get him to do what she wanted. This was truth.

"Reese is set to deliver a baby any day. She has seen more than her fair share of violence. Lived with it in ways the rest of us will never fully understand. Veronica, too.

And Belle." Arden shook her head. "She made a vow to catch the bad guys. To build a life working for safety and justice. I know how committed she is and how determined she is to do the right thing. Yet day after day, it gets worse." She dropped back into her chair, an even starker reality hitting her. "We've fought and fought, and if this morning is any indication, we're losing."

Ryder said nothing, instead turning to stare out the window. The kitchen door looked out over the driveway and the stables beyond, blocking any further view of the property. Even if he'd been looking in the right direction to see Tris and the police, who even now worked around his body seeking clues, Ryder would still be too far away.

Would still be separate.

And could still walk away.

Arden wondered at that and what he might be thinking as he stared out over that vista.

Was he reconsidering his decision to come here? To come to them. Or maybe he was feeling as hopeless as she was.

As if surrender was increasingly the only option.

"You're not losing." His voice was low and scratchy, as if he were searching for something from the deepest part of himself. "You won't lose. None of us will."

"So you're in? You'll use your op to set a trap. For whomever the bad guy actually is."

"Yes."

"Then let's get to work."

Rick thought of Shayne, warm and snug in her bed, and tamped down on the idea of going to her. Of pulling her close and nuzzling that soft spot in the groove of her neck and simply breathing deep. He could practically smell her, the light citrus of her shampoo and those subtle, feminine overtones of honeysuckle.

Damn.

He fought to get himself under control, banishing the image and the mental sense memories as far away as he could. When had she become such a temptation? Such a force?

And why now, when he was at the pinnacle of all he'd worked for? He couldn't lose his head. Or his focus.

Not now.

Even if all he wanted to do was bury himself in her for a few hours and clear his head. He *needed* to clear his head.

Needed to forget the image of the surprised cowboy, his sightless eyes staring up at the midnight sky.

Needed time to regroup and figure out what to do about Durant.

And most of all, he needed some damn time to think about what he was going to do. And just who might have some insight into what he'd been up to.

The text had come an hour ago.

WE HAVE FRIENDS IN COMMON. WE SHOULD MEET.

He took a risk, running the communication on Shayne's personal laptop. The hacked piece of Bureau software he'd covertly added to her machine—the one that could identify the sender—had been a lifesaver before, but it had turned up nothing. And Rick had let it lie, half curious, half spooked at its origin.

Until the second message came.

THE MEETING WASN'T A SUGGESTION.

The text had given the address of an obscure nature park a few towns north of Midnight Pass and an assigned meeting place.

Rick considered his work up to now with the various drug cartels down in South America. The work had been direct and relatively easy once he'd earned their trust.

Or what passed for trust among the illicit deal-making crowd.

But the fact remained, he had a service to offer and they had a product to trade. It worked and rather smoothly at that.

Which made the nameless, untraceable texts that much more ominous. Impulse screamed at him to ignore the instructions. He wasn't set up yet. Wasn't in a position to run or put his final retirement plan into place.

Which meant he was going to the meeting.

And would hope like hell whoever was at the other end was in the mood to make a deal.

Ryder kept his distance, his focus on Belle Granger Reynolds as she issued orders over a dead body. Dead men might not tell tales, but the actions of those working over them told a hell of a lot.

And once again, he acknowledged to himself, Belle was a damn fine cop. Thorough, thoughtful and, as evidenced by her serious blue eyes, never willing to forget the sadness and absolute waste of life that was violent death.

Arden had said she'd underestimated what he lived with. He'd inwardly laughed at the Venus on a clamshell idea, but the broader thought stuck.

Were cops born or made? What drew someone to the

life? And what made him determined to seek justice for others, regardless of whether they deserved it or not?

This was his life.

His chosen profession.

What did that say about him? That he reveled in the macabre? Or that he stood for justice.

Likely both, he mused.

"She's pretty amazing."

Ryder saw the depths of love that welled off of Tate Reynolds like a gushing oil derrick and knew a lost cause when he saw one. "She is. A fine cop and an even finer person."

"If I wasn't so inclined to agree with you, Durant, I'd slug you for good measure just for looking at her."

Ryder held up his hands. "My interests are solely professional. There are few that have Belle's dedication and compassion. It's a powerful combination."

Tate's emerald green gaze softened. "That it is."

Ryder turned fully to Reynolds, pulling his gaze from the body. "I'm sorry about your ranch hand."

"So am I. Tris was a good man."

Ryder considered how to play it. This wasn't his jurisdiction, despite his overarching interest in Reynolds Station. Nor did he want to come off as a voyeur or, worse, an instigator.

In the end, he didn't have to when Tate picked up the thread. "We had our doubts about him at first. Kept to himself and uncomfortable with a lot of attention. We all kept an eye out, but over the past year he more than proved himself as loyal and hardworking."

"Your men have any idea why he'd be targeted like this?" Ryder asked.

"Targeted like what?" Tate frowned, considering Ryder's question.

"Execution style." Belle had moved up beside them, her face grim, mouth set in a straight line. "No fighting. No struggle. I'd lay odds he knew his killer or was intrigued enough with what was being discussed he never saw the shot coming."

"You're sure?"

Belle laid a hand on her husband's arm, staying close to their small conversation circle. "Yeah, babe, I'm sure. Tris was either a part of something or he walked straight into it. There's no evidence of a fight or a struggle. Someone got the jump on him and he was comfortable enough to let them."

"You think it was another hand?"

"Do you?" Belle's gaze was sharp. "Was he having issues with anyone? Any fights recently?"

"Geez. No. That's not what I meant. But you said he knew his killer."

Belle shook her head. "*Know* might be a stretch, but he didn't fight so he had some passing acquaintance or no reason to fear his assailant. Let me finish up here and then we'll all sit down and discuss my theories. We can map out a plan for questioning everyone after that. For the time being, I need them all here. All in the bunkhouse except for the few that have to be out on the property for any reason."

"I'll shift duties to Fitz and Barnes. Both are rock-solid and can handle the work today. We'll gather the rest up."

Ryder saw Belle already itching to get back to her co-workers, so he hitched a thumb behind him in the general direction of the ranch. "You need some help with that, Reynolds?"

"Yeah, I do."

Ryder didn't miss Belle's look of gratitude as she pressed a kiss to her husband's cheek before walking away.

Ryder let himself into the small field office they kept on the south end of Main Street, the events at Reynolds Station weighing heavy. Murphy paced beside him, equally tired, and Ryder considered the day they'd both had.

Before he'd gone with Tate to round up the ranch hands, Ryder had asked Belle if he could let Murphy near the body. She'd agreed and after he'd gathered Murphy from his protection duty at the house, Belle had given them leave to review the scene. Although Ryder had little hope the exercise would pay dividends in the bunkhouse, he didn't want to lose the possibility of a clue.

In the end, Murphy had scoured the bunkhouse top to bottom and other than an unerring path straight to Tris's bunk and personal locker, nothing else had stuck.

Leaving Ryder even more convinced another ranch hand had nothing to do with Bradshaw's murder.

"You're a champ." Ryder dug out a few bones from his desk and presented them to his partner before giving Murph the all clear to take his spot on the large dog bed that dominated the corner of the small office they shared.

Ryder booted up his computer and let the familiar screens cycle through, his mind wandering as the mundane routine played out before him. He'd have preferred to let this wait until morning but the idea was fresh in his mind and he wanted to get it all down.

His time in the bunkhouse had given him an idea.

The ranch hands were as attuned to what went on

at the ranch as the Reynolds family. More so, in some ways, especially with what went on behind the scenes day-to-day.

Arden had been spot-on with her assessment. There were some things you simply didn't tell the boss. Even the more loose-lipped hands among the Reynolds Station employees had clammed up when it came to their impressions of Tris or what went on when the work stopped. Although he'd ultimately left the questions to Belle, he realized he could use their camaraderie and loyalty to each other to his advantage when he built his op.

But it was Arden's other words that had played over and over, forcing him to acknowledge the woman had planted a rapidly growing seed.

You've wanted to set a trap for the bad guys. So set it.

Could he use the staff at Reynolds Station to bring his sting to life? All along he'd seen the op as something run on the far side of the property, closest to the border, with minimal involvement from anyone associated with Reynolds. The FBI handled their own and didn't need or want outside interference.

But things had changed and there was no way he could manage it all without bringing someone else in.

Ryder reread his planning notes before shifting to review the various points he'd earmarked on his aerial maps. Each spot he'd pinpointed had been tied to border crossings, but he'd done little with the trail someone would have to make *through* the land to exit on the other side. That thought had grown clearer and sharper as he'd considered the placement of Tris Bradshaw's body and how his killer would have escaped the property.

"You come in, you gotta go out," he whispered to himself as he cross-referenced a few spots on the map with some photos in his files.

If Statler was innocent—and a persistent part of him desperately wanted that—then his boss would be unscathed by the makeshift op designed to catch drugs moving through the property. Rick would have no idea he'd been one of its intended targets, his agents handling the take and processing the cache, as per Bureau procedure.

And if not...

If Statler took the cache himself and moved it through the property, then they'd know who he was working with.

And how he was doing his dirty work.

We've given you the perfect cover.

Ryder had learned long ago there was little that was perfect about police work. It was a daily slog to keep the bad guys in sight and fight the continuous blight on humanity. Only now things seemed different.

He was different.

Arden had given him hope that there might be a real opportunity to deliver that strong, decisive, winning outcome he craved so badly. Midnight Pass deserved better and the Reynolds family sat at the top of that list. And if his plan worked, he'd have a real chance to do something about that blight.

And hell, if he played his cards right, he might even get the girl, too.

Chapter 10

Rick sat in his car, rereading the text message summoning him to the small nature preserve. His gut had been screaming all day to find another way but in the end he'd come.

Not showing up was *not* an option.

Faceless bastard.

He'd worked damn hard to get to this point and every thing was coming together. The transfer to south Texas has been all he'd hoped and more. The relationships he'd built with the cartels were paying dividends and he was finally in a position to get the big score.

Losing ground simply wasn't an option.

Even if an untraceable ghost had hacked his phone.

He'd finally given in and risked possible exposure by running the last message that hadn't popped on Shayne's computer through a program at work, hoping like hell he could get a trace, but nothing.

So here he freaking was.

The gun on his hip and the knife at his ankle were little solace facing the unknown. But they were something.

What bothered him more than the physical threat was that his faceless contact had sought him out. Not in a way that suggested he had intel on the Bureau.

Oh no. In a way that suggested his opponent knew full well how Rick spent his free time. His extracurricular contacts and the rather lucrative side hustle he'd set up for himself.

The dark sedan that pulled up beside his own car signaled the wait was at an end and Rick took a harsh breath, ready for the mystery to be over. The car idled momentarily before a large bruiser got out of the driver side, followed by an elegant, slender man in a dark navy silk suit from the passenger side. The motions were clearly choreographed, the bruiser-slash-bodyguard in position before his boss alighted from the car.

Rick knew the drill well. More, he recognized it for the clear statement.

Screw with us at your own peril.

He'd reserve judgment on exactly who was getting screwed and stepped from his own car.

It was showtime.

"Mr. Statler." The well-dressed man spoke first, his voice as crisp as the points of his collar and as smooth as the white-blond hair slicked back off his face. "Thank you for joining me."

Rick mentally flipped through the images he had regular access to at the Bureau. Assassins, criminals, crime heads, known associates of each. He cycled through them all and kept coming up blank on the sharp-dressed man with the Eastern European accent—was it Ukrainian? Russian?—and his bodyguard.

His own training failed him as he struggled to assess the threat.

Why couldn't he identify the man? Was it possible there was a threat operating in Texas they were completely unaware of?

And how the hell did the guy find a way to contact him?

"I see your—" the bastard hesitated, "—*concern*, and I'd like to allay your fears."

"Then get to it."

The comment was calculated to show his lack of concern but the slight smile that tilted the man's lips suggested Rick had missed the mark.

Once more, his frustration at being on his back foot swirled acid low in his stomach.

"I'm here to make a deal. My associates have informed me you're a sharp businessman. Surely you will see the value in working together."

The lack of facial recognition only added to the tension and Rick's thoughts shifted gear abruptly.

What if this was a sting instead?

The man was unrecognizable as an existing threat operating in the region. Was that because he was a decoy? A messenger designed to draw Rick's extracurricular activities out into the open?

"I'm afraid you have me confused with someone else."

That small smile hovered once more, sharper this time. And way more poisonous than the last. "I'm quite sure I don't."

Rick held his tongue, the weight of his gun at his hip

offering little comfort or solace as he stared across the small expanse between their two cars.

The man extended a hand toward the walking trails that speared off from the parking lot. "Come. Let us walk a bit. Alexander will stay here and watch our things."

He'd be lucky if Alexander didn't stay behind and bug his car, but Rick heard the clear order beneath the invitation.

Hell, might as well go with it. At this point he wanted it all over with anyway.

"That one's rather difficult." Rick pointed toward the trail farthest to the right. Although he'd never been, Rick had checked the trails on his maps of the area and knew there were several drop-offs on the last one. Drop-offs that would give him a chance to defend himself and get the upper hand should things turn ugly.

And if they didn't…

Well, he'd still get the pleasure of seeing the man's Italian leather loafers muck their way through decomposing leaves and the sogginess of late winter rains.

Win-win.

The man nodded his head. "As you like."

Although they took off casually toward the trail, Rick had no illusion he wasn't being carefully watched. Or that he could pull much in the way of going on the offensive. But he could—and would—defend himself if things went sideways.

"You and I have a few friends in common."

"To my earlier point, I'm afraid you've confused me with someone else."

The man had kept a suitable distance as they started off on the trail but he came to an abrupt halt, the back of his hand slamming into Rick's chest. "Games don't become you."

He'd passed the point where he had anything to lose. Just barely. It was the only reason he hadn't reacted to the hand on his chest. "Neither does illusion or prevarication. What's this about?"

"You've crafted an interesting relationship with some business associates of mine down in Colombia. I believe I can make you a far more lucrative deal."

Up until now Rick hadn't said anything to get him caught. Sure, showing up was suspicious, but he'd yet to say anything that, if recorded, would suggest he was managing opportunities outside his job.

Asking for more details would change that.

Did he dare?

Or did he attempt to cut his losses and get out.

"Who said I was looking to make a deal?"

"Sharp businessmen are always looking to make a deal. Especially of the sort I'm offering."

Although he'd braced for a violent outcome, as prepared as he could possibly be, the smooth cadence and steady walk of the man beside him hadn't yet suggested a capacity for violence. Nor had he been checked for any weapons by the big bruiser driving the car.

What was the play?

"Perhaps I haven't been appropriately persuasive." The thick accent couldn't hide the subtle menace swirling beneath. "Something to ensure you know I'm serious."

"Most serious individuals I know introduce themselves by name. They ask for a phone number before presuming their messages are welcome. And they don't expect meetings without that proper introduction first."

His companion on the trail said nothing, simply continued moving forward with a lilting, sinuous walk that only reinforced the serpent-like quality that seemed to pervade his aura. Nothing ruffled him and if Rick weren't so wary and on his guard, he might have taken a few pointers. The guy was pure ice, and as a man who'd made his living focused on hiding every ounce of emotion, Rick was seriously impressed.

Until he was slammed against the nearest tree, one long sinuous hand wrapped around his throat, his vision wavering as those long fingers tightened around his vocal cords. Rick reached for the gun at his back, stilling only when the tip of an ugly blade rested just above his straining throat muscles.

"I appreciate bravado as much as the next man, but I've had enough."

The words remained smooth, as if the effort to hold Rick still required no exertion whatsoever, but the suggestion of collaboration or equality had vanished. "The relationships you've built have run their course. I'm offering you an opportunity to retain your position and your extra income stream, yet all I'm getting is the not-so-subtle insinuation that I'm wasting your time."

Rick fought for air, the edges of his vision wavering. His mind raced between pulling the gun and taking his chances and recognizing just how neatly the bastard had gotten the upper hand.

"Fine." The word eked out on a long, wavering breath.

Those fingers tightened another notch as the tip of the blade pricked like a laser-focused point of fire. "Excuse me?"

"I'd like. To know. More." Rick wheezed out the last few words, the pressure of the blade reducing in tandem with the iron, clawlike grip of fingers.

As abruptly as the assault started, Rick was shoved hard, his feet losing purchase as he stumbled over the tree roots at his feet. Facedown in leaves and muck, he was still calculating the distance to his gun when he heard a distinct click.

"Now, Mr. Statler. Let's make a deal."

Ryder drove through the gates of Reynolds Station, the early morning sun glinting off the eastern windows of the ranch house. He hadn't had a chance to say goodbye to Arden the day before. The time he'd spent with Tate rounding up the ranch hands and then the need to get back to the office ensured they hadn't seen each other after the intense time in the kitchen.

And he wanted to see if she was okay.

Which was ridiculous because her family was around her so of course she was okay.

Only he had to see for himself.

The briefest concern that 6:00 a.m. was too early was allayed as Ace Reynolds headed out of the barn, waving as he caught sight of him. Which meant he'd make nice with Arden's brother even though all he wanted was to get to her.

"Agent Durant." Ace greeted him first. "Early morning?"

"I'd say the same for you," Ryder said as he stepped out of his SUV and opened the back door for Murphy, "but I have to believe you're always up at this hour."

"Damn near every day of my life." Ace grinned, the easy visage at odds with the serious nature he'd already observed in Arden's oldest brother. "Goes with the territory."

"I guess it does."

Ace's smile fell. "Belle update you already?"

Ryder shook his head. "Not yet. I just got here."

"Then you're in time for breakfast. Tate's on KP duty so you're not getting much more than nearly burned bacon and scrambled eggs."

"He does make the best coffee of any of us," Ace added as almost an afterthought.

"Thanks." Ryder nodded. "Since I'm not the one cooking it sounds like heaven."

Or would be if he shared it with Arden.

Proof positive that he really was further gone than he wanted to admit. Yet even as the knowledge flowed over him, he was hard-pressed to worry about it or shake it off or make excuses for it.

Which was a kick in the ass he'd think about later.

They stepped into the kitchen as a unit, the smell of bacon veering dangerously close to burned scenting the air. Murphy's tail beat extra fast, but his training kicked in and he moved to the corner of the kitchen, out of the way.

Even if those brown eyes remained vigilantly focused on the direction of the stove.

"Every damn time, Tate," Belle groused as she dragged a large tray out of the oven. "The oven has a handy-dandy timer, baby. You need to learn how to use it."

Totally unapologetic, Tate shrugged. "I like it extra crispy."

The moment she had the tray settled on the counter, Tate leaned in and kissed her with a loud smack. "Besides, I was too busy dreaming about last night to remember the timer."

"Eww, enough. Seriously, you two." Arden rubbed a

hand over her face as she poured a mug of coffee, still unaware of Ryder's presence. "It's way too early."

"Ryder." Belle's eyes twinkled as she pulled out of her husband's embrace. Whether from the early morning kiss or her opportunity to surprise Arden, Ryder wasn't sure.

"Durant." Tate nodded, his greeting way more accepting than the past visits. Clearly their time questioning the ranch hands the day before had paid dividends in the trust factor.

A factor that seemed nonexistent as Arden whirled on him. "What are you doing here?"

"Murphy and I came to see you. All of you," he added.

Even sleep tousled, her hair up in a messy knot, she looked gorgeous. A thin-strapped tank top—this one in hot pink—came just to the top of her waist over a tight-fitting pair of black yoga pants. Although he had frequently admired the comfort trend favored by women the world over, Arden Reynolds wore the outfit as if she were born for it. Lean and strong, her strength matched the warm color riding high on her cheeks.

It was a far better sight than the gaunt hollows beneath her eyes as she'd sat at the very same table yesterday.

"Oh," she finally said, shooting a glance toward Murphy before meeting his eyes once more. "Well, good morning."

"I hear there's scrambled eggs, bacon and coffee to be had."

"Nearly burned bacon." Arden tossed a look over her shoulder at her brother as she handed Ryder her recently filled mug. "But hey. It's bacon."

She hadn't had a sip, but the intimacy of the gesture wasn't lost on Ryder and he took the mug, staring at his reflection in the dark brew. Before he could say anything, she'd already turned back to the coffeepot, pouring a fresh mug for herself, the moment gone.

So Ryder sat down, ready to eat whatever Tate had prepared.

"I expect you'd like to know about the report I filed last night," Belle started in, all business.

Ryder gave the coffee one last glance before looking up. "I'd like to hear what you're comfortable sharing. But that's not why I'm here."

"It's not?" Arden asked, one lone eyebrow reaching toward her hairline as she sat down, gesturing to Murphy to join her. "I figured you'd want to know what's going on with Tris."

"I'd rather know what's going on with you." He kept his gaze pointedly on hers even as he continued. "With all of you."

"We're fine." Arden glanced at her assembled family before focusing on scratching Murphy behind the ears. "All of us."

"You discovered a body. You sure you're alright?"

If the question caught her off guard, she didn't show it, her focus on the dog as she pressed kisses to his head and kept steady pressure on his fur. For his part Murphy was in heaven, even as Ryder saw the move for what it was.

Emotional escape.

"I'm fine." She pressed another kiss to Murphy's head before sitting back and meeting Ryder's gaze directly. "More than fine. I've had a good rest and time to process the situation."

"So you're good then?"

"Yep. Better than good. I'm great."

Belle shot her sister-in-law a mild glance, devoid of any clue as to what she was thinking, as she took the two plates her husband handed her and passed them down the table. Her words told another story. "The sooner we get a handle on who did that to Tris we'll all really be fine."

Since "that" was violent death, Ryder was all in to help. And now that he was here, the idea of a daily check-in with the Reynolds family might just be the order of the day.

Even if he was going to have to find a way to make the hell of sitting three feet away from all that bacon up to Murphy. "How can I help?"

"This isn't the FBI's jurisdiction," Arden poked in as she picked up the lone slide of bacon on her plate. "This is a local matter."

Nope, Ryder mentally shook his head. *So not fine. Or good. Or anywhere near past what she'd discovered on Reynolds land.*

"And I'm a local citizen in a position to help."

"You run Tris back at the office last night?" Belle ignored the brewing fight and picked up where she'd left off.

"Didn't find much. He popped on a few drunk and disorderlies several years back, but I suspect you've already found the same."

"He disclosed those on his application," Ace said, catching sight of his wife at the entrance to the kitchen, her sleep-filled gaze taking them all in.

"What did I miss?" Veronica asked.

"Nothing new since last night." Ace walked over and handed her his mug, and she proceeded to down half of it. Once again, Ryder thought of the simple gesture of Arden handing over her mug and marveled at the ease of it all.

Even if Arden was still staring at him as the early morning interloper instead of someone she'd like to share breakfast with.

He'd observed his sisters' marriages, of course. All three of them had found solid, steady men to share their lives with. And he'd had a few relationships of his own that had progressed to semisteady morning intimacy. But there was something different about this. Something simple and basic, steeped in a fundamental courtesy of sharing space with one another.

It was the simple that struck him the most. That way with one another that indicated deep comfort and ease.

Had he ever had that? Really had that?

His sisters might have found their way into good, strong adult relationships, but it hadn't been because of their parents' loving, understanding touch. Steve and Debbie Durant been as ready to fight as show any semblance of a loving relationship and he'd grown to adulthood assuming marriage was an ongoing balance of managing the rounds in between the day-to-day mundanity of living.

Only he hadn't seen a single hint of that here.

Inside these walls were love, care, support and, once again Ryder settled on the word: ease.

Even with the daggers Arden was presently shooting at him sideways out of her eyes, he wasn't uneasy. He'd been made to feel as if he belonged and that was something he was going to need some time to process.

An attraction to Arden Reynolds was one thing. Hot blazes left to burn out of control could be a lot of fun while they lasted.

But it was the other thing—that thought that had poked and prodded and nagged at him for the better part of a few weeks that finally broke the surface—causing the real concern.

Given too much more time together, he might just

fall in love with her. With her entire family, while he was at it.

For a man who did just fine with his dog and his independent life, that should have struck a whole hell of a lot more fear than it did.

Even if it did come with a heaping pile of nearly burned bacon.

Lying didn't sit well with her and the well-rested comment had been a steaming pile of bs. She'd barely slept for the second night in a row, but Arden would rather eat an entire plate of Tate's most burned bacon than admit it.

Which was dumb because no one expected her to be fine after discovering a dead body. A *murdered* dead body and of one of their own employees, no less.

They looked out for their own and the fact that something had happened on the property didn't sit well with any of them. It had been easy to cast an eye toward Tris and anything he might have been personally involved in, but it was hardly fair to leap to the conclusion he was at fault and not turn the questions inward.

They all knew they had issues with their land and its placement so close to the border. Any property as vast as theirs was bound to have some security issues, but no amount of work to cut off interlopers had seemed to work.

Was Tris a victim of one of those interlopers?

Arden had gone over and over it in her mind. She was more than willing to leave the detective work to Belle, but it didn't stop her from considering the angles.

From considering what they needed to do.

Allowing Ryder onto their land to run his op had been a start, but Tris's death had proven that they needed

Ryder Durant far more than they'd initially believed. His help. His focus on fixing the problem.

And his protection.

She and her brothers did just fine taking care of what was theirs, but even they were no match for the festering wounds of violence that seemed to seethe beneath the surface in The Pass. Hadn't the past year proven that?

She'd barely seen Hoyt since the day before. He and Reese had holed up in their bedroom suite, begging off as tired for dinner last night and still upstairs this morning. As concerned as they all were about the danger that hovered nearby, Hoyt was beyond anxious as he worried about his pregnant wife and unborn child.

What must this all be doing to him?

To think that he was bringing new life into the world, even as the world he'd built for himself seemed to have cracks all the way through it.

"Is there any significance to where Tris was shot?" Veronica asked the question, her morning haze apparently burned off by her coffee guzzling. Arden admired the readiness to take on the day even as she struggled to understand it. A person had to wake up slowly, damn it. Slow and steady and without the presence of a gorgeous man and his dog in their damn kitchen.

As if to punctuate the thought, Ryder leaned forward beside her, his profile hazed in the golden early morning light that came in through the kitchen windows. He'd shaved and all it did was give her a clear line of sight all the way down that smooth jawline.

Arden wanted to chalk it all up to hormones. He was a wildly attractive man, that hard jaw and broad shoulders only proving her point. But it was more.

Way more.

His attention and affection for his dog. His determined focus on his work. Even the way he'd confided in her his concerns about his boss and then understanding Arden's need to protect Shayne if things went sideways.

Ryder Durant was the whole package. One that was far more complex and complicated than the cocky grin and hot body suggested. One that kept her on her toes and, more than that, kept her thinking. And that hadn't happened for a very long time.

Maybe not ever.

"Significance how?" Belle and Ryder asked the question of Veronica nearly in unison, something humming and arcing between them across the kitchen.

Like a dog catching a scent, Arden thought as her flights of fancy over Ryder's jawline—of all things!—subsided.

"This is a massive piece of property," Veronica continued. "Yet Arden found Tris within hours of his being killed. That's got to be deliberate, right? If someone was really determined to hurt him, wouldn't they have hidden Tris where he'd have been hard to find?"

"But someone was determined to hurt him." Ace was quiet as he moved up behind Veronica's chair, laying a hand on her shoulder. "Badly."

"Yeah, but you're on to something, V. Whatever Tris walked into, and that's a big if," Belle warned, "the fact remains he wasn't hidden somewhere. A fight with another ranch hand or even a local that turned deadly? The other person would have found a way to hide his body."

Arden fought the shudder as the image of Tris, laid out with a gunshot wound, filled her mind's eye once again. More proof that his death had imprinted itself in her thoughts and likely would never leave. "Only he was laid out in the open, for anyone to see."

"To find," Belle said gently. "To find, sweetie."

And she'd been the one to find him. To happen upon a man who not only trusted them but had given his time and attention—and now his life—to Reynolds Station.

They owed him something better than that.

Hell, she thought as the swift anger followed on her lingering sadness. They were all owed something better than that.

Chapter 11

Ryder tossed Murphy's favorite ball in a wide field out behind the Reynolds paddock. His partner's daily training always included time for a sense of fun and relaxation and over the years of working together, Ryder had found that the exercise relaxed him, too. The simple act of tossing a ball and watching his dog run to fetch it, tail wagging in high, wide arcs, never failed to make him smile.

Even if the smile came a bit harder today.

Veronica Reynolds had made a stunning—and impossible to ignore—point.

Someone had wanted them to find Tris and find him fast. The placement of the body wasn't random, nor was it an accidental discovery, brought on by weather or some other natural occurrence.

It was a message.

Murphy's happy *woof*! around the ball in his mouth—his version of a greeting—had Ryder turning. Arden was behind him, still in her yoga outfit but with a matching, formfitting jacket in the same shade of hot pink as her tank.

Ryder took the ball and tossed it again, Murphy taking off in a running leap after it, his infatuation with the game still showing no signs of fatigue. Ryder wanted to collect his thoughts but Arden beat him to the punch.

"You didn't say anything in there. Before," she clarified. "About your suspicions about your boss."

Although he couldn't hear any whispers of judgment, Ryder felt them all the same. "Nothing's changed. That's between you and me right now."

"Even if it puts my family in danger?"

Murphy returned, triumph quivering off him as he dropped the ball at Ryder's feet.

"The danger's here whether we like it or not. But me playing a hunch?" Ryder tossed the ball again, the hard, slobbery rubber flying off his fingers with all the force of a rocket. "That's all I'm doing, Arden. Playing a hunch."

"A hunch with my family's lives at stake."

He whirled on her then, the steady calm he was desperately trying to keep vanishing like mist. "A gut feeling I can't back up with everything at stake!"

"You sure about that, Ryder? Because I don't see your home under attack. Your family worried sick about a faceless threat or the possible danger to a child not even born yet!"

He had to give her credit—she gave as good as she got. And even as he knew there was anguish and frustration in the rising crescendo of her argument, he was helpless standing in the face of her fierce protectiveness.

Helpless because he understood the consequences now. Breakfast with the Reynolds family had only brought into sharp relief what he'd already suspected. Or rather, on the deepest level, had already known.

He was falling for her.

And even though he barely knew her, losing her now that he'd found her was simply not an option. Nor was the risk of losing any of her family.

He'd lost so much already.

"Do you know why I do this job? Why I'm driven to do this?"

The heat and fire that had propelled her outside faded, her voice going soft with what he guessed was surprise at the abrupt change in conversation. "If you're anything like Belle, you were born that way."

A harsh laugh erupted on its own, the sound bitter on the morning breeze. "I wasn't born that way, I can tell you that. I was a little aimless and a lot bored after college. Austin's a fun town and I did enough to get by in school. I was happy to be out from underneath my family's thumb and I'm lucky that I remember things. Enough to get my degree."

"But?"

"But it was time to graduate and make a life and I ended up following my buddy. Pete was a good guy, always talking about growing up in Fort Worth. It sounded nice enough and I didn't have anywhere else to go so that's where I went. He had dreams of being a detective and I lined right up with him. Figured I'd do a few years on the force. Learn a few things. Figure out what I wanted to do. There wasn't some big grand plan for my life."

"That's not the man I know today."

"That's because I *became* this man. A few years in, I was doing okay. I'd found my niche. I'd done traffic duty and worked a beat and then I got involved with the K-9 dogs and things began to change. I saw a purpose I hadn't before. It became my focus, like Pete wanted to make detective."

"Did he?" Even as she asked the question, Ryder sensed she already knew the answer.

"He made an undercover op. Working inside a local dealer's turf. He was supposed to play a low-level guy. Get some basic intel and get out."

Without giving her the room to ask any more questions, Ryder rushed through the end. "He got caught up in it. Couldn't separate the job from the drugs and was set up as part of his initiation. The dealer caught wind there was a narc in his midst and made Pete pretty quick."

"Ryder, I'm sorry."

"I knew something was going on. At the time. I knew it. It was only a few weeks into the op but the Pete I knew became someone different. He was trapped and it all happened so fast. I didn't have anything to go on but my gut but I knew there was a problem. And I let it happen."

"But it's not your fault."

"It will always be my fault."

"But it isn't. It's sad and horrible and I'm sorry that he got caught up in something he couldn't handle, but that's not on you."

Ryder glanced up at the sky before dropping his eyes back to the ground. There was no way to make her understand. So it had to be enough that *he* knew. That he understood. "It will always be on me."

He glanced up, and his gaze lasered into hers. "So no, Arden. I don't have a calling and I wasn't born this way. I was made. And I'm damn well going to do my job and see to it that the scum on the streets loses every damn node on the supply chain."

As determination pumped through him—that resolve that drove him each and every day—Ryder saw something else. A reality that had his heartbeat thundering and blood rushing through his ears in great, galloping waves.

Arden.

He saw her in clear, sharp relief, even as the house behind her, the driveway beyond and the early morning air went fuzzy. Distorted. Because all he could *see* was her.

Without checking the impulse—or even giving it a consideration—he took the last few steps toward her. Reaching for her shoulders, he pulled her against him wrapping himself fully around her. His mouth came down on hers, his heart slamming even harder as he pressed his chest to hers and could only marvel as he received a matched reply.

Lord, he wanted this woman. In every way imaginable and likely a million more he'd not even thought of. In his arms. In his bed. In his *life.*

A myriad of emotions pumped right back at him through her kiss. She embraced him fully, her arms wrapping around his neck as tight as a vise. She met him, her lips as eager as his, her tongue matching his thrust for thrust. Only where he'd have expected something life-affirming, all he found instead was a raw grief, layered over seething frustration.

With one last press of his lips against hers, he lifted his head. "Arden?"

The vivid blue of her eyes had been clouded in the kitchen, obscuring her thoughts. But now that same sky blue was full of all the emotion she'd hidden earlier. He'd have ignored it and given her some measure of privacy but for the sadness that layered beneath.

"Tell me about it," he said softly. *Tell me what you keep locked so deeply inside.*

He braced for tears.

And got raw fury instead.

"Why the hell'd you stop kissing me, Durant? I don't need your sympathy or your pity. And I can take on whatever it is you carry and then some."

Arden shoved Ryder's shoulders as hard as she could, the motion enough to unbalance him. He stumbled backward, righting himself as Murphy danced around his legs with his ball.

Served him right.

Damn man came into her kitchen, looking as fresh as sunshine and smelling like a bar of soap mixed with the lightest hints of dog fur. Who knew soap could be delicious? Or appealing? Especially when layered with hints of Labrador.

He'd stared out of those damn soulful eyes that would give the calves a run for their money, drinking her coffee and talking to her family like it was an ordinary, everyday occurrence.

Ordinary?

Yes, ordinary. And *welcome*, a small voice whispered beneath the rumbling anger.

And then he told her the saddest story she'd ever heard, about a young man who'd gotten in over his head and who'd paid a terrible price.

A price Ryder somehow felt was now owed by him.

Anger she could channel. Great, lapping waves of it

could be used and twisted and turned to achieve her goal. But pity and sympathy?

She'd had a lifetime of both when her father's crimes had come to light and she'd vowed to never take any more.

Only here she was, angry and now sad for his friend and, based on their early morning kitchen conversation, struggling to understand how she'd been set up along with Tris.

Because she had been.

Or her family had and she was the unlucky one of them to make the discovery. That had become frightfully clear. The poor man had been a pawn, like some sort of warning shot over the bow. Aimed directly at Reynolds Station and those who made their home there. Which would have meant something if they knew who'd fired the shot.

Instead they had to ruin all that wonderful, lovely, early morning kitchen goodness talking about murder.

"I don't pity you." He tilted his head just so, his stare penetrating before it shifted, his gaze roaming over her face. "Nor am I going to apologize for the sympathy. I know what it is to experience the ravages of violence done to another. Don't you get that?"

She wanted to keep pushing. Wanted to keep swatting at that gentle comfort and ready understanding. Only now she knew how he'd suffered, too.

Ryder pressed on, unaware of the struggle that raged inside of her. "It's like a part of you has been dragged from a deep sleep and you can't get back to that warm, soft, safe place."

The flash of anger that had propelled her from their kiss faded as quickly as it came, leaving nothing but a dull, throbbing emptiness. "Do you ever get back? To sleep?"

"Truth?"

"Always."

"No. Not all the way."

The pity she'd accused him of carrying shifted, rebalancing the load so that it now weighed her down. Ryder had seen a lifetime's worth of violence in his line of work. While she'd observed Belle over the past year and knew the woman didn't spend every single day—or even every week—battling evil head to head, she did see it.

Experience it.

Live with it.

That was the real heroism in cop work. The willingness to stare into that underbelly over and over and still come out hoping you could make a difference.

But it was *more*, Arden acknowledged, thinking of Belle's devotion to her job and her equal devotion to shaking it off each time she came home.

It was believing that you *did* make a difference.

How was that possible? To get up each and every day, knowing what you might face, yet doing it anyway.

"Why are you so damn hard to read?"

The words drifted to her on the breeze, half mutter, half curse, before Ryder bent down to toss Murphy's ball once more.

"Excuse me?"

"You heard me." Ryder kept his attention on eighty pounds of dog currently racing across the wide expanse of yard, even as Arden knew he was acutely aware of her.

Just as she was of him.

"Yeah, I did. And all I can say is right back at ya."

He whirled then, his moves faster than Murphy's leap

on the still traveling ball. "You're a piece of work, you know that? You stay on my ass, convinced I'm holding back something. Something that happens to be my job and the safety of my coworkers and the completely irresponsible idea of acting solely on impulse in a way that could ruin a man's career. So I spill my damn guts to you and you're still here, hiding from me. Hiding from your family. Hell—" Ryder broke off, scrubbing a hand over his face "—hiding from yourself."

Somewhere deep down, Arden knew he wasn't speaking of the situation with Tris or any danger at the ranch. He wasn't even talking about the lingering fear Rick Statler might not be who he said he was.

Ryder was talking about her.

Her reticence to share her past. Her even bigger wall of reserve, unwilling to consider anything between them beyond flirting and a few meals.

And he was right.

She'd been hiding for years, behind her calm facade and piles of namaste and *practice*, desperately seeking some sense of balance and deeply rooted comfort that had eluded her. That had always eluded her.

Even before Dan and the baby that wasn't meant to be.

Neither had helped, but they hadn't been the root cause.

Whether it was feminine intuition or simply being the last child in a marriage that had cracks from the start, Arden had innately understood the chinks in the armor her mother and father both wore. Long before her mother's cancer diagnosis and her father's near ruin of the business, there had been warning signs.

Her brothers hadn't seen it. Not in the same way she had. Oh, on some level they knew—they'd have needed to be beyond oblivious to have missed all the signs and the lingering tension that never fully faded—but they didn't understand what it all meant. Even now she'd wager she could ask them if they'd had a simple, easy childhood and to a man, all three of them would say yes.

None of them had understood that their mother had felt trapped in the ranch house, in love with a man who couldn't love anyone as much as himself. And fearfully raising four children she hoped beyond measure would turn out different.

Betsy Reynolds had gotten her wish there. Not a single one of them had followed in the footsteps of their father. In fact, adulthood had been a steady, determined march to a different path.

A different life.

Maybe she was hiding, just as Ryder had said. And maybe she could have more if she'd open herself up and take what was clearly being offered. Only she had no idea how to do that.

And questioned if she ever would.

The early morning visit to Reynolds Station and the terse, heated words with Arden had done little for his mood. Even now, as he drove back over the bumping two-lane, away from the Reynolds property and into downtown Midnight Pass, Ryder seethed with the frustration.

And the lingering memory of Arden's face as she stood nearby, clad in that electric pink. It should have been a happy, vibrant color, and instead it had seemingly mocked the pain and the hurt he'd put on her face.

Yet here you are, hiding from me. Hiding from your family. Hell. Hiding from yourself.

Oh, he'd been more than happy to drop the bombs, one by one, a perfect strike attack.

Yet he rarely turned that same honest assessment back on himself.

The turnoff for town came up and Ryder slowed for the stop sign, his gaze drifting to Murphy through his rearview mirror. Assuming he'd worn his partner out with the play, he was surprised to see those soulful brown eyes watching him from the back seat.

"What?"

The eyes arched a few notches higher, even as Murphy kept his chin firmly in place on the back seat.

"Yeah, yeah. I know. I'm an ass. I have feelings for the woman and I've got a funny way of showing her. Jabbing at her soft spots."

Murphy let out a slight, low grumble before punctuating it with a sigh, his agreement—and assessment of Ryder's behavior—obvious.

On a hard curse, Ryder swung through the intersection and turned his SUV around, bumping his way back to Reynolds Station. The round trip didn't take more than fifteen minutes and by the time he'd headed back through the ranch entrance and down the long driveway, his mind was already on how to fix things.

And the small flicker of hope that had flared that morning in the Reynolds kitchen when Arden had handed him that coffee mug and continued to spark to life each time he remembered the kind, casual, *caring* gesture. It was something, right?

It had to be.

He pulled back into the space he'd vacated and jumped out of the car, Murphy obediently waiting for him to open the back door instead of leaping over the seat. Ryder's gaze searched for her when Murphy let out a sharp bark and took off for the paddock. Arden was saddled, cantering around the large oval as she exercised a pretty bay stallion with a large cloud of white on its hindquarters. Murphy jumped up on the rail, his front paws on one of the metal rungs, his tongue lolling to the side. Ryder would have winced at how much of an eager marshmallow the dog looked if he didn't feel the exact same way himself.

Minus the tongue lolling since he'd had the good sense to keep his teeth firmly closed lest his own fall out.

She looked gorgeous. Why did that always sucker punch him? He'd already half convinced himself she had a solid streak of Greek goddess threading through her DNA, but watching her on the horse proved it. Arden sat high in the saddle, her back straight and her thighs bunching and flexing against the equally powerful sides of the horse's body.

Of course, he knew she could ride. The woman had been raised on a ranch and she'd even been on a horse when she'd discovered Tris Bradshaw's body. But he hadn't seen for himself.

Hadn't seen the taut muscles of her shoulders, now bare to the sun, flexing as she deftly maneuvered the horse's reins. Hadn't imagined how sexy all that sheer competence was as woman and horse moved as one.

And he certainly hadn't imagined how hard his heart could crack in two as he thought of the harsh words, lobbed directly at her, that he'd dropped before leaving.

Her discarded jacket hung off one of the paddock rails and he leaned against it, the lightest hint of soap wafting up to him on the breeze.

What was it about this woman?

And why at this time?

He was in no place to have feelings for someone. Not in the middle of one of the most dangerous ops of his career and certainly not with someone intimately involved in the time and place and circumstances.

Only that's all he could think of. Whether he was with her or without her, he wanted to be *intimately involved*. In every way that mattered.

Arden slowed the horse and redirected them both toward the fence. The horse seemed unfazed by Murphy's presence and instead, moved right up to the place where man and dog both stood. Mounted, she stared down at him, her gaze unwavering. "You came back."

"I did."

"Why?"

"I didn't finish what I had to say." Ryder shook his head. "What I meant to say."

"You don't think you said enough?"

"Not enough of the right things."

She seemed to consider his answer, though her poker face ensured he had no clue if that was a good thing or a bad thing. On a soft sigh she dismounted, the motion as smooth and lithe as the rest of her. With a light pat on the horse's rump, Arden gave the bay room to move off, continuing the exercise without a rider.

"I'm sorry to interrupt the workout."

"Charlie knows what to do. He'll be fine. And probably glad in his own horse way not to be stuck waiting for us to have a discussion."

"You and I don't seem capable of discussions."

Arden boosted herself up on the paddock rail, climbing over in a heap of legs, dropping down beside him. "No, Durant, we sure don't."

"Believe it or not, I'm actually pretty good at it. You know. Talking to people without pressing them too hard or probing into thoughts they'd prefer to leave unsaid."

"Could have fooled me."

"I know. And I'm sorry."

"And that's why you came back?"

"Sort of." When she only lifted an eyebrow he added, "I came back because of the coffee mug and because I hadn't finished doing this."

Her brows shot down in confusion at his mention of the coffee a fraction of a second before they shot back up in wide-eyed surprise when he pulled her up close, his mouth claiming hers once more.

All the things he couldn't say, or worse, continued to fumble over, seemed to vanish as their mouths met. Subtle hints of coffee still flavored her tongue, along with that special taste that was uniquely Arden. She was as volatile as a summer thunderstorm and as potent, too, and their kiss was as much gentle acquiescence as it was heated battle.

Over and over again, they fought each other for dominance. For submission. For completion.

How was it possible he found all of it in her? She was his match in every way possible and once again, it floated through his increasingly distracted mind that the circumstances weren't ideal to press this and see where it went.

Yet there was no way he could stop himself.

No way he could stay away.

He could have stayed right where they were for hours but the subtle pressure of her palms on his shoulders had him lifting his lips from hers. Her eyes were filled with passion-glazed confusion and he could only assume his own reflected the same bewildered look.

"What does a coffee mug have to do with any of this?"

His own confusion lingered a few beats longer before a smile he was helpless to hold back split his cheeks. "You gave it to me."

"Where?"

"Before. In the kitchen. You handed it over like it was as natural as breathing."

"You kissed me over a mug?"

"No." He pressed a light kiss to her lips, unable to resist. "It was the inspiration to come back over and kiss you. The thoughtfulness behind the gesture. The simple way you thought of me."

"Well, sure. You were there. And it's courtesy."

"I know." Lord, he was messing this up, but since his insistence on seeing something through often overrode his common sense, he opted to see it through. "It's stupid of me to make such a big deal about it. But it's not a kindness I'm accustomed to." He stopped, recognizing a deeper truth. "Or something I even realized I was missing."

She lifted a hand, pressing her palm against his cheek. "It's not stupid. It's nice. It's even nicer to know something you did was appreciated so much. Thank you for telling me."

Gently, she pressed a kiss against his jaw, drifting her lips over the firm line of bone toward his ear. "Thank you for coming back."

Ryder studied her, committing each line of her face, each curve from cheek to jaw, even each sweep of her eyelashes to memory. The hasty words between them from earlier came back to settle, heavy in his chest. "You accused me of pitying you before."

"I did," she affirmed.

"Do you really think that?"

"Do you think it?" Arden cocked her head, the light of battle filling those ocean depths of blue. Only she didn't drop her hands from his shoulders or shift her body away from his. In fact, she moved imperceptibly closer, her hips flush to his and that warm, heated flesh from her ride rapidly heating him through the sleeves of his dress shirt.

"I won't take back what I said but I am sorry if I hurt you in the careless way I spoke."

"Do you think I'm hiding from something?"

He refused to lie to her, but he didn't need to be an ass about his opinions. It was with that in the forefront of his thoughts that he spoke, hoping he could find the right words. "Yes, I do. I think you're hiding from the pain of something that hurt you very badly. I'd like to be there for you. When you're finally ready to come back into the light."

The memories that dragged so clearly at her heels filled her eyes, clouding them with a sheen of pain. It tugged at him, bone-deep, and made him wish he could change it. All of it.

Only he couldn't. He could only be there, patient and strong, as he waited for her to step out of the darkness.

"What if I'm never ready?"

"I think that's the wrong question."

The thick sweep of her lashes drifted downward, before her gaze shot back up to his. "What's the right one then?"

"Not if. It's when will you be ready." He touched the tips of his fingers to her cheek, a light caress over such soft skin, before drifting down to cup her jaw. "And know that I'll be here when you are."

Chapter 12

Arden led her class through their practice, watching for form and position, listening to proper breathing and keeping an eye out overall for anyone struggling. Her mind drifted along with her gaze, in and around the darkened room, as she took in the eight women and three men who'd joined her for today's session.

Though she took her responsibilities as class instructor seriously, there was no sense of responsibility that could keep the rabbiting thoughts from hopping through her mind.

He'd come back.

Whatever else she had to do today, that lone thought had pushed out every other one.

That and the memory of kissing Ryder Durant in front of the paddock, his trusty dog beside them. His incredibly *hot* kisses, she amended to herself. Hot kisses that had warmed her far more effectively than the early morning ride on Charlie.

Had anyone ever done that before?

The coming back part, although the kissing was pretty incredible, too.

But the fact he'd come back had meant more than she could say. That and the fact that he seemed determined to stick around.

It's when *will you be ready.*

And know that I'll be here when you are.

Her family cared for her, of course. One of the biggest points of pride she'd always carried was the love she had for her brothers and the love they gave her in return. Amazingly, the women who had come into her brothers' lives had only added to that, as they all became a family.

She could still remember a conversation she'd had with Belle shortly after her now sister-in-law had come back into Tate's life. Belle had told her how appealing it was to see how close Tate was to his family, and how much they all mattered to one another.

And now that love remained strong even while their lives changed. It was good change, even though she had been afraid of it. Happy for her brothers but struggling to understand where she fit. Where her life was going.

And then Ryder Durant had come back. And told her he had the will to stick.

Which left an even bigger question for her to puzzle her way through. Did she dare let him in? All the way in?

Could she actually share the things she'd kept buried away for so long? Could she open herself up and share her memories of the baby she'd ached for but would never hold?

But he'd come back, that small, hopeful voice inside whispered.

It shouldn't mean anything but it did. And the intensifying feelings she couldn't quite dismiss or think away or worry her way through had seemingly gone into orbit with his return this morning.

Compartmentalizing her thoughts, Arden focused on the last ten minutes with her students. Those moments of relaxation, meant to quiet the mind and calm the spirit, were always the part of her practice she treasured most. Eyes closed, breathing quietly, a person had no limits to who they were or could be or might become. In that moment, every bit of it was inside of them.

Even as she believed it—completely and absolutely— she'd still lost a sense of herself over the past few years. She'd recognized the need to turn inward for her strength, yet somehow hadn't found all she'd been seeking.

Or hoped to find.

Why had it taken her so long to recognize it?

Vowing to think about that later, too, she closed out the practice, her gaze meeting each of her students as they all resumed a sitting position. She lifted her arms high above her head, pressing her hands together palms first. With gentle movement, she brought her hands where they pressed together above her head downward to rest against her heart. "The light in me greets the light in you. Namaste."

Her students responded in kind, their own soft smiles reflecting back to her.

It was completion.

A sense of belonging.

And, yet again, that knowledge all you needed was inside of you.

Lighter than she'd felt in much too long, Arden reveled in that feeling. She belonged here. In this time and in this moment.

Her students busied themselves with rolling their mats and returning any pieces they'd borrowed from a collection she kept at the front of the room, from elastic belts to wooden blocks to stuffed bolsters of fabric. It was only as she finished rolling her own mat that she saw Shayne hanging behind.

"Arden, do you have a few minutes?"

"Shayne." Arden smiled, determined to keep her behavior as normal as possible, even as her heart punched up in a thick, heavy beat.

Which was ridiculous. This was Shayne, for heaven's sake. They knew each other. And had known each other for years. Was she really going to let Ryder's suspicions get in the way of that?

But what if Shayne was in trouble?

Although Arden considered herself a strong judge of character, she'd gotten minimal vibes off of Ryder's boss the other night. A large man, Rick Statler had come off like a decent guy and totally into Shayne. There'd been a few tense moments between Rick and Ryder, but Arden could hardly make the leap to devious-bad-guy-operating-from-the-shadows over the rather obvious show of male dominance.

"I needed that." Shayne smiled, rubbing it a small spot on the back of her hand. "I've been stiff this week."

"Everything okay?"

"Oh sure. Everything's fine."

Based on the small lines of worry that fanned from Shayne's eyes, Arden didn't think everything was fine, but opted to give the woman a bit of breathing room. "I've been feeling a bit stiff myself. The weather hasn't helped, but that's nothing new. The constant threat of storms usually make me feel a little creaky in March."

"My mother always called it the privilege of getting older." Shayne rubbed that small spot a little bit harder, as if all she wanted to say was focused in that tiny space.

"I like that." Arden couldn't hold back the wry smile at remembered grumbles as she led her own mother through practice in the living room. "My mother had a slightly different view."

"Oh?"

"For all her delicate nature in public, my mother had a rather salty view she shared with a chosen few. Her fondest moniker for Mother Nature was Queen Bitch."

Shayne did laugh at that, a spontaneous sound that still carried some weight beneath it. A point that was confirmed a few moments later when Shayne broke into tears.

On a gentle smile, Arden extended a hand toward a row of benches she kept at the far end of the practice room. "You want to talk about it?"

Shayne nodded and Arden offered her a tissue from a small box she kept at the end of the bench once they sat down.

"I know this is silly." Shayne sighed hard, plucking a tissue from the box. She waved the tissue before bringing it up to blot at her eyes. "I can't believe I'm crying."

"Just get it out. Whatever it is, I'm sure it's not silly."

"You haven't heard me yet." Shayne dabbed at her eyes again. "It's about Rick."

That thick beat of her heart only rumbled harder and Arden made a point to breathe, slow and even, so she didn't give away how her own thoughts raced. "What's the matter?"

"I'm happy and I'm convinced it's all going to come crumbling down."

"Come down? How?"

"He's got a big job. And he's gone a lot. I knew that going into things, but lately it's begun to bother me."

Although Arden hated to give Rick Statler the benefit of the doubt, she forced herself to look at the situation objectively. If Ryder hadn't shared his suspicions, she'd have no reason to question Shayne's relationship. And Ryder had gone out of his way to say that he had no real evidence against Statler beyond a gut feeling that refused to settle.

"You've got a pretty big job, too, running your own consultancy. Managing a business and all the travel you do. I'm sure you've talked about the pressures of your work, too." Arden waited through Shayne's ready nod. "Did something else happen to upset you?"

"It's my expectations. I know it is. It's me." Shayne shook her head and Arden sensed the woman was rethinking her upset, despite her continued acceptance of blame. "Isn't it?"

Arden had observed through the years that relationships were rarely that black-and-white and it concerned her that in the midst of her obvious pain Shayne was already trying to brush her feelings off as silly and singular. Even without Ryder's suspicions echoing through her head, that alone would have set her instincts humming.

"Maybe yes, maybe no. You're entitled to feel how you feel."

"He's just so secretive."

Not absent. Or distant. But secretive.

Arden didn't say anything. Instead she reached for Shayne's hand to give the woman the gentle support she needed to get through her frustration.

"I know secrecy is part of his job and I didn't think

it bothered me, but there's something. Well—" Shayne stilled before rushing on "—sinister about it all. I don't know how to explain it."

"I know those in law enforcement carry a heavy weight. Is it possible that's the problem?"

"I don't know." Another round of tears thickened Shayne's voice. "I thought I could handle dating someone who had such a dangerous job but maybe I'm not cut out for it."

"Did something happen?"

"Last night." Shayne's blush rose up beneath the tears. "We were a little amorous on the couch. He'd been distant all night and I thought maybe it was just the stress of going back to the workweek. But I—" Tears choked up her throat once more. "I did something or touched him wrong or, oh, I don't know! He rose up off the couch like he'd been burned and slammed out of the house."

"Has this ever happened before?"

"No. And I thought things were going so well. We talked all week and were looking forward to an entire weekend together. We had dinner plans Friday and then were just going to spend a quiet weekend. Only he ended up getting called out on emergency meetings both days."

Even if she didn't have Ryder's suspicions echoing in her head, the emergency meetings would have struck a chord as a picture of Rick Statler came into view.

Big man. Big job. Big responsibilities.

How easy would it be to position ongoing absences through the lens of work? Especially if a pattern of absence was established from the start of the relationship.

The sense that had dogged her since Ryder's abrupt behavior change at Friday's dinner expanded and grew.

She had little tangible proof save her screaming instincts that said Shayne Erickson was in trouble.

Ryder dropped Murphy back at his apartment and was already heading out of town toward the address Arden had texted him. She'd seemed insistent they meet and even more insistent they do it outside of the Midnight Pass city limits. He had a vague recollection of the road-side sign for the Mexican restaurant called Manuel's Kitchen and an even vaguer sense of the town of Mesa Creek about a half hour away.

When he pulled into the parking lot, her car was already there, parked in a nearly full lot that suggested Manuel did a brisk lunch business.

Ryder saw her immediately, her hot pink of earlier traded for a softer lavender that clung as intimately as her morning ensemble. She had a booth in the back, affording them a degree of privacy in the midst of the boisterous lunch crowd, and was already waving him in. Before he could check the impulse, he bent over the booth, pressing his lips to hers. The sweet mingling of lips—so simple and easy and welcoming—had his head swimming.

And reminded him that he was in more trouble than he could have imagined if this was his reaction to her a mere four hours since he'd last left her.

Ryder's ass had barely hit the booth when Arden dived in. "I saw Shayne today. She was in my late morning session."

"Did she say something?"

Arden held up a hand. "Can I ask you something first? About work."

"Sure."

"I know part of your job is running ops and catching bad guys. But how often do you have work emergencies that pull you away."

"Away where?"

"Anywhere."

"I wouldn't call it rare, but I would say it's not common. You might get called in on an emergency meeting if the big brass is coming in or if another team needs help on an op. So I can't say it never happens, but I have a decent handle on my schedule."

"Does it happen very often two days in a row?"

"Come on, Arden. What's this about?"

For all her eagerness to share, Arden sat back, her expression shuttering. "You can't leap to conclusions or get Shayne into trouble."

He knew he shouldn't take it personally. She was worried about her friend and it wasn't like the federal law enforcement community was going to bolster anyone's faith if Statler's rat bastard behavior was all Ryder suspected. But damn it, he'd given his word. And he wasn't some green agent, just out in the field, trying to play hero with his career.

"I already told you Shayne's safety is my priority. I won't see her get hurt because I can't keep a confidence, Arden."

"I know." She took a chip from the basket at the center of the table, breaking off a small piece and setting it on the plate in front of her.

"Do you?"

His voice had dropped into a low growl, but even with the thick pulse of lunch conversation humming around them, he knew Arden had heard him.

The pieces of tortilla chip had piled up on her plate, a

mindless, nervous gesture that matched the tension lining her face. He appreciated her struggle and even more appreciated the quality of her character that she wanted to preserve a confidence, but he couldn't—nay, *wouldn't*—sugarcoat things. While he had no interest in forcing a rash gesture, if Shayne Erickson was in danger, waiting was the last thing they should do.

"She's upset and having doubts about her relationship."

"Come on, you met Statler. Wouldn't you have doubts, too?"

"I'm serious, Ryder."

"Me, too." Ryder stilled, the chip he'd taken from the basket halfway to his mouth. "I am serious. What's his appeal?"

"What's anyone's appeal? That's why people fall in love with each other. If we all liked the same person the whole thing wouldn't work very well."

Ryder shook his head. "Play this out with me. They've been together what, a few months?"

"Yeah, a few. Five or six at the most."

"And he's working all the time. Or gives her the line that he is, right?"

Arden took another chip, breaking off the pointy end. "Yeah, sure."

"Why get serious? If you want casual, he's clearly her guy. But serious? With some dude who always has an excuse to go away. What's in it for her?"

"Love, Ryder. She's in love with him. She's the one in the relationship."

"Is she?" Ryder gave it a few beats, well aware Arden was quick enough to pick up on his thoughts. "Or is she part of all this?"

"No way." Arden shook her head, her arms folded in mutiny. "She's the one we have to look out for."

Ryder sat back, considering Arden's ready defense of her friend. And wondered if her friend was part of the problem. How likely was it Shayne was smack in the middle of all of it?

"Why don't you believe me, Ryder? I think Shayne's in big trouble."

"I do believe you. It's Shayne Erickson I might have the problem with."

Rick reread the text message and swallowed back the bile that rose up in his throat. He'd thought to come to work and take solace behind his desk and his duties, looking for all the world like a man on the rise.

What he was, instead, was screwed.

Although he'd avoided using his work computer to look up his newest business partner, it hadn't been too hard to stir up some telling whispers on the dark web. Right off of Shayne's computer the night before while she was out of the room.

One Vasily Baslikova was one nasty bastard and somehow he'd figured out damn near every bit of Rick's business venture with the boys down in Colombia. Rick had been tempted to call on his contact at the cartel but he knew a wasted cause when he saw one. Baslikova and his organization had somehow infiltrated the cartel and based on the man's intel and his willingness to get his hands dirty, Rick had quickly assessed who was in charge. His cartel lead was nothing more than a puppet, if the guy even lasted that long.

And if Baslikova found out Rick was trying to make a deal, the bruised ribs and memories of a cocked gun he was currently sporting would progress to something far worse. All he'd worked for would vanish.

He would vanish.

It was time to shift loyalties and prove to his new partner that he deserved his cut of the action. The only ace he had at the moment was the fact that he could manage federal presence at the border. Because no matter how powerful Baslikova and his organization was, there were some places they still risked their livelihood.

And that's where Rick would win.

He was the inside man and as long as he kept up his end of the deal, he could keep padding his retirement fund and stay alive long enough to ultimately enjoy it.

The bigger issue was Shayne.

She'd put on a brave face but he'd promised her a weekend together and hadn't delivered on it. Beyond their Friday evening together, he'd slipped away to kill that cowboy on Saturday and then again yesterday for the meet with Baslikova. And even last night, he'd been distracted and in far more pain than he could let on.

He still wondered if the cowboy was a mistake, but he needed a diversion over at Reynolds Station. The bullets, gun and silencer were untraceable to him and the cowboy had been an easy mark. Rick had gambled, letting the man know he was a friend of Belle's and wearing his FBI gear as a cover. The use of Belle's name had done the trick, but the dumb hick had even bought his stupid claim that he was there to collect some soil samples.

Crouching down and focusing on the ground had allowed Rick to set up the shot, firing as he stood.

The dumb sucker had never seen the bullet coming.

Just like Shayne hadn't seen their dismal weekend coming, either.

He'd see the hurt reflected in her gaze when he'd moved away on the couch. Had recognized the confusion at his abrupt mood change. If he had any hope of keeping her around for when his retirement finally kicked in, he needed to make amends.

Keep her around?

Once again, it struck him how necessary she'd become. Even in the midst of his sullen bastard routine the night before, he'd wanted her. He'd hadn't been able to act on it, his damn ribs making it hard to move, but he'd wanted her all the same and he still had the raging hard-on to prove it. She was like a reward at the end of the day or a grand prize that said all his efforts had been worth it.

But prize or not, there was no way he could let her see the purple flesh over his ribs or the still-weeping wound on his neck where Baslikova's knife blade had dug in. The gym pullover he'd worn to her place had hidden both and he'd added a high-necked muscle shirt to avoid her catching sight of the knife wound.

Tapping a query into a search bar, he quickly pulled up a florist in Midnight Pass. Roses might be trite but he had no doubt that his friends at Blooms and More could help him make it up to Shayne. Navigating through his order, he hit Send and sat back to consider his next move.

His new friends had made it clear they needed an opening on Thursday night at the border to move a cocaine shipment through The Pass and on up to Houston. Which meant he needed to find the good men and women of his department a convenient diversion.

Turning back to the computer, he pulled up some of the intel his team had gathered over the past few months. The small-town gang that was making trouble in the northwestern part of the county could be interesting. Or the human trafficker who'd been making his move down in Harlingen could work, too.

Rick reread them both and it was only on the second read through that he got the details he needed. Noah Ross had opened the trafficking case when he was still down in The Pass and Ryder Durant had worked the intel with him when he'd first joined the field office. Durant's sharp-eyed stare still stuck in his craw, and Ross—well hell, that situation had gone from bad to worse. Captain Boy Scout was still sending emails from Dallas, just often enough to show professional courtesy and not often enough to seem suspicious.

But Rick knew better.

Ross wasn't ready to give up his old jurisdiction, no matter how much work his new office threw at him. So Rick would use it to his advantage.

If Ross wanted to come back and play in The Pass, he was going to let him. In fact, he'd serve it up on a shiny silver platter.

Opening up his secure email program, he tapped back a response to Noah's latest note. As he hit Send a half hour later, he'd already figured out what to do with Durant, too. It was time to get both of them out of the way.

For good.

Chapter 13

Arden considered the hard line of Ryder's shoulders as he loomed over the table opposite her. He was formidable, and that wasn't an idea she'd associated with him before. Strong, yes. Sure of himself, absolutely.

But formidable?

Formidable was a bull in heat, restrained during mating season. *Formidable* was dead summer, the sun high in a Texas sky, draining as much out of the hands as it gave back to the land. And *formidable* was a business, rising from the ashes of disgrace, building its way back to profitability and success.

Apparently, it was also Ryder Durant.

And with that, Arden recognized a simple truth. The man was a formally trained federal agent. While he might sit behind a desk for much of his job, he was a trained professional who could turn lethal at times. She allowed that knowledge to wash over her as she stared at the man opposite her.

A dress shirt stretched across impressively broad shoulders. His sharp eyes were focused and direct. And his hands, where they rested on the table, were strong.

He was a man who looked every inch the badass agent. And from all she'd come to know about him, he didn't simply look the part. He *was* the part.

With their waitress in sight, beelining for their table, Arden held off on expanding her comments about Shayne until they'd both ordered and were alone once again. She hadn't called him to meet her because she was looking to get Shayne in trouble or cast aspersions on the woman's character.

But she also knew Ryder.

Not only was it his job to help, but it was his innate kindness and willingness to protect others that defined who he was. What if he was right?

What if Shayne was up to her eyeballs in this?

She was a smart woman. She ran her own business and she had a good head on her shoulders. While Arden herself had been fooled by a charming man—and had years of self-berating to show for it—was it possible Shayne was in on whatever Statler might be up to?

If Statler was up to anything.

Which was the problem with all of it. They kept playing a game of "if" and had very little else to go on.

The moment their waitress was out of earshot, Ryder picked up the thread. "Why do you think Shayne's in trouble?"

"She was part of my ten o'clock practice and she seemed okay throughout. But at the end, she asked to talk to me, and she was crying." Arden walked him through the things Shayne had shared. The strange way Rick had recoiled from her touch and the mysterious disappearances chalked up to work emergencies.

Ryder listened throughout, offering little response beyond head nods, but in his focused attention Arden recognized a shared commitment to keeping her friend safe. Even with his doubts, he didn't jump to conclusions or make assumptions.

Their waitress returned with their orders, setting down heaping plates of enchiladas for her and a burrito for him, and headed off to deal with the busy lunch crowd. Ryder's laser-sharp gaze hadn't wavered through Arden's recounting of her conversation and was equally as pointed after their waitress was out of earshot.

"Does Shayne have any family here?" Ryder asked. "Anyone you can encourage her to go to?"

"I'm not sure. I know she's referenced siblings before but I'm not sure if they're in The Pass or not. She moved back here a few years ago. She's a consultant and came here to set up her business. She's said a few times that she liked it here because she'd lived here as a kid."

"Where did she move back from?"

"I'm not sure. East Texas, I think. Or maybe even Louisiana."

"Do you know her well enough to convince her to go to her family for a few weeks? Get out of here and away from Statler's reach."

Out of his reach?

Whatever Arden had believed after her conversation that morning with Shayne, the immediacy of Ryder's reaction still left her unsettled. "You think she's in that much danger?"

"I think she could be. Especially if she really is clueless to all that's going on. And Statler's disappearance, based on what Shayne told you, coincides with Tris's murder."

Although their ranch hand hadn't been far from her thoughts for days, the reminder of his death slapped her back to reality with a swift emotional punch. "You think he did that? You believe he was the one to kill Tris?"

"I think we have to consider him a suspect. Especially if he's disappearing at odd times and flinching away from Shayne as if hurt."

"Could Tris have hurt him? Maybe he got some punches in at his attacker in self-defense."

"It's hard to say. The body didn't show any signs of trauma, and despite what the movies want you to think, punching a full-size man with any level of force leaves a mark on the one throwing the punch." Ryder lifted his fork and knife to cut into his burrito. "I still don't like the timing."

Arden dug into her own lunch, the rich scents of cheese and sauce wafting up to her as she put a small bite on her fork. It was only as a second thought hit that her fork clattered against her plate. "Do you think he killed someone else later in the weekend, when Shayne said he was gone?"

"I don't know what to think. But at this point, I'm not willing to rule anything out."

Ryder followed behind Arden the entire drive back to Midnight Pass. Although he struggled with the increasing urge to put distance between them to avoid putting her in harm's way by association, he couldn't bear to let her out of his sight.

The rest of their lunch had passed by with minimal

conversation. She'd left him much to think about as he tried to objectively assess Statler's purported actions and the question of Shayne Erickson's guilt or innocence. His zeroing in on Tris's death had obviously left her shaken as well. And after she'd connected Rick's second disappearance with the idea of another possible death, she'd lost her appetite.

Ryder had wolfed down the rest of his lunch while she moved food around on her plate and then had escorted her out of the restaurant. Under better circumstances he had every expectation the food would be amazing, but he still couldn't quite remember what he'd eaten or how it had even tasted.

So here they were. One more red flag between them that suggested a relationship was the last thing he should be thinking about.

Because Statler had seen them together.

And Arden was a friend of Shayne's.

And Ryder hoped like hell he could keep them both safe.

It was only when she turned off for the road that would take her back to Reynolds Station that Ryder beelined back into town. Although he was pushing a line talking to people outside the Bureau about federal business, he needed support. Someone he could trust.

He figured Belle Granger Reynolds could give him both in spades.

It was only five minutes later, after being directed to her office, that he began to rethink the impulse. He stood just outside her closed office door and heard the distinct sounds of retching from the other side. Since the front desk had already announced him, he could hardly leave, so he tapped gently on the door.

"Come in." The words were faint and matched the even fainter visage that greeted him once he walked in.

He had a split second to check his words before he opted for the honesty he'd come expecting in return. As soon as the door clicked shut behind him, Ryder asked, "How long have you been pregnant?"

"Not sure." Belle shot a miserable, glassy-eyed gaze toward the trash can as if considering a return visit. "I'm a newlywed. I have a lot of sex."

"Does your husband know?"

"About the sex?" she shot back, deadpan. "I'd hope so since he's been the beneficiary of it all."

"I mean the baby."

She shook her head, the motion only making her skin go an even pastier shade of ghostly white. "I was going to tell Tate tonight because I took a pregnancy test at lunch. Which came back positive by the way. But as of right now, no one knows."

"I'll keep it to myself."

"If this keeps up, it won't matter. Everyone in a twenty-five-mile radius will know."

"That's some powerful morning sickness."

He got a wan smile for that one. "The sickness will confirm it to my immediate family. My immediate family will confirm it to anyone who will listen in the surrounding county. Good news travels fast and all."

"You looked okay this morning?"

"The problem seems to sneak up on me at lunch. Every morning I want to eat whatever I can get my hands on. And every day for a week the thought of lunch has had me doing this. I thought it was a stomach bug and then the stress of Tris's death and then the lightbulb finally went on this morning."

Ryder figured the worst was behind her when she pulled a sleeve of crackers from her desk drawer and gestured toward him. "Would you like one?"

"I'm good." He considered mentioning the burrito he had for lunch, then thought better of it as the mention of any type of food beyond the dry, square cracker she nibbled could possibly set her off again. "I had lunch with Arden."

"Oh?"

The twin lights of interest and speculation bloomed across her face before he cut her off. "I need some help and I wasn't sure where else to go."

Belle's pretty blue eyes narrowed as angry heat fired away the ghostly pallor of her cheeks. "You want to know something, talk to Arden yourself."

"Stand down, Mama Bear. I did talk to Arden. That's why I'm here. On a professional matter."

The heat remained high in her cheeks and Ryder took some small relief that her unintended confusion over his visit might have pushed the nausea toward the back of her mind. "What's up?"

"I need a confidante. A professional one."

"Because of my sister-in-law?" When he only nodded, she gestured him to sit down. "Then catch me up."

Ryder shared all Arden had told him about Shayne's concerns and upset after yoga class. He deliberately waited until the end of the telling to share his own mounting suspicions about Statler. But the methodical detective beat him to the punch.

"That's a lot of time Statler's unaccounted for this weekend," she said.

"Which only adds to my suspicions."

"Rightfully so. The county coroner's backed up and

we don't have an ETA on when he'll get to Tris. We can pull in a local doctor who'll consult on cases for us. I can go that route."

"Gunshot wound's pretty straightforward." He could imagine the body where it lay on Reynolds property. Even more distressing, he could imagine Arden coming up on that scene all by herself, discovering a valued member of their ranch family taken down in cold blood.

Sweat broke out down his back, cold and clammy fingers crawling over his spine. For all he'd seen in his career, both in person and through textbooks and classes, hadn't prepared him for the raw, pulsing fear that gripped him each time he thought about her finding the body.

Whether Statler was ultimately at fault remained to be seen, but someone had perpetrated a sick and twisted crime on Reynolds land. And Arden had been far too close to it for comfort.

Especially his.

Belle's matter-of-fact approach pulled him back to their conversation. "The gunshot wound is the argument my boss made as well. Autopsy or no, the case is rather straightforward. But it wouldn't hurt to have some examination of Tris's extremities. Any visible struggles or defensive maneuvers. And I'd prefer a tox screen sooner versus later. I can't and won't shut this case simply because you have a theory or the town wants to wrap things quickly."

"I wouldn't want you to, either."

"There's always a possibility Tris got into it with another hand. Or someone down at one of the local watering holes on Saturday night."

Ryder waited a few beats before pressing his advantage. "But you don't think so."

"No. I don't." She tapped her index finger on the desk. "He was seen in the bunkhouse as late as nine that night and Arden found him a little before seven the next morning. And your theory explains a lot, too. Why the scene was so clean. Efficient, really."

"Cold and clinical is how I'd put it."

"I've been over and over the pictures and you're on to something with that. Whoever did that to Tris, did it in cold calculation. There was no emotion and certainly no visible motive other than ending a life." Belle leaned forward. "And based on what you're telling me, if this bastard is trying to divert attention from himself, what better way to do it than to get everyone else distracted around him?"

"Once again, Detective, you're reinforcing all the reasons I came to visit."

Belle sat back, the warm smile that seemed to define her nowhere in sight. "And now my sister-in-law is in the thick of it all. Tate's whole family, really." Her eyes grew distant as her lips thinned to a straight line. "And with a baby on the way."

"Two babies, as it were." Ryder moved closer, leaning over the desk to lay a hand over hers. "I'm sorry for bringing this trouble to your door. More than I can say."

"I know. And I'd like nothing more than to see my family put all of this behind them. But this blight? This horrible, terrible affront to our way of life? It won't go anywhere if we don't do something."

"Spoken like a true warrior."

She tapped the crackers. "And a mother who is determined to bring her child into a place far better than the one I can offer right now."

Ryder knew there'd be hell to pay if he was wrong

or had even slightly miscalculated Rick Statler's character or behavior. It was a risk—one that he'd already accepted—because there was no way he was rolling the dice on this and hoping like hell his boss was a good guy.

The Reynolds family deserved better. Hell, the entire Bureau deserved better.

He'd made a vow to work for the betterment of society. For the good of people and country. And as restitution for Pete's death. Anyone who dared to violate that, for any reason, was enemy number one.

"You'll help me?" Ryder asked Belle.

"I will. Best as I can tell, there's only one thing to do." Conviction laced every syllable. "We need to set a trap."

Arden had spent the better part of the afternoon helping out in the field with Ace, Tate and Hoyt. She'd come back from lunch with Ryder restless and frustrated and knew she wouldn't find the solace she was looking for in another yoga practice on a mat in her room.

The work had done what she'd hoped—it had tired the muscles and gave her some blessed hours in the sunshine—and it was only now that they rode back toward the stables that Arden found some small sense of equilibrium. Hoyt rode beside her, his clothes gritty with dirt and his hair stuck up at odd angles all over his head from where his fingers had tunneled through all afternoon.

"Are babies supposed to be this hard to wait for?"

Arden couldn't hold back the smile as she turned to her brother. "You're excited to meet him or her. Of course it's hard to wait for."

"I know everyone's upset about Tris and I'm upset, too. But no matter how much I try to tamp it down, I can't sit still. I feel like Christmas morning and the day before the SAT tests and my birthday all rolled into one."

"Anticipation and fear." She leaned over and patted him on his knee. "A potent combination. And one that you shouldn't tamp down on just because of Tris. He was a good man and we're going to find out who did this. We're going to catch the bastard."

Hoyt shook his head. "I like the sound of that. Implacable and lethal. A combination I've always been able to get behind."

Her brother was a former member of Special Ops, so she figured that was one the highest compliments he could give.

"And we will find the person responsible," Hoyt added.

"We will. I know we will."

"Even with all that's going on. I had no idea I could be this happy."

Arden studied her brother, from the dazed look that filled his green eyes to the lopsided grin to the giddy set of his body, still active and excited and seemingly unfazed by a full day of strenuous labor.

She couldn't say where the words came from. Whether it was the simple joy she saw hovering around him and beaming from within—something she'd not seen before Reese had come into his life—she had no idea. But a small part of her—the quiet part she didn't give a lot of space to—even wondered if it might be hope. And then the words were out, springing forth with all the memories she couldn't hide from any longer.

"I remember that. How excited I was to have the baby. How I could picture him or her in my arms, their small fingers curled around mine. It's hope, Hoyt. And it's joyful and wonderful and absolutely life-affirming in every way."

Her brother came to a halt, pulling gently on Stinkbug's reins and reaching for Marigold's to slow them both. Once they were at a complete stop, the horses' training so innate they both understood the requirement to wait, Hoyt focused on her fully. "What's this now?"

"I remember that happiness. Somewhere along the way I buried it or just plain forgot it in the pain of what came after, but I remember it." She leaned over and placed her hand over his where they held tight to the reins. "We don't get a lot of moments in our lives to simply be joyful. You need to take this. With both hands and hold on to it. Hold on to Reese. And hold on to that beautiful baby who will be here before we blink."

"You never talked about it. I mean, I was away when you were dating Dan and then after—" He took a breath. "After I was back everything happened so fast. The stuff with Dad and the ranch, then you guys breaking up and then the baby. It seemed like…" He stopped and laid his hand over hers. "I thought the subject was off the table. I didn't ask you about it out of respect for your feelings. And now I realize that was wrong."

"No. No it wasn't. The subject *was* off the table. For a long time. And I don't know. I've been thinking a lot lately. About that time. About the way all our lives are changing. About you having a baby. I'm tired of running from the past and being so sad about it all the time."

"Would Ryder Durant have anything to do with that?"

With Tate she might have made a joke or with Ace she might have remained stoic, making sure the eldest Reynolds didn't go all alpha big brother on the situation. With Hoyt things had always been different. The youngest of her three brothers, he was also the one she could confide in. The one she could talk to without fear he'd go racing off to defend her in some way.

Or that he'd only see her as his little sister and not as a fully grown person who could make up their own mind and determine their own life choices.

"Honestly? I'm not sure. He's certainly made an impact in a short time. But I'd like to think I was on my way to understanding and acceptance all on my own."

"Maybe it's why you've even given Durant a chance."

It was a novel thought and one she hadn't considered in all her mental machinations over the past few weeks and months. "You think so?"

"Seeing as how you're as stubborn and pigheaded as the rest of us, I'd say that might be a very real possibility. Haven't you watched me, Tate and Ace fumble around for the past year like a bunch of fools? Fools who couldn't appreciate the relationships sitting right in front of our faces."

She smiled at that, the image of her brothers falling in love, one by one, like life-size dominoes falling to the ground. "Now that you mention it."

"We're deep thinkers, Arden. And we have a stubborn streak the length of the Rio Grande. Sometimes it takes each of us way too long to work through a problem." He patted her hand once more. "As someone who nearly would have missed out if not for the unbelievable good luck of a defective party condom, I'd say make the most of your time with Durant. Give it some time to grow."

"Does Reese know you're telling the broken condom story?"

He tugged the brim of her hat, effectively blocking

her vision. "I'm telling it to you, bozo, not the whole damn town."

She tugged the hat free, allowing it to fall toward her back, still secured by the ties at her throat. "Smart move of you, too."

That same carefree happiness still hovered around him, but something more serious limned Hoyt's features in the late afternoon sun. "I'm not saying an unplanned pregnancy is for everyone and I know Reese and I got lucky the way everything has worked out for us and between us. But all I'm saying is if you have an opportunity to embrace joy—" he leaned in to press a kiss on her cheek "—take it."

Chapter 14

Hoyt's words still loomed large in her mind as Arden came down for dinner.

Embrace joy.

What a profoundly simple thought and one she'd determinedly avoided for years. Like a muscle that hadn't been worked in far too long, the idea of going after what she wanted in matters of the heart filled her with some pain, but the sense of movement and action was a soothing balm.

She'd call Ryder tonight. The weird way they'd left things at lunch required a follow-up anyway and it would be good to talk to him. Share her thoughts. And see where this heat and attraction between them might go.

More than that, to tell him she *wanted* to see where their attraction might go.

Resolved to action, she took the last turn into the family room that sat off the kitchen. They'd always taken turns with the cooking but with Reese's impending delivery everyone had pitched in extra to help out and take any burden off of her. Which made the distinct scents of tomato sauce and garlic bread a surprise as she neared the kitchen.

Hadn't they'd agreed on tacos that morning before everyone headed out in their own direction?

The heaping spread on the table—yep, lasagna, salad and garlic bread—reinforced those hadn't been phantom smells wafting through the living room. And the large take-out bags still visible on the counter from Mama's Trattoria in the next town over filled in the rest of the gaps.

"Who ordered in?" Arden asked as she walked over to peek at the large metal tray of lasagna steaming on the counter.

Reese smiled from her seat at the table. "Ryder did."

"Ryder?" Arden took a full turn away from the counter but didn't see him. "When did he get here?"

Veronica busied herself at the counter, pulling down plates. "About ten minutes ago. With Belle and the food. The two of them want to talk to us."

"Everything okay?" That steady hum of anxiety that had kept her company since the conversation with Shayne ratcheted up a few beats. "Did they say anything?"

"I'm not sure what's going on." Veronica moved to the table and began setting a plate for each seat. "Belle asked us to give her a few minutes to go out to the barn and talk with Tate, and Ryder went with her. She said they'll be right back and we can all talk."

Arden moved to the windows and saw Ryder throwing Murphy's ball. Just as he had that morning, the dog raced across the open lawn with happy barks echoing in his wake. Belle wasn't beside him so whatever was going on with her didn't include Ryder. Still, her curiosity grew.

What had been important enough to include takeout and a family meeting?

Ryder caught sight of her through the window and waved, gesturing her outside. Veronica had already moved up beside her and placed a warm hand on Arden's back. "Go on out. The table's set and I can put out a few water glasses."

Embrace joy.

"Thanks." Impulsively, she pulled Veronica close in a tight hug, then stopped where Reese sat at the table, dropping down and wrapping her arms around her sister-in-law's shoulders. With a quick kiss on Reese's forehead, she stood back up and headed for the door.

The fresh scents of March greeted her. They were far enough south in Texas that even though spring didn't officially begin for a few more weeks, new life had begun to scent the air. The trees had the evidence of new shoots and the grass was soft under her feet as she tromped over to Ryder and Murphy.

"Hi." She didn't hesitate. Didn't wait. She simply went up on her toes, wrapped her arms around his shoulders and pulled him in for a kiss.

He responded in kind, placing his free hand around her in a tight hold while he held the one dirtied by Murphy's ball out to the side. His lips were cool from the early evening breeze that whipped around them, but quickly warmed under the heated welcome.

When he finally lifted his head, Ryder's dark eyes flashed in the dying light. "Hi yourself."

Murphy nipped around her heels and Arden bent down to give him a proper greeting as well. She rubbed his ears and ran her hands down over his back before dropping a kiss to his head. "Hello to you, too, sweet boy."

Ryder's gaze drifted over his faithful companion. "He's a goner, too."

Arden stood back up and took the ball from Ryder, tossing it for Murphy. He was already off like a shot before the ball had left her hand and raced toward the far side of the paddock where she'd lobbed his slobbery toy.

"Is that what you are? A goner?"

"I am." The cheeky smile that she so associated with him faded a bit, his eyes growing serious to match. "I think I've been a goner since that day outside the coffee shop. All that self-righteous fury I'd leave my dog tied to a post outside did me in."

Arden remembered that day, too. She'd walked to the coffee shop after closing up her studio and had found Murphy sitting outside, tied to a pole. Although he looked well cared for and could hardly have been left roaming the sidewalk while Ryder ran inside, something had stuck in her gut. Was it that Murphy had been alone? Left behind?

She had no idea, but Ryder's cocky smile as he'd come back outside with his coffee had only added to the moment, adding to her confused fury. "That wasn't very kind of me. I can see how well Murphy is cared for."

"Now you can. You couldn't at the time. It stuck with me, you know. That ready defense." He moved in close once more. "You don't particularly care for it when people come to your defense but you're always quick to support and protect others."

"My flying off the handle is attractive?" She settled a hand on his chest and stared up into his eyes.

"It is." He leaned down and pressed a kiss to her forehead. "The care you have for others. You feel a responsibility and you act. It's powerful, Arden. Compelling." He added one more kiss. "And yes, wildly attractive."

Tate's and Belle's twin voices floated toward them as they came out of the barn. They were entwined together, her arm around his waist and his around her shoulders—their usual position when they were together—and Arden took heart from the clear support they offered one another. It hadn't been this way always—far from it. They'd nearly missed this, their own stubborn focus on fighting what was between them keeping them apart for far too long.

To look at Tate and Belle now, all that had vanished as if the past had vanished, too.

It was something to think about, she mused, as she, Ryder and Murphy followed them into the house. Maybe your past didn't have a hold on your present or future.

Or maybe an even better notion. It didn't *have* to.

Ryder felt the change in Arden down to his marrow. The warm woman who'd greeted him outside had changed somehow. She was still Arden, of course, but something was different. She was settled in a way he'd never seen before.

Settled in a way that made him think this was the old Arden, trying to resurface. Before whatever it was that had sent her curling inside herself, living half a life. Back before she'd been hurt beyond reason.

Her teasing about their initial meeting hadn't been far from the truth and his memory of the moment was genuine. Despite her ready skepticism of him, she'd been a vision to behold. Her defense of his dog and Murphy's safety had impressed him from the very first words they'd spoken.

Of course, he hadn't minded the view, either. She was

clad in one of her yoga confections, a bright, vivid spot of color on an admirably sunny day. But she'd been all he could see. He'd gone on the defensive at her hostile tone, but had still felt that sly, stealthy attraction bubbling and brewing underneath. It had only grown stronger in the ensuing months, their brief introduction at New Year's on the town square reinforcing his attraction and then the past few weeks with her and her family.

He was interested.

More than interested, if he were honest with himself. Despite the bad timing and the deeply concerning issues at work, he wanted her. Physically, yes, but also in a way that went well beyond the carnal.

He wanted her in his life. With him, building a family together.

Just like the examples he saw all around him.

Tate and Belle walked into the house in front of them and, based on the near bouncing of Tate in his thick cowboy boots, he could only guess Belle had shared their pregnancy news out in the barn. What must that feel like? To know that the love you had for someone could actually make a tiny new human. That you'd welcome that life together, with a shared vision of the future.

He gestured Arden through the door before him and watched the graceful sway of her hips as she walked through. He was jumping the gun, of course, thinking about babies and forever.

But even as he attempted to squelch the thoughts, he couldn't erase the warm feelings that settled deep inside.

The idea of marriage and fatherhood had always lived in the distant future somewhere. Was it possible that time was becoming a distinct possibility? That attraction had finally sprouted into something beyond the physical? A glance at Arden and then, further, around the room to take in her assembled family had the distinct notes of *yes* forming in his mind.

And his heart.

"Mama's Trattoria?" Ace asked as he strode into the kitchen, beelining for his wife. "What's all the good food for?"

"Ryder and I have called a family meeting," Belle answered from where she still stood, safely captured beneath Tate's arm.

"You know what this is about?" Ace asked his brother. When all he got was Tate's bewildered, dumbfounded smile his gaze shifted to Ryder. "Does anyone?"

"I think I do," Ryder said, his tone easy, "but why don't we get some dinner and then we can talk."

Arden shot him a curious look but didn't say anything, just did as he'd asked, helping herself to the feast spread out on the counter. Heaping portions of pasta and salad loaded with garlic and vinegar were passed and paired and in minutes everyone had a plate and was seated at the table. Ryder kept a careful watch on Tate, amused when the man nearly dumped his can of soda on his salad instead of extra dressing.

Yep. Belle had definitely told him about the baby.

Once they were all seated, Reese surprised them by speaking first. "I love a good mystery as much as the next person, but since I'm liable to pop at any minute, can you end the suspense?"

Ryder nodded at Belle, his silent communication— *this is your show*—accepted with a subtle nod in return.

"Tate and I have some news."

Belle's smile was soft and warm and overwhelmingly maternal but it was Tate's bellow that brought home the joy and happiness her announcement in the barn had created. "I'm going to be a father!"

The curiosity that had captured everyone gave way to whoops and cries as everyone stood back up from the table, quick to offer hugs and happy, heartfelt congratulations. Ryder took his turn, hugging Belle and slapping Tate on the back, unwilling to let it break that he'd already been privy to the news.

Even if Arden's sharp gaze suggested she wasn't fooled. A point proven once they all sat back down. She leaned in, her breath warm against his ear, when she said, "Innocent face or not, you're not getting off the hook that easy, Durant."

"I wouldn't expect to." He shifted before she could, planting a quick kiss on her lips. The move was enough to bring the smile back into her eyes, a point she reinforced by laying a hand on his knee and squeezing.

There *was* something there.

A lot of something, he acknowledged to himself. Which made the second part of their dinner—and the other news he and Belle needed to impart—that much harder to bear.

By unspoken agreement, he and Belle allowed the talk of babies and nurseries and the proper age their child needed to be to get a puppy dominate the meal. It was only as the plates were cleared and the coffeepot turned on that Ryder felt that hand on his knee once more.

Arden spoke up. "You two play a mean game of poker, but I think it's time to tell us the other reason for dinner."

"Tell them, Belly," Tate nodded, encouraging. "They need to know."

Belle leaned in and pressed a kiss to her husband's

cheek before turning her attention to Ryder. "It's the good agent's case. Let's let him fill you in."

Arden fought wave after wave of emotion as she listened to Ryder's recounting of all that had happened since they'd left each other at lunch. The suspicions about Rick Statler. The perceived danger for Shayne Erickson. The plan Ryder and Belle had hatched to bring it all into the light.

And a baby in the midst of it all.

Her brother was going to be a father. From the expression on Tate's face—wide-open and full of emotion—it was clear he was still processing the news. From wild excitement to rawboned terror to a sort of overall bewilderment that twisted her heart into a gooey knot.

All in the midst of talk of betrayal and the very real potential for violence.

It was madness to think of drawing Rick Statler out in the open. And, she surmised as Ryder recapped the situation, their only option.

While it was easy to assume from Belle's life's work that she had a love of danger and putting her life on the line, Arden knew it for the wrong assumption. Her sister-in-law believed in the rule of law and the importance of rooting out crime wherever it might lurk.

How stunning to realize that, once again, it seemed to lurk around Reynolds Station.

"You both seem to think this is the only course of action. To draw Statler out." Ace looked first at Ryder, then at Belle. "There's no other way? No way you can't get the venerable FBI to police its own?"

She wanted to take Ace's side—how easy it would be to

make this all someone else's problem—but she couldn't. This was *their* problem. Their land. Their danger.

Theirs to handle.

Which meant that ignoring it was not only futile, but it was a betrayal of what they'd vowed to each other so many years before. This was their land and they'd protect it.

Ryder was simply caught in the middle.

"Not if they don't know how deep the betrayal goes."

Everyone turned to look at Arden, but it was Ryder who captured her sole focus in return.

"You think that's what's going on here?" Ace volleyed back. "A conspiracy."

"I think we have to take Ryder's professional assessment that sharing this news is dangerous. Just like Statler," Arden added for good measure.

Hoyt spoke before Ace could. His interference meant more to Arden than she could say, especially since his position up to now had been solely focused on his wife and child. "How can anyone know if he's got allies in the Bureau? Even if he's acting alone, there's no way we can fully rule it out."

"My father acted alone," Reese spoke, her hand covering Hoyt's. "And he did an immeasurable amount of damage. I can't imagine how much worse it would have been if he'd had a partner. Or a team behind him."

Reese's willingness to go there—to talk about the sins of her father—was enough to shift the tone at the table. And when Ace next spoke, some of the bluster had left his demeanor. "Do you have any reason, at this point, to think Statler is working with someone?"

"No, I don't. Other than the possibility that Shayne Erickson is his conduit on the outside."

At the quick upset around the table, each of Arden's

sisters-in-law decrying the idea that Shayne could be involved, Ryder held up a hand, looking at each woman in turn. "That right there. That defense of her. It goes a long way in the plus column. But we can't rule it out. Even if she's not intentionally involved, Statler may be using her computer and network when he's at her home to access his contacts."

"And you've got absolutely no one at the Bureau who can help you?" Tate asked.

"There is one person I can reach out to for help. I've been hesitant to drag anyone else in, but I think it's time to call for some reinforcement."

"Noah Ross?" Belle asked immediately.

Arden vaguely remembered mention of the man who'd held Ryder's job during the crisis with Reese's father the prior year. Belle had spoken highly of the agent and the man had come to Reynolds Station a few times asking questions.

"He knows The Pass and he knows the Bureau," Ryder said. "Most of all, I trust him."

"Where is he now?" Now that she knew his return was of interest, Arden couldn't help wondering where the man had gone.

"He was given a promotion and moved to Dallas last year. That's what opened the spot for me in The Pass."

Belle's gaze grew sharp. "Ross is good so I've no doubt he's qualified, but who gave him the promotion?"

"The top brass, I'd assumed." Ryder stilled. "Or do you think that his promotion was engineered?"

"A little bit of both, maybe? What if we—"

Tate laid a hand on Belle's shoulder before she could finish her thought. "I think you and Durant have a phone call to make. We'll clean up here."

"Are you sure?"

Tate reached out and laid a hand on Belle's stomach before leaning in and pressing his forehead to hers. "We've got a lot to look forward to. Let's catch this bastard and put it all behind us."

Without considering her actions, Arden reached out and took Ryder's hand, resting their joined fingers against her knee. "I'm with Tate. Do what you need to."

Ryder's focus on her was absolute. "Once we do this, I can't go back."

"Then we'll deal with what comes."

Ryder's hand tightened on hers. "Even if I'm wrong, I can't change it."

"Then we'll still deal with what comes." She leaned in and pressed her forehead to Ryder's, the gesture similar to her brother's. "But Tate's right. This needs to end."

They barely knew each other, their time together limited to some of the most volatile days of her life. Yet even with that knowledge, Arden knew she'd follow Ryder Durant into hell and back.

Knew even more that he'd do the same for her.

That was what she needed to hold on to. That somehow, some way, this good man had been brought into their lives. In the midst of turmoil and upheaval, he was the one in a position to help them.

Ryder pressed a kiss to her lips before standing and following Belle from the room to make their call. And as Arden watched them go, she knew something else.

She would give him whatever help he needed in return. She'd ensure her family did the same.

Because despite her best efforts at resistance, Ryder Durant had increasingly breached every defense she possessed.

Chapter 15

Ryder climbed the stairs to the upper floor of the ranch house, moving in the direction of Arden's rooms. Reese had sleepily given him directions from her perch on the couch, Murphy curled up at her side, while her feet settled on a huge ottoman. Everyone else had remained in the kitchen, lingering over coffee and the Italian cream cake Belle had ordered on a whim as they were buying dinner.

Only Arden had disappeared.

Ryder had been unsure if it was an invitation to join her until Veronica had suggested Arden's disappearance had been to give Shayne Erickson a call under the guise of setting a lunch date.

So here he was, navigating his way through the surprisingly large ranch house, working his way toward the wing that belonged to Arden.

She'd spoken before of how she and her brothers had

crafted a life together and had been clear that one of the reasons they'd made it work was because they took care to have space that was their own. Looking at it now, he could see what she meant. Although they came together at meals and during key points in the day, they also had their space. An area to call their own.

And enough room to maintain their individuality even while they proved over and over that they were a tight unit.

He'd had that. Or believed he had when he'd joined the Bureau. It had been his crowning achievement after he'd vowed to make something out of Pete's loss. Only the suspicions over Statler had put a hole deep in those beliefs. They'd blown straight through what he understood about the camaraderie and commitment of his fellow team members.

And painted good men and women with the brushstrokes of doubt.

Without warning, exhaustion washed over him, like a rogue wave on the beach. One moment he had his footing and the next he felt ready to drop from the weight and the pressure, with no hope of ever regaining his balance.

No hope of standing upright on the shore, ever again.

He stood before a partially opened door, the subtle strains of music floating from the depths of the room. Arden sat on a couch in an outer area obviously used as a sitting room, her legs curled up and her phone on her lap, her blue gaze lost in thought as she focused on something across the room.

That gaze drifted toward him and she beckoned him in with a welcome smile. "You found me."

"Reese gave good directions, but even with them, this

is quite a place." He slipped into the room, extending a hand to the doorknob. "May I close this?"

"Yes, please do."

Ryder looked around, the space a mix of what he would have expected of Arden's private quarters and also wildly different than he could have conjured up in his mind. The beige overstuffed couch she currently sat on, with the fluffy, multicolored throw pillows was exactly what he'd imagined. The abstract art displayed on a solid purple wall behind her, not so much.

Yet, somehow, it worked.

Sort of like her. She could be the earth mother yoga instructor, the accomplished horsewoman or the business owner of one of the most successful ranches in Texas. All were her.

And still, like that abstract art, he got the sense that he'd never stop seeing new things each time he looked at her.

"I talked to Shayne."

"Oh?"

"I feel bad. I suggested I was interested in hiring her consulting services for an upgrade to my business network."

Ryder took the seat next to Arden, maintaining a respectful distance. He had the oddest remembrance that he hadn't sat this far away from a woman since the night he picked up Deb Forney for the junior prom. They'd ended up a lot closer as the night wore on, but with her parents in the same room at the start of the evening, he'd felt equally as awkward then as he did now.

Was it because Arden's family was just downstairs?

Ignoring the strange stabbing memory of lingering

teenage embarrassment, he tried to focus on the conversation. "Is that what she does?"

"Yep. That's why she has the flexibility to take my daytime sessions. She works for herself and is doing quite well from what I gather. She's even set up shop in a new business development a few towns over."

"Good for her."

"Once she gets going on bits and bytes and packets and upload-download speeds, I sort of zone out, but she and one of my other regulars talk about all of it often. He's a recent retiree from communications engineering and seems excited to have someone to talk shop with."

An image of the woman he'd met Friday night filled in the gaps in his mind. As he'd observed, Shayne had been keenly aware of the conversation, but admittedly he'd kept his focus on Statler and the determined way he and Rick had verbally circled one another. Like Arden, Shayne had attempted to defuse the situation with polite chitchat and social niceties.

Which further indicated she was aware of the tension.

It was only now that he thought about it that he considered Arden's description of Shayne's work. "So she's good at networked communications. Computers and mobile phones, too?"

"I suppose." Arden stopped and tapped her mobile against her thigh. "Come to think of it, yeah, she is. She and Ted talk about that stuff regularly as we're warming up and waiting for everyone to arrive."

"Which means she could be helping Statler."

"Or she could be totally unaware her rat of a boyfriend is using her stuff."

Once again, Arden's defense was at the ready. Although he couldn't fully turn off his training, that complete and absolute defense of her friend gave some weight to the Shayne-Erickson-is-innocent column. "That, too."

She exhaled a heavy sigh before shifting to face him more fully on the couch. "Okay. For the sake of fairness, let's play it out both ways."

"Innocent caught in the crossfire and helping hand giving Statler the access he needs?" Ryder asked.

"Yeah. Those." Arden tapped her phone again before setting it aside on a nearby end table. "What could he access through her systems he couldn't get at work?"

"Not a hell of a lot. Personal communications but that's about all. Any authentication into work tools, even from a personal device, is logged and tracked."

"So she can't be involved." Arden's smile was triumphant.

"I wouldn't say that."

"Prove it to me then."

"There's a lot of damage Statler could do on devices not registered to himself. Everything from basic contact with a piece of scum to drawing on an extensive network via social channels. There's been a lot of work to crack down there but I know our e-team is overworked. And the bad behavior happening in social channels is incredibly hard to police."

"Because there's so much of it?" she asked.

"That and because it changes constantly."

"Okay. What else then?"

"Statler's been trained in all the counterterrorism exercises we all are. Ways to hide intel online. Ways to use public programs to hide nefarious deeds. Too much of this crap is out in public view."

"All of which he could be using Shayne's devices to manipulate."

"I suppose. Now. I've got a question for you." Although he truly appreciated her ready defense of her friend, Ryder couldn't leave the subject alone. "You mean to tell me a woman who makes her living on computer networks wouldn't know if someone was messing in hers?"

"What reason would she have to look?"

At his sudden silence, his mind whirling with Arden's supposition, she moved closer and rested a hand on his knee.

"Come on, Ryder, think about it. They're dating and totally into one another. He makes some comment like he has to check his email or quickly log into work for something. Would you think otherwise?"

"Maybe." At her skeptical stare, he relented slightly. "I guess not. But at the same time, you run a business. Would you let someone on your work systems?"

"To do something innocuous like respond to an email? Of course I would. It's easy. Simple." Her gaze roamed around the room before she seemed to settle on her point. "It's like offering someone a drink of water or allowing them to use the restroom. It's so average and normal there'd be no reason to give it another thought."

Ryder laid his head back against the couch, his eyes drifting closed as he considered her arguments. And she'd made some damn good ones. He wanted Shayne Erickson to be innocent. For the woman's own sake as well as Arden's. Only the longer he sat in that room with the vivid purple wall and the even more vivid woman who'd decorated it, he couldn't keep his attention focused on the problem at hand.

Or hold back the sheer exhaustion that had come of

wondering what sort of viper had nested in the office down the hall from him.

"Does it matter right now?" The mumbled thought was out before he could stop it, but it was the soft hand that drifted from his knee to his arm that kept him steady.

Grounded.

And suddenly, desperately hopeful that she felt as much as he did.

Opening his eyes, he found hers searching his. And in them he saw the truth.

He'd fallen hard. Harder than he'd even realized until that moment. And this was the woman he not only wanted, but that he'd been waiting for.

"I care about you, Arden. More than I can say. And if you're not ready for this, or for us, I can handle it. But I think about you. How it could be between us."

"I think about that, too." The hand on his arm drifted closer until it lay pressed against his heart. "I want to be with you, Ryder. I want you to make love with me."

He laid his hand over hers, where her palm still nestled against his chest. "I want that, too."

That sensation of being washed away hit him once more, only this time Ryder felt it for an entirely different reason.

She was here.

And she was his.

Arden knew the leap she was taking and knew it was as inevitable as taking her next breath. As essential, too. But she wanted him and she wanted to be with him and nothing else seemed to matter. Not the small voice that kept whispering that she'd get hurt. Not the slightly louder voice that pressed at her that she hadn't told Ryder the full truth about her past. About the time she'd carried another man's child.

But it was the biggest voice of all that threatened to pull her under. The one that whispered along her spine with cold fingers, taunting her by saying that she and Ryder had nothing. That they'd come together on a riot of emotion and intense moments because of what he did for a living and for the violence that seemed shockingly persistent at Reynolds Station.

Heat… intensity… emotion. They were a powder keg beneath their smoldering attraction.

Then she looked at him.

And nothing else seemed to matter.

His eyes were dark, his pupils wide with desire, as his gaze searched hers. Even his voice remained as steady as the hands planted on her shoulders. "You're sure this is what you want?"

"Yes."

Her darkened bedroom lay beyond the sitting area, and in a matter of moments, he had her lifted and in his arms, carrying her to the large four-poster that she made faithfully each morning. The soft, butter yellow duvet and flowered pillows should have seemed at odds with the determined masculinity that had suddenly entered her personal domain, yet somehow, he fit.

Just like he'd increasingly begun to fit in her life.

His biceps bunched against her body as he lowered her to the bed before following her down. His lips found hers, firm and seeking as his hands roamed a path down her rib cage. She met his strokes with touches of her own, her hands sweeping over his broad back that was as strong as the chest that lay pressed to hers.

He was so *solid*.

So safe.

She knew so much awaited them outside this room, yet in that moment she could barely conjure up an image of any of it, so lost in him and his touch. So determined to take all she could from this moment.

Suddenly urgent with it, her hands shifted course as she gripped the hem of his shirt and dragged it up, exposing all that amazing warm skin beneath. Branded with the heat of his body and emboldened to continue with the smile that crested against her lips, she pulled up and up before breaking the connection of their mouths by pulling his shirt over his head.

"Anxious to get me out of my clothes?"

She smiled at him as his shirt slipped from her fingers to float somewhere beside the bed and wondered how she'd ever thought that cocky visage hid someone vapid and empty. Oh, how she'd been humbled to learn otherwise.

And how happy she was to have been proven wrong.

"Damn straight, Agent Durant."

His eyebrows winged up. "Are we back to that?"

"Can we be if I tell you it's a turn-on?"

A heavy laugh escaped and he pressed his weight to her before wrapping her up and rolling them so that she lay atop his chest. "Darlin', with that sort of incentive, you can call me anything you want."

Carefree and happy and feeling lighter than she had in years, she settled herself over top of him, balancing her weight so that she cradled his body at the perfect spot. She felt the insistent press of his erection—felt her own body react at the tender pressure—and went to work on her own clothing. Although the material of her workout gear was thinner, the skintight fit ensured a bit of struggle as she tried to wiggle her way out of the top.

"Are you trying to kill me?" His question had determined edges as she heard him grit the last few words between his teeth.

"I'm trying to get naked," she huffed out as she struggled with the skintight top as it stuck to her skin and the light sheen of sweat he'd already helped generate.

"Keep wiggling like that against me and I'm afraid this is going to be a very quick trip."

In a heartbeat, the absurdity of the moment hit her and Arden was helpless to hold back the laughter. Large, rumbling waves of it seemed to start in her stomach and work their way up her chest before blasting out in wondrous hilarity.

"It's not—" Ryder broke off, holding her hips still as he shifted beneath her "—funny." That last word came out on a harsh moan and Arden only laughed harder with the joy of it all.

"Oh, but it is." Shifting to give the poor man a bit of breathing room, she sat beside him on the bed. Her workout tank was halfway up her torso, the material bunching just beneath her breasts in a thick lock of spandex she couldn't quite get undone.

"What are you laugh—" He broke off, a wry smile breaking through. "You a bit stuck there?"

"Yes."

"What will you give me if I get it undone?"

"Last time I checked, it was a willing and naked woman," Arden huffed out as she tried to get a better grip on the bunched material, "but if you leave me like this too much longer I may take the deal off the table."

His eyes narrowed and Arden saw a naughty light

spark in those dark depths. "Now I consider myself a smart man." He ran a finger over her stomach, lightly tracing her muscles so that they contracted on a hard wash of need. Who knew they could be so sensitive? Or that a touch like that could make her nipples ache so suddenly as they pressed against such confining material?

"But I'm not sure I should let you off so easily." That tantalizing finger continued to make circles over her skin before moving determinedly up, circling one of those hardened peaks.

"According to you," Arden breathed out hard as his finger circled once again, "you're the one dangerously close to off."

"Perhaps I was too hasty." With his free hand he took both of hers where they still held the traitorous material and shifted them down, locked in his hold. And with that other hand, he continued that glorious tracing exercise.

Up, over, down, around.

It was a pattern she recognized and in a matter of moments, was able to follow, pressing her body against his with each increasingly sensitive stroke. It was only when his mouth replaced his finger that she thought she'd come off the bed.

Hot, wet heat closed over her, through the material of her gear. What had been too tight and too confining suddenly felt like heaven as he added the heat of his breath all while moving his tantalizing fingers to her other breast.

Lost in the moment—lost in the beauty of what he did to her—Arden felt the last vestiges of fear fall away. Fear she wasn't good enough. Fear this wouldn't last. Fear that this was all the output of a wild stretch of time that would sort itself out or burn itself out—whichever came first.

None of it mattered.

Because even with the prospect of it all falling to ashes, she couldn't help but think she'd found something to rise in its place.

Ryder struggled to keep the needs of his body in check, pushing them to a corner of his mind as he held his full focus on Arden. She was so sweet—so responsive—and all that had come before her faded away to nothingness. With her, he was new.

This was new.

What they made was new.

And he was renewed by it.

Unknowingly, the past few years had taken their toll. The work he did, the people he came in contact with, the death of his friend before he joined the Bureau. Even the relatively new fear that his boss was a raving lunatic with a vendetta against the department and the world.

All of it had left dark spots deep inside of him, most of which he hadn't realized were there.

Only none of it could compete with the woman he held in his arms. The woman who took pleasure from his touch.

The woman who he wanted to be his.

The only woman he'd ever met who could stand against that darkness and wash it away.

It was really that simple. For all that he'd been through and all that he'd seen, she made him new again. And she made what was between them a sort of life-affirming beauty he had no idea until recently he was even missing.

Much as he'd have loved to stay there, pleasuring her mindless, his body had other, more urgent ideas. Levering himself up, he gripped the sides of her workout shirt and easily pulled it from her body, freeing her breasts to his gaze. A rosy hue shaded her chest and he saw her arousal matched his own.

"Now that wasn't so hard." He gazed down at her, looking his fill, before she shot back as he knew she would.

"Easy for you to say. You weren't the one tied up in polyester."

"Tied up, you say?" He nipped at her jaw with quick kisses. "Are you suggesting something, Ms. Reynolds?"

"As if," she snorted.

The response was exactly what he was looking for and he snagged her from her comfortable perch beside him on the bed until she was pressed beneath him. "Who's got the high ground, now?"

She smiled up at him, her mutinous expression turning thoughtful.

Unbearably smitten by the soft look that had come into her eye, he tapped a lone finger gently against her forehead. "What's going on in there?"

"I didn't know sex could be like this. Easy banter and sexy talk and—" She broke off, slight little lines furrowing over her eyebrows. "And, well, fun."

Although he had little regard for her slimy ex, the sheer wonder in her tone had Ryder thinking the man should have been tied up and flayed for his inability to satisfy this woman as she deserved.

"I mean, I know it's fun. And it's way better than a root canal. But I didn't know. I mean—" Arden broke off and blew out a light stream of breath. "I didn't know you could talk through it. And enjoy it all at the same time."

Even more charmed by her than he could have expected—and he'd expected a lot—Ryder stilled and laid a hand against her cheek. "When it's with the right person every bit of it's good."

"Yes." She smiled, laying a hand against his jaw in a move that mimicked his. "It's all good."

Whether it was the quiet after the laughter or the simple fact that their desire had peaked once more, that tender moment shifted as both of them were gripped with a renewed urgency. Her hands shifted to the opening of his slacks, flipping the button and slipping the zipper down until he felt her hand take firm hold of his body.

Stars winged through his mind as he fought to hold on against the onslaught of pleasure brought on by her firm grip and he quickly laid a hand over hers to still her movement.

"You really are trying to kill me."

"You say the sweetest things."

"I do even sweeter ones."

Before she could even think to answer him, he slid from her mind-bending grip, then moved with speed down the length of the bed. He freed himself from the last bits of his clothes before reaching for her. In one swift move he had her workout pants and panties in his grip, dragging both down her legs in one long, efficient swoop of material.

He resettled himself over her and it was only at the last minute that he remembered a condom was in the back pocket of his slacks, nestled in his wallet and hopefully awaiting use. It might be dumb to project his desire on an inanimate object, but he'd done it all the same as he'd placed the condom there the prior week after spending time with Arden.

She registered his movements as he began to slide

back down the bed, capturing his shoulders. "Side drawer." She tilted her head. "A recent addition."

Ryder reached over as directed toward the bedside table, sweetly amused by the blush that suffused her neck and rose up over her cheeks. It was only when his hand closed over the box that he added, "I could say the same about the recent addition to my wallet."

"You planned, too?"

"I hoped." He pressed a kiss to her lips. "Fervently."

"Then what are we waiting for?" Her hand closed over his, tearing one of the small foil packets off the strip from the box before he tossed the rest in the direction of the end table.

In moments she had the condom rolled over his body and had shifted, welcoming him to that warm, waiting place between her thighs. "I need you, Ryder. Now."

All his plans to make this last were tossed aside in the riptide of need caused by those simple words. By the sheer desire as she spoke his name. And as she pressed upward beneath him, taking him even deeper into her body, he was lost.

Absolutely lost to her.

Yet as he began to move, Ryder realized the truth.

It was only in the lost that he'd been found.

Chapter 16

Arden shifted, her eyes popping open at the realization that she'd rolled into a solid wall of male perfection. Her mind went on instant alert, even as her body willfully snuggled in closer, still sated and warm from a night spent with Ryder.

Her face had seemingly been taken over as well.

Her mouth was creased in a huge smile, which, if she were anywhere close to a mirror, would likely register both cat-n-cream satisfaction and sheer, mindless happiness.

Good heavens, the man had been a revelation.

She'd had sex since she'd been with Dan. Not as much as she'd told herself she *should* be having, but she'd had pleasant evenings with men whose company she'd enjoyed. Men who had given her temporary pleasure in the course of dating for a few months. Men who'd been, well… Pleasant.

There was nothing *pleasant* about the way Ryder Durant made love.

Mind-bending, maybe. Aggressively satisfying. No, she dismissed that one. He wasn't a juicy steak she'd dived into with gusto.

Although he had been delicious.

And she melted once more at the memory, entirely respectful of her boundaries. He'd clearly handed her the reins, determined she'd decide how far they'd go last night.

And oh, where they had gone.

Pops of electricity went off beneath her skin as she remembered his hands moving over her. Soft, floating touches at times; solid, firm touches at others. He treated her as if she were precious but not fragile, and until last night she'd never really understood the difference.

Did she ever get it now.

Last night she'd had an equal partner in bed. One who'd enjoyed her company as much as she did his. One who'd pushed them both toward the outer limits of pleasure and beyond.

One who'd loved her so hard she'd woken up with a smile on her face.

That hadn't happened in... Well, ever.

"Is it morning?" His deep husky tones drifted over the top of her head before racing down her spine in a sexy wave.

"Almost. This is a ranch, so I'm afraid to break it to you but everyone here gets up early. But—" her gaze drifted to the small alarm clock she kept on the edge of her dresser "—4:00 a,m. is early even for us."

"You talk like early is a bad thing."

"It can take some getting used to."

"I'm an early riser myself." His hand roamed down her skin, the lightest of touches, but it was a clear telegraph of his affection. "I enjoy getting my day started."

Like a cat preening under tender, steady strokes, she arched into him, her hands heading off on an exploration of their own. Warm skin was firm beneath her fingertips, his muscles tensing with sensitivity beneath her light touches.

For someone who made her living understanding the needs of the human body and how it worked, it still fascinated her to feel how he responded to her. How her own flesh responded in return.

Need, yes. Desire, absolutely. Yet even with all that, there was something else. He was sexually exciting yet she also took away the same sense of comfort she had with her family or offering a hug to friends. How was it possible those things could coexist?

Yet they did. Sexual desire and satisfaction, coupled with the safe and the welcome. With belonging.

"Did I lose you to the Arden Reynolds Method of meditation?"

She heard the smile in his question and couldn't work up much beyond mild curiosity. Especially with all those amazing muscles beneath her hands. "I have a method?"

"A particularly cute one, as a matter of fact."

She shifted so she could look at his face, curiosity warring with the desire to lie there for, oh, about the rest of her life. "What do I do?"

"Your eyes go first."

"My eyes?"

"That blue is so sharp it always makes me think of the sky on a summer day."

"You're being poetic and silly. My eyes are just blue."

"There's no *just* about it. They're sky blue and when you get angry they grow distinctly darker."

Now she did move up on an elbow, curiosity getting the better of her. "You've paid attention to this?"

He leaned in and pressed a kiss to her nose. "I've paid attention to you. All of you."

"So what do you see in my 'sky blue' eyes."

When he only rolled his own eyes at her verbal air quotes she added, "Seriously. What do you see?"

"Like I said. Your eyes go first. They go from focused and sharp to sort of hazy and unfocused. Like you're here but you're not."

She tried to conjure up what he meant but since she was the one apparently day meditating she had no idea what she looked like. Or that she even did it, for that matter. "I'm always here."

"Your body may be but your mind travels places, sweet thing. I've seen it."

"Okay. What about the rest?"

"You take these deep breaths. They're light but it's like something evens out and your breathing keeps the rest of you going while your mind wanders."

"You make it sound like some woo-woo sixties astral projection or something."

"Or something." He leaned in and pressed a quick kiss to her lips. "Where were you?"

"When?"

"A few minutes ago. Your mind was a million miles away."

Lost in thought, she understood. Meditation was a whole other kettle of fish but she felt too good to argue the point. Or even attempt to make a point. Because with all that warm skin and flexing muscle beneath, she was increasingly losing interest in thinking at all.

"You," she finally said, when it became evident he was waiting for an answer. "I was thinking about you."

"I think about you a lot, too. And after last night," he added with a wink, "a lot might be an understatement."

She smiled at that, the same one she'd woken up with, before pressing on. "I was thinking about how easy last night was. How—" She stilled, suddenly realizing he might not want to be compared to family or friends.

That he might want to keep what was between them separate and far from any suggestion of family or permanence.

Wasn't that where things had gone all wrong with Dan?

His eyebrows bunched as that dark gaze narrowed. "How what?"

"Nothing. It's silly and it's nothing."

"I don't think so." The warm, emotional blanket that had enveloped them since waking vanished, replaced with a cool blast of air.

And reality.

They'd slept together one night. And here she was, thinking about things she had no business thinking of. Getting serious about things she had no right to assume.

Something flashed in his narrowed eyes. Although the room was dim, the only light coming from the sitting room where she'd left on the lamp beside the couch, Arden could still see the hurt.

And wondered how she'd managed to snap herself out of her early morning bliss with such shocking efficiency.

"It really is nothing." She kept her voice light and breezy, fighting the urge to roll away until she couldn't hold back any longer. Slipping from beneath his arm, she shifted to the edge of the bed and reached for her thin robe that lay over the footboard. The material didn't cover much but it would offer some protection against the dark eyes that suddenly saw too much.

"Arden?" His voice was low and calm.

She busied herself with tying her robe closed. "Hmm?"

"What are you doing?"

Well aware she couldn't keep a poker face after the stream of emotion that had just whipped its way through her, from satisfaction to near-giddy happiness to awash in misery, Arden grasped at what was handy. "Like I said before. It's a working ranch and we're up early."

"I thought you said 4:00 a.m. was early, even for you?"

"We're up. Might as well get the day going."

She made it all the way across the room when he spoke again. "Was it something I said?"

"Of course not. It's just time to get up."

"Bull."

That lone word hovered in the air between them. His voice had remained low but the whip-quick response had her head snapping back to him with equal force. "Excuse me?"

"You got my meaning."

Tugging on the tie of her robe, she tried not to use the thin material as armor but was desperate enough to grasp at the lone straw she had. "I'm not sure I did."

"No, I think you did." Ryder got out of bed, his naked body haloed by the light spilling in from the sitting room. Arden cursed herself for being at all captivated by his leanly muscled form, especially since she was the fool who'd just leaped out of those sculpted arms.

The even bigger fool who'd believed she could shut down on him and not have him notice.

He stood near her, close yet not touching. Even at that distance she could feel the heat of his body and fought the deep, deep desire to crawl back into his arms and stay there.

"What is happening here?" he asked.

She'd once seen the world-famous bats in Austin take flight from beneath the town bridge. The spectacle had been all she'd been told and more, made even more potent by the swift and immediate power she'd sensed in the air. The initial panic that had fluttered in her chest as she'd realized where her thoughts had been after only one night with Ryder suddenly took on that same shape and form.

Urgent.

Unyielding.

And demanding space to take wing.

"You want to talk bull, Ryder? I'd say you're dangerously close to overplaying your hand. We had a great night. Amazing, if you want to know. But now it's morning and you have a killer to catch and I need to get the hell out of here and start my day."

Arden turned on one bare foot, self-righteous anger propelling her toward her en suite bathroom. She'd nearly made it—had almost crossed the threshold—when that quiet, steady, implacable tone caught her once more.

"What did he do to you?"

She stopped and pressed a hand to the doorway but didn't turn around. "This isn't about anyone else."

"Not anymore. Now it's about you. But before. It was about someone before."

Pain, white-hot and searing tore through her chest, at

odds with the soft, gentle conversation she'd shared with Hoyt as they'd wrapped up work the day before.

Embrace joy.

Hadn't that been her goal? Wasn't that the reason she'd welcomed Ryder to her bed? Celebrated his presence, even.

How humbling and terrifying to realize just how wrong she'd been. And how she'd never be free of the pain and the sorrow that had settled into her soul the day she'd lost her baby.

Just like all the words of wisdom and grace she gave to her students—she had none for herself.

Just like the dogs she insisted others take on to enrich their lives while hers remained empty.

And just like watching her brothers find love—find their futures—where she had none.

While she might not believe there was room for any of those things in her life, one thing remained certain. Ryder Durant was a good man. And at a bare minimum, he deserved an explanation.

Still unable to look at him, she remained where she was. "If I tell you, will you go?"

"Arden—"

She cut him off. "Will you go?"

Silence stretched between them, long, agonizing seconds before he finally relented. "Yes."

Pressure built in her chest as her heart thudded and she grasped at a few deep breaths to center herself. By the time she'd turned, Ryder had dragged on his slacks and stood facing her.

"I told you there was someone in my life. A relationship gone bad. All the way bad, like he wasn't the person I thought he was."

"Did he hurt you?"

"If you mean physically, no. He was a jerk and my brothers would have loved a collective shot at him, but he wasn't abusive in the way you're asking. Insensitive and unnecessarily cruel, but that was more of the self-ishness I'd ignored."

The news might not have pleased him but she did see an easing in his shoulders as the battle-braced tension faded from his stiff form.

"I told you about my father and the history with the ranch. Dan and I were together during that time and the months after when my brothers and I were working to put it all back together. With all the traveling I was doing and lack of sleep, I made a mistake with my birth control pills. Took the wrong pills at the wrong time and got pregnant."

The tension was back in his stance but this time Arden saw the surprise that he couldn't hide. "Where is the child?"

"I lost the baby about four months into my pregnancy. Dan was long gone by then and all of a sudden, the life I'd begun to believe so strongly in was gone, too.

"That baby was my miracle and then it simply wasn't any longer."

"Arden, I'm so sorry."

He moved a few steps closer before stopping. Whether it was respect for her boundaries or something he saw in her face, Arden had no idea. But suddenly it was essential he not come any closer.

If he did, she might be lost and risk the emotional security she'd worked so hard to maintain.

"I was sorry for a long time, too. Then I was mad. Only after that did I finally accept it."

"To hell with that. You had something awful happen and the one person who should have stood with you abandoned you at the most crucial moment."

"That's why I became strong all on my own. Dan was the proof you can't really depend on anyone else."

"That's not true." He held up a hand but didn't step any closer, still respecting those invisible boundary lines she'd thrown down. "You can't possibly believe it's true."

"Of course it's true. Isn't that what your friend taught you? The drug deal gone bad? Wasn't that the same thing? Someone you trusted who abandoned you. Isn't that what Shayne's going to learn soon? That the person she trusted with her body, the person she allowed into her home, betrayed her. My father was the same, with his betrayal of his family. And for what? A few bad years on the ranch?"

Even as she made her list, she knew there were some who found their way out. She wasn't even surprised when Ryder landed in the same place.

"Your brothers. Your sisters-in-law. They're proof it's not true. Look at Reese. Look at what she endured."

God, how did she make him understand?

How could she possibly make him see that even if she did believe in love—even if she did believe in *him*—there was no way she would make herself that vulnerable again. Losing her child had cursed her with an awareness of just how fragile it all was.

And how the only way to stay above it was to keep it at arm's length.

"They're the lucky few. And even with finding each other they all suffered betrayal before that. Reese with her father and brother. Belle with Reese's father. Veronica with her ex-husband."

He did move this time, so quickly that Arden barely had time to blink. One moment he was in front of the bed and the next he was pulling her close, all that warm skin and strong muscle surrounding her.

"Lucky? No. They made their lives. Remade them, really. They found love and they used it and molded it and shaped it into a future. A new, better future than what had come before."

Words buffeted her mind—excuses, really—but she no longer had the energy for them. Or for arguments. Or for trying to convince him why she was different.

So she stood there, wrapped up in all that warm strength, cocooned yet not taking anything from it. Her arms remained at her sides, her stubborn refusal to take. Her voice remained silent, now that she stood at her immovable line.

All the time they'd spent together, it had all been working up to this.

"I need you to go now, Ryder."

"Arden."

"Please."

Ryder opened the passenger door of his SUV for Murphy, the predawn darkness feeling as weighty as a thick, wet blanket. After staying close to Reese, Murphy now stretched and frolicked in the cool morning air.

Air that his canine seemed to love, but which felt clammy over Ryder's skin, the air redolent with heavy dew.

What in the freaking *hell* had happened?

He'd asked himself that as he'd backed away from Arden's stiff form. As he'd struggled back into his clothes and moved through the darkened ranch house. As he'd collected his dog from where he lay sentinel beside Reese, the woman curled up on the couch watching an old sitcom rerun. Hoyt lay sprawled in the corner of the couch beside his wife, yet even in sleep his hand held hers.

If Reese had thought anything, she didn't say it, but the softness in her hazel gaze, illuminated by the flickering TV, said she knew.

And in the simple comfort he saw between her and her husband he nearly lost it all right there. Nearly fell to the ground, broken and battered because all he wanted stood silent and alone in that room upstairs.

How had he missed the signs so completely? He knew that Arden struggled with her past but he'd believed she was coming out of her shell. Hell, he'd *seen* it with his own eyes. He'd seen her relaxing and embracing more and accepting more.

And then last night.

They'd been amazing together.

Sex had been one more transformation between them. Giving and taking, accepting and receiving pleasure from one another.

Until she'd shut down.

Ryder bumped over the long driveway off the ranch and headed back toward town and his own apartment. Work still waited for him and it required his full focus. Maybe if he could get through this—figure out where Statler's loyalties lay and put his op into motion—then he could concentrate on Arden.

On what was between them.

And on what it would take to convince her that they were worth the risk. That what they had between them was real and tangible and not going to evaporate in the poor choices of another. Because there was no way he was ready to let her go.

The hands-free function on his SUV interrupted his thoughts, the dash lighting up just before the insistent ring of his mobile kicked in. A call this early always put him on high alert and for a split second his mind rejoiced that it was Arden, calling him back to the ranch house.

Only it was Noah Ross calling, his colleague's name filling the readout. He hadn't seen Noah since the man was transferred out of The Pass, and even though Ryder and Belle had been discussing reaching out to Noah, they'd ended up using their time last night to finalize their plans.

But now?

Ross might be the answer to solving Ryder's suspicions of problems at the Bureau.

But it still didn't explain why the man was he calling.

Scrambling for those last few seconds of calm to clear the pain from his mind, Ryder gave it one last ring before hitting the answer button. "Noah."

"Durant. Sorry for the early morning call."

"Not a problem. I'm already up."

"Good. I'm in town and camped out at a motel up in Mesa Creek. Would you come on up and meet me? I've got a few things I want to talk to you about."

Ryder had a split second to decide his approach, even as everything in him recognized a kindred spirit in his fellow officer. "I think I know why you're here and hiding out twenty miles outside of town."

Ross's feedback was terse and to the point. "Figured you did."

"Murph and I are on our way."

* * *

Ryder found the motel easily, the row of chains forming a welcome line at the entrance to Mesa Creek. He'd had twenty minutes to think how to play this with Ross, well aware that no amount of trust for the man could protect him if things at the Bureau were more off the rails than he'd expected.

Or if Ross was dirty.

Statler had transferred Noah, making a big deal of the move as promotion. Which it was, but it had the secondary benefit of getting the man out of The Pass. Which either meant they were in league with each other or the promotion had gotten the ever-sharp-eyed Noah out of the way.

It was the same argument he and Belle had batted back and forth, as they'd considered if it made sense to call Noah with their suspicions about Statler. A discussion they'd never closed with a conclusion.

Yet here Noah was, nearby and calling Ryder of his own accord.

As he jumped out of the car, then gave Murphy the command to come, Ryder knew the time had come to make a leap of faith. "And hope like hell this leap goes better than last night's," he muttered to himself, the words even more bitter than he'd expected as they lay on his tongue.

He'd struggled to keep Arden from his thoughts as he'd traversed the miles up to Mesa Creek, but she'd remained persistently in his mind. Clouding his judgment? Or giving him much needed clarity to make a decision?

"Who the hell knows," he added, well aware that progressing to talking to himself wasn't the best of signs.

Murphy let out a light yip of happiness as Noah Ross

emerged out of his room and in moments was dancing happily around the agent, reveling in seeing his long-lost friend.

Was it a sign? A confirmation? Or simply time to lay his cards on the table.

Ryder realized that it really didn't matter. He needed help and he refused to believe that betrayal was the only thing that awaited him or that duplicity was the only possible outcome.

Noah gave Murphy one last pat on the head before standing to his full height. The man was tall and lanky and had a build Ryder had always called "Upstanding Texas Man" in his mind. He could just as easily have pictured Noah Ross walking the dusty streets of Fort Worth or Laredo or Abilene, keeping the peace as town sheriff a century and a half before, as he could see him today—one of the FBI's most well-respected officers.

With that last thought in mind, Ryder stuck out his hand, rewarded with a strong, solid handshake. Neither of them said a word, just moved inside the motel room and closed the door. Only after it was closed, did Ryder say what was on his mind.

"You're here about Statler."

"You mean the poison in our organization?" Noah asked. When Ryder only nodded, he continued on. "Damn straight I am."

Chapter 17

Arden knew she needed to leave the house, but after two days she hadn't conjured up a good enough reason to go. The flaming disaster of a morning after with Ryder had blazed in her mind for the past forty eight hours and she vacillated between absolute misery and self-righteous fury when she thought about all they'd said to one another.

Even if that fury faded each time she was reminded of his cool, although not-quite-calm logic in the face of her arguments.

They made their lives. Remade them, really. They found love and they used it and molded it and shaped it into a future. A new, better future than what had come before.

Did he really believe that?

She'd asked herself over and over if he did, each time coming to the same conclusion.

Yes, he did believe it.

He wasn't the one who seemingly struggled to see them in a relationship. Or to see a future for them. And she'd been drawn to that certainty. Like moths and flames, she'd flown into all that glorious light.

Wasn't that the very reason she'd told him about the baby in the first place?

Yet once she had, all the pain she'd carried inside came rushing back, burning away all the progress they'd made. All the hard work she'd done to see a new life for herself fading away in the face of the remembered pain.

And killing the tender shoots of understanding that had grown up between them since he'd confided in her with his work.

On a hard sigh she got up from the couch in her sitting room. She'd dropped down there after her morning shower, and only now that she glanced over at the clock did she realize she'd wasted half the morning, the readout indicating she'd sat there gazing at nothing for over an hour.

"Enough."

The admonition came out harsher than she intended, the word nearly a shout into the quiet of the room. Rushing toward the door so she wouldn't find a reason to turn back and climb into bed, she was halfway down the hall when she heard the first sound of anguish.

Running even harder, she headed down the stairs and into the living area, nearly at the door to the family room when the heavy cry came once again.

"Reese!" Arden rushed into the room where her sister-in-law was bent over and holding on to the back of the couch. "Are you okay?"

"I'm fine." Her cry of pain was at odds with the reassurance and Arden rushed over, one hand on Reese's lower back as her other came tight around the other woman, taking Reese's hand in a firm grip.

"Come on now. Let's get you into a chair."

"I was in the chair. Standing up is what made me cry out."

"I've got you." Arden walked the woman toward the edge of the couch, the large, overstuffed arms high enough Reese could prop there without needing to put all her weight at a lower center of gravity. Arden nearly had her there, too, when another cry came, this one harsher than the first two.

A cry that Reese reinforced with a hard squeeze on Arden's free hand.

"Have you called Hoyt yet?"

"He headed out early to get a few things done."

"Not today, I'm afraid. The two of you are going to have a baby." Arden heard the giddy joy in her own voice as she reached for the cell phone that lay in arm's reach on the coffee table. "Come on, sweetie. Call him."

Reese's pretty hazel eyes went wide in her face. Arden didn't miss the pain that hovered in their depths, but it was mixed with clear excitement and happiness. "You really think it's going to be this morning?"

Arden realized that Reese only continued to stare at the phone and figured she needed to take matters into her own hands. She dialed Tate's number first and hoped her brothers were out together.

"Reese, honey. You doing okay?" Tate's voice came, smooth as silk, through the phone.

"It's me. Hoyt with you?"

Her brother's jovial tone came winging right back at her. "Yup. You think I'd let him out of my sight?"

"That's the answer I was hoping for. Get our daddy-to-be in hand and get him back to the house. It looks like Casa de Reynolds is going to get a new member today."

"We're fifteen minutes away." Tate said before he let out a whoop and a holler and disconnected the phone. Arden was hard-pressed to hold back one of her own before she set the phone back on the coffee table.

"They're on their way back?" Reese gritted her teeth around what Arden assumed was another contraction.

"I guess you heard but about fifteen minutes away."

"Good."

"Why?"

"Because my contractions are about five minutes apart."

Despite the early start, Arden's estimates on the baby's arrival took longer than any of them expected, and Casa de Reynolds had to wait a full twenty-four hours before welcoming a new member to its fold.

But oh, welcome they did.

Dark hair, soft and downy, covered the sweetest little head Arden had ever seen. Even now, running on zero sleep and nothing but pride, Arden could picture her nephew peeking from the blanket he'd been swaddled in and just smiled from the sheer elation of it all. His cheeks plumped sweetly around a little bow mouth and Arden still pictured the stubborn set of her brother's jaw, perfectly mimicked in his son, outlined neatly against the blanket.

Hoyt was a father.

He'd stumbled out to the waiting room to tell them all, shell-shocked and overjoyed and full of pride to announce the arrival of his son. William James Reynolds.

A nod to their great-grandfather who had charted the course of their family the day he settled his land in The Pass and built the Reynolds legacy. And a memorial to Reese's brother, given with the solemn promise and deep understanding that those we loved were never forgotten.

It was that legacy she thought of now as she turned through the gates of home.

She'd lived here her entire life. She knew what her forebears had built and what it all meant. She felt it in her own blood and understood the power of heritage. But only at that moment in the hospital, staring down at her nephew as she had her turn to hold him in her arms, did she finally understand the deep truth of it all.

Life went on.

In all its joy and sorrow, all its moments of shocking and profound gratitude and the deepest struggle and mourning, it continued.

All she could hope was that Baby William had a strong and steady foundation to traverse all the hours of his life. A foundation that they'd all have a hand in crafting.

Unbidden, Ryder's words came back to her.

They made their lives.

Remade them, really.

They found love and they used it and molded it and shaped it into a future. A new, better future than what had come before.

He'd spoken of her brothers and their wives, but in it, Ryder had given an illustration of what could be between the two of them. A life remade. Rebuilt from ashes that didn't have to hold them back any longer.

That didn't have to hold *her* back any longer.

With images of William's sweet, firm chin still lingering in her mind, nestled against the baby blue of his hospital blanket, Arden finally understood what Ryder had meant. What Hoyt had meant a few days ago when he'd told her to embrace joy.

Where all her life had been leading her up to now.

She had a future. One that was bright and shiny and waiting for her if she'd only reach out her hands for it. She loved Ryder Durant. He might have come into her life unexpectedly, but that didn't make his presence any less powerful or any less meaningful. He'd changed her plan. *All* of her plans.

With love.

Jumping out of the car as she'd barely cut the engine, Arden raced for the house. She'd call Ryder. Right now she'd call him and tell him. She'd apologize, too. Because she was sorry for all she'd put them through.

Sorry for even missing one more day with him after all they'd already shared together.

A happy and purposeful sort of determination lit fire beneath her feet, step by step as she raced for the door, love beating in her chest. A determination that she'd later realize had the power to shut out the rest of the world.

And did when a sharp prick registered in her biceps.

A wicked, painful reminder that it was a mistake to forget her surroundings when a killer remained on the loose.

Ryder walked into his favorite sub shop on the main drag through Midnight Pass and once again ran the plans he and Noah had built in his mind. They'd done little else over the past three days and he forced himself to think about all the areas they might have forgotten. He mentally considered every possible booby trap, missed angle and open switch he could come up with.

And after nearly seventy-two hours of little sleep and coffee-fueled adrenaline, he had to admit even his considerable trepidation couldn't hold him back.

They were ready.

He'd juggled his planning sessions with Noah as well as his day job, making it look to Statler that he was on his game and focused on the upcoming op the department was planning. All the while, he built his con, email by careful email, suggesting a large shipment was coming through Reynolds Station in a matter of weeks.

The intel was deliberately vague and hard to trace, and Ryder used all he'd learned about The Pass and its various land formations around the border to drop disparate clues. All while he and Ross hunted for the source of Statler's contacts.

It had been difficult, time-consuming work, made that much more challenging by the need to cover himself every step of the way. He and Noah had agreed to run the op on their own, considering but ultimately discarding several qualified team members. Between a fear for their lives and the concern there was no one they could fully rule out as beyond Rick Statler's influence, they made the decision to take all the risk on themselves.

Which meant the few hours he did manage to sleep, his dreams were a mix of "op-gone-bad" scenarios interspersed with just how poorly he'd messed things up with Arden.

He *would* fix things between them.

In his quiet moments—the ones not fully fueled on adrenaline and anxiety—he believed he'd find a way past her barriers and an adult lifetime of reluctance to be vulnerable ever again. In his more anxious moments, he wondered how he'd fouled things up so badly. In either, he'd yet to figure out a solution.

The rumble of his stomach reminded him his goal at the moment was lunch, and a glance down at his watch showed it was after two. He hadn't seen Statler yet today and had hung close to the office in hopes he could plant today's seed. Despite casually asking around, his boss had been hard to find and Ryder had finally given up, heading out to grab lunch.

Murphy remained obediently at his side and Ryder bent to tie him up outside the sub shop when his partner let out a hard yip of happiness. Glancing up, he saw Belle heading their way, her smile bright as her arms swung at her side. Even as the pain of his fight with Arden threatened to pull him under in another wave of misery, he couldn't ignore Belle's pretty, fresh face and happy smile.

"Well look at you, Detective Reynolds." Ryder waited until she was closer, then bent to kiss her cheek. "Pretty as a picture."

"I'm happy because I got a new name today."

"Oh?"

"Forget Detective Reynolds. I'm Aunt Belle to you."

Another shot slammed Ryder in the gut, but he ignored it in favor of the joy and happiness radiating toward him on the sidewalk. "Reese had the baby."

Belle nodded, her smile never dimming. "A healthy boy, born at four forty this morning."

This is a ranch so I'm afraid to break it to you but everyone here gets up early. But 4:00 a.m. is early even for us.

His stomach rolled once more, the pitch having nothing to do with his hunger and everything to do with the lingering memories of Arden that refused to abate. "Sounds like Hoyt and Reese got their own early-rising little rancher in the making."

"They do."

"Can I buy you lunch? I was just grabbing a late one myself."

She patted her own stomach. "I've been trying to be good since this is usually the morning sickness witching hour but I feel too great. So yeah, I'd love a sandwich."

Belle gave Murphy one more solid pat, ruffling his ears in a way that always made the dog's eyes roll toward the back of his head in satisfaction before giving Ryder the room to put on the leash. Her phone went off, the ringtone drifting on the air, and Ryder paid it little attention until her hand came over his forearm, gripping him tightly.

"I'll be right home. I've got Ryder with me and he's coming, too."

She shoved the phone in her pocket, all the rosy color he'd seen so recently in her cheeks vanished in the bright afternoon sun.

"What is it?"

"Arden. She's gone. Tate found her keys kicked under the bushes near the kitchen door and no sign of her ever getting inside."

He didn't need any additional details, nor did it matter. He knew why she never made it home. Knew it to the innermost marrow of his bones and the very depths of his soul.

"I'll drive. We'll call Noah Ross on the way and fill him in."

Arden tried to swallow around the thick, dry taste in her mouth and nearly choked for her efforts. A wave of panic rushed her as she struggled to swallow and she forced herself to calm down, breathing in deeply to slow her pounding heart rate.

Where was she?

That panic threatened again, but she breathed through it, gently in and out, and tried to think.

The image of a small bundle, wrapped in blue, filled her thoughts.

William.

Reese had had the baby. Happiness had her breathing easier until the rest of her memories caught up with her. The drive home. The realization about Ryder and how much she loved him.

And then nothing but blackness as she tried to unlock the kitchen door.

Unbidden, an image of the sweet puppy she'd seen a few weeks ago with Ryder filled her mind's eye. Newman. She'd pushed the puppy away, just like she'd pushed everything else in her life away. Anything that might cause attachment, she'd held at arm's length. And now she didn't even have a dog standing guard at the door, a waiting sentinel to alert anyone to her whereabouts or to scare off a would-be intruder.

"Arden!" Her name was hissed from across the dimly lit room and Arden came up with a start, surprised to realize she wasn't alone. "It's me. Shayne."

Arden rolled to the side, her neck stiff from where it lay flat on some sort of mattress without a pillow. But she could see across the room her friend, tied to a chair. She lifted her arm—or tried to—and realized that, like Shayne, she was tied up, too. "Where are we?"

"I don't know. Oh, Arden—" The words came out on a weepy rush as Shayne's face crumpled, her lank hair falling around her face. "I had no idea. None at all. But it's Rick. He did this to us."

Arden saw the hurt in her friend and felt the anguish arc across the room between them.

And in that moment was beyond sorry that she'd been so right about Rick Statler.

Ryder had known something was wrong. He'd known from the start, working to find a way to uncover the poison that had taken up root in his office. Despite their arguments about Shayne's innocence or guilt, the rest of Ryder's instincts had been spot-on.

"What did he do to you?"

A small sob crept up Shayne's throat and Arden heard her friend take a moment to swallow around the tears. "He's been strange the past few weeks. At first I chalked it up to us getting closer and him panicking a bit that our relationship had grown serious, but—"

"But what?" Arden asked gently.

"But he's become someone I don't know. Worse, he's made me realize I never knew him to begin with. He tied me up. Drugged me yesterday and last night. He—" She broke off on another sob. "His eyes were so mean."

Although Dan had never been a criminal—nowhere close—Arden knew that bone-deep sense of betrayal. That realization that someone you believed in and trusted and depended on wasn't who you believed they were. It hurt, but far worse, it was an embarrassment. That you could be so very wrong about another person.

How much worse would it be to realize that along with betrayal was a monster lurking beneath the friendly facade?

Shayne's voice quavered once more and this time she

didn't make any attempt to hold back the tears. "He's awful, Arden. He's someone I don't know."

Although Arden wanted to tell Shayne what Ryder already suspected, she held back. She had little reason to believe her friend was guilty—especially tied up and locked in a room along with her—but she couldn't be too careful, either. For some reason, Statler had targeted her.

Which meant Ryder was his main goal.

She took a modicum of heart from that thought because it meant that Statler would keep them alive until he could contact Ryder.

And then any whisper of hope plummeted once more when she considered that it meant Ryder was in serious danger. One he likely had no idea was even headed his way.

"I'm sorry, Shayne." Arden's eyes had adjusted to the light and she could make Shayne out more clearly than when she'd first woken up. Her friend's small form was attached to a chair, her legs tied to the base, while her arms were strapped behind her. Arden had no idea how long she'd been gone but even an hour like that and Shayne would have to be in terrible pain. "Take me through it from the beginning. What did he do to you?"

"I was at home finishing up a call when he showed up. He has a key so I didn't think much of it." A grim smile ghosted Shayne's face, but the tears were gone, replaced with anger and a hell of a lot of grit. "I'd nearly wrapped up the call and was already imagining an afternoon quickie. He'd been tense and on edge the past few days and I thought how good it would be for us to be close. To make love and wash away the past few days."

Her mouth turned down in a deep frown. "I am so damned stupid."

"No, Shayne. No you're not."

Suddenly frantic with it, Arden struggled to sit up. Images filled her mind, one after the other on a rapid sort of loop. Her brothers and their wives. Baby William. Murphy and his wagging tail. The horses in the corral.

And Ryder.

Embedded through it all was Ryder.

It wasn't normal to expect betrayal and it wasn't fair to assume that you were stupid because you thought the best of someone.

Arden used that anger to their advantage, focused on the moment at hand.

"Look at me." She waited until Shayne lifted her head, then pressed on. "You're not stupid and you're not to blame. Rick played you and he's been playing the FBI, too. They have no idea what has been lurking in their midst."

Resolve lit Shayne's features and she straightened in the chair, as far as her bonds would allow. "We have to do something."

"Do you have any wiggle in those restraints?"

"A little, maybe. I tried for a while when he first tied me up but my arms have gone numb."

"Okay. Let me see what I can do."

Arden's arms were numb, too, where they lay behind her on the bed but she moved a bit, testing just how strong they were. There was minimal space but she felt the slightest give on her right wrist and set about seeing how far she could pull her arm even as spears of pain traveled up and down her biceps, straight into her shoulder.

Ignoring the discomfort, Arden tapped into her steady training and the focus that came with her daily yoga practice. Calm and slow, she treated the problem like a difficult yoga move, flexing her muscles with and against the bonds. She'd nearly given up when she felt a bit more give on that right knot. It wasn't much, but she used it, flexing and shifting to work her wrist through the narrow hole. Pain zinged up her arm once more as she made the last tug on the bond, but was rewarded with her arm slipping free.

"Got it."

Shayne had remained quiet as she worked, but now spoke up. "You're amazing. Seriously, is there anything you can't do?"

"Ask me that after we're out of here." Arden scrambled up from the bed, leaving the other end of the rope dangling from her wrist as she raced to Shayne. She kneeled behind the chair, frantically working the bonds that bound her friend's wrists.

Whatever danger might await them—and she was fast coming to believe Shayne wasn't a part of it—they'd do better with their mobility intact.

Her fingers trembled as she undid the thin rope at Shayne's wrists, rubbing the cold hands as her friend's arms fell from the bonds to lie limply at her sides.

"Can you move your arms?"

"They hurt," Shayne gritted out, "but yes." Arden came around the front of the chair, going to work on Shayne's ankle restraints as the other woman worked the feeling back into her upper body.

"Bastard," Shayne muttered. "Seriously, what was I thinking?"

"You can't blame yourself for falling for someone."

"How could I have missed it, though?" Shayne dropped her head, her gaze focused on the ground. "How could I miss something so big?"

"Psychopaths have a scary ability to blend in. My sister-in-law was married to one and I've heard the stories. Veronica had no idea what her ex-husband was into or how depraved he really was."

Arden thought about that now. In all the times she and Veronica had spoken about Veronica's time in Houston, never once had Arden thought less of her. Or thought her stupid and misguided. She'd been lulled into a false sense of security by a bad man. It was how she handled herself once she was out that Arden truly admired.

And it was that grit and gumption that had made Veronica willing to take a chance again with Ace.

All things she'd tell Shayne when they were free and clear of here. Free and clear of Rick Statler.

But for now they had to focus on the freedom part of that equation.

"Can you walk?"

"I think so."

"How long have you been here?"

"I'm not sure exactly. He nabbed me at lunch. Or late lunch, really, since I know I looked at the clock around one and he hadn't shown up at my house yet."

Arden looked around, curious where "here" even was. "He got me late morning. Does that mean you've been here twenty-four hours already?"

"He had me sedated until this morning. I was on that mattress where you are." Shayne scrunched up her face. "He fed me this morning. Or I assumed morning since he had breakfast from a fast-food place. He kept me tied up but on a rope long enough to go to the bathroom."

The tears that had flowed off and on faded as anger took its place. "Then the bastard tied me up again to that chair and shot me up with something else. When I woke up you were there on the bed."

With Shayne's feet free, Arden stood back up, assessing the room. They were in some sort of hideout, the room spare with the bed she'd been laid on, Shayne's chair and a bathroom visible at the edge. As she'd have expected from a man with Rick's training, beyond the rope that had been used to tie them up, there wasn't anything either of them could use as a weapon.

Arden's gaze alighted on the chair. Unless…

"Shayne. How are your arms feeling?"

"Getting there. The feeling is almost back but my head feels like it's going to explode from the sedative."

Shayne muttered a few more curses under her breath and Arden was happy to see the spark she'd always associated with her friend.

Anger was good.

Anger was something they could use.

Anger was the best weapon they had to take on a monster.

Chapter 18

Belle set up the Reynolds kitchen as their central base of operation, and Ryder and Noah had filled in, focused on marshaling whatever information they could find. Belle did the same, calling in her most trusted coworker to run point on local MPPD intel.

They all knew what they were dealing with and running anything through formal channels ran the risk of tipping Statler off.

And he'd be damned if he was going to give the man any advance warning.

Ryder scrubbed a hand over his face, his beard scratchy beneath his fingertips. His gaze landed on Murphy, where the Lab lay on the floor beside the kitchen door. He'd taken up position there, his head on his paws and his large eyes tracking the movements of everyone who came in and out of the room.

While they'd set everything up, Belle had conferred with Tate on how to tell the rest of Arden's family what was happening. Although there had been some debate on whether or not to tell the new parents, common sense and the bonds of family won out. Despite the tired excitement of becoming parents—and her own nearly twenty-four hours in labor—Reese had insisted Hoyt leave immediately to go to his family and find Arden.

Ryder had thought the decision to tell them more than fair—and one he'd have made himself—and he couldn't deny how much he appreciated having a former member of Special Ops back in the kitchen helping him and Noah.

And if the man had pulled out his phone and looked at a photo of his sister holding his new son more than a few times, Ryder would grant him that, too.

A man needed to know what he was fighting for, after all.

Veronica had opted to stay with Reese at the hospital and Tate and Ace paced steadily behind Hoyt's chair where he huddled with Noah, reviewing aerial maps of The Pass.

"What if he took her farther than the county line?" Ace asked.

"We can spread out the search but he can't have taken her far." Noah tapped his screen. "He's been in and out of the office, which means he needs to stay close to keep up the facade of engaged employee. And his last call into the team was triangulated inside city limits."

"You have the coordinates?" Tate asked.

"No specifics. He works off a new technology beta that encrypts location. Damn bastard volunteered for it, in fact. Beyond knowing the last cell tower pinged, we have no other detail."

"Damn it." Ryder slammed out of his chair, stalking through the room. "Every freaking detail, he's thought of."

Noah's voice remained calm but no one missed the storm clouds flashing in his gaze. "He's planned this, Ryder. Carefully and over a long time."

"Which means he's left a trail," Belle said. "It may be faint and buried, but it's there."

"I've found part of it. My promotion never sat well with me." Noah grimaced, his lips turning down in a sneer. "I know my value and my work, but the way it went down never felt right."

Belle smiled at that. "One day you were here and the next you weren't."

"Exactly. It was abrupt and poorly handled, even though it had great, booming, hearty congratulations layered over top. Hell, IT or human resources didn't even know I was moving until I showed up in Dallas and that was one of his biggest blunders."

Having moved in the last year himself, Ryder understood the requisitioning process and the general paperwork that accompanied an office shift. For Statler to have overlooked that was one more chink in the armor. Even with that truth, there was something Noah said that kept echoing through his mind.

Careful planning. Long lead time. Agency resources. Resources…

"The safe house. Damn it, that's it!" Ryder moved around behind Noah's chair to point to an area on the map. "There. Edge of the county about three miles from the border. We established a safe house there about six months ago."

"There's no way he's that brazen." Noah exhaled, before shaking his head. "Or maybe he is."

"You have intel on the location?" Hoyt asked.

"Perimeter cameras," Ryder said. "And we can activate internal cameras if needed."

"Can you access them here?"

Ryder appreciated where Arden's brother was going with it all. "We can, but if Statler is using the location, our looking in on the internal cameras will alert him for sure."

"What about the perimeter?" Belle asked from where she leaned against the counter. She'd been rather quiet since they returned to the house but Ryder hadn't missed the way she considered every angle, offering up something smart each time she spoke.

"I can have one of my IT leads in Dallas get me into the perimeter cameras unnoticed. We'll handle it as a regular comms check." Noah had his phone in hand, his gaze landing on Ryder.

Ryder nodded. "Make the call."

"Is that a camera?" Arden pointed to a small hole in the upper corner of the room. The point was so tiny she'd have missed it if she hadn't been staring so intently at the ceiling, desperately trying to figure out how to get them out. She and Shayne had been out of their bonds for at least an hour and still no sign of Statler. Which suggested he was in town, lying low and trying to convince everyone he was some good, upstanding guy who worked for a living.

Ryder had been right all along.

That thought had kept her steady company with each step she'd paced. He knew there was a rotting, festering poison under the surface of Midnight Pass and he'd been determined to root it out, with no regard to himself.

Hadn't that really been at the heart of it all? The continued problems she and her family had dealt with over the past year had all stemmed from that festering rot. The multiheaded hydra that wouldn't die because there was someone in connected places ensuring it wouldn't.

Worse, ensuring it could thrive.

Shayne moved closer, her gaze following Arden's. "Where?"

"There. In the corner, just above the crown molding."

"I'm going to go look at it." Shayne moved closer, studying the ceiling. "If it is a camera Rick's either not using it or not using it right now. We've been up and walking around out of those restraints and he hasn't showed up."

There was a logic to Shayne's argument and Arden figured they might as well use it to their advantage. She moved in the opposite direction from Shayne, searching the room for any more signs of surveillance. By the time she and Shayne re-met on the other side of the room they'd identified four between them.

"Do you think he set these up?" Arden asked. "Like some sort of Peeping Tom where he can watch his vict—" Arden quickly corrected herself. "Guests."

"I don't know what to think anymore."

Arden moved back to the center of the room and stopped, then turned a full circle. There had been something nagging at her subconscious that she hadn't been able to define. For all intents and purposes, the room looked normal. It was painted and had clearly had some sort of decoration, giving the sense that some care had been taking on creating a space.

Only when she looked closer, all she saw was the bed, the chair and the overhead lights. The windows had been stripped of curtains and curtain rods, but there were base screws and hooks to hang the rod still in the wall.

"He's changed something here." Arden moved to the windows. "Look up there."

Shayne joined her, before exhaling a heavy breath. "He's using this space but he's made changes."

"Damn straight he has." Arden nodded, moving closer to the window and eying the brackets. "Is it possible this is some sort of FBI house?"

"A safe house, you mean?"

"Sure. Something the government keeps. Only he's using it for his own purposes."

Heavy clapping came from the doorway, punctuating the silence Arden had unwittingly begun to take for granted.

It was silence that had suggested she and Shayne still had time to get away.

Only time was up.

Ryder stared at Noah's screen, something dark and oily unfurling in the very depths of his stomach as he watched Rick Statler turn into the driveway of the safe house. Noah's contact had activated the perimeter cameras and the one on the mailbox caught the turn-in, with several loaded in nearby trees then capturing the short journey down the safe house driveway.

"Hell and damn, you were right." Noah shook his head. "Every time I think the bastard can't be that brazen, he proves me wrong."

"He's proved us all wrong."

"What's the play?" Hoyt spoke for his brothers, but Ace and Tate hovered nearby, anxious for action.

"We can't bring civilians into this." Ryder eyed Noah. "Hoyt maybe with his background and training."

"Try to stop us." Ace moved up, his expression as bleak as any Ryder had ever seen. "She's our sister. Our family. There's no way in hell you're going after her alone."

"I can't let you go." Ryder shook his head. When Ace looked ready to change his mind with fists, Ryder moved in, laying every card he had on the table. "I love her. More than I can tell you. More than I ever thought possible. I can't drag you into this. What would she do if we got her out and hurt one of you in the process?"

"Well we're sure as hell not sitting home." Tate spoke for all of them, but there was a softness in his tone that belied the harsh words. "We get it, man. Really, we do. And we've all been there. But you're not doing this alone."

"Nothing about this has followed protocol." Noah stood from the table. "Why start now?"

"Then let's get ready to head out. We can finalize plans in the car." Ryder didn't have time to question his decision or argue. So he nodded at Noah and motioned for Murphy to join them.

Hell, Ross was right.

Why start following the rules now?

Statler moved forward from his position in the doorway, his smile dropping as the clapping stopped. "You figured me out."

"You're using a government safe house to hold us?" Arden shot back, unwilling to show any sign of cowering weakness. "What kind of moron does that?"

Statler's face clouded at the insult but he kept his cool. "The kind who isn't a moron at all."

"You can't possibly think this is a good idea."

"I know it is. No one knows where I am and I control who comes and goes here. Why use anywhere else when this place was purpose-built for holding someone when necessary."

"I thought safe houses were meant to keep people safe," Arden shot back.

"Or keep prisoners in. You know, we the good and faithful executors of Uncle Sam's wishes like to keep our options open."

"Good and faithful," Shayne spat the words. She'd vacillated between anger and fear and tears over the past hour and had firmly come down on the anger front since Rick's return. "You're neither."

"Tsk tsk." Statler laid a hand over his heart. "You wound me, baby. I've been nothing but faithful to you."

"You've lied to me since the day we met!"

Rick marched over to her, his face set in soft lines. "I've been good to you, too," he crooned as he got closer. "You're my girl."

Shayne never wavered, nor did she telegraph her movements. But it was only when Rick was in range that she lifted her hand, slapping him on the face with a hard crack that reverberated through the room.

"You're mad." Statler's voice was singsongy as he grabbed Shayne hands, his grip like a vise over her wrists. It was only as he gave them a vicious tug that his voice turned equally cold. "And I don't like temperamental women."

Shayne cried out at the tight grip, crying even harder

when Statler retained her wrists in one hand and back-handed her face with the other.

Arden watched the byplay, unable to turn away, as she bided her time. Her immediate instinct was to jump in and protect her friend, but they needed to use their freedom to their advantage. They were two against one. There was no way Statler wasn't carrying a gun so they had very little time to overpower him before he decided to use it.

But as Rick lifted his hand once more to strike, Arden couldn't stay still. On a war cry, she rushed the couple, pushing every bit of strength she had into her forward movement.

Ryder stilled at the edge of the property. There was no way of knowing what eyes Statler had on the perimeter and they'd agreed to stop just south of the property line, out of range of the surveillance equipment.

Nothing about the situation sat well with him.

He wanted to get inside and get to Arden. Every bit of his training and understanding of how to handle high stress situations had seemingly vanished. In its place was a driving, desperate desire to get to Arden.

"You see anything?" Ryder hadn't had any luck with his own long-range binoculars and hoped Noah's position three hundred yards away was more informational.

"Nothing."

"Negative as well," Hoyt affirmed, his position about five hundred yards past Noah added another knife to the gut.

Those negative responses on his comms only reinforced that need to get inside.

Beside him, Murphy quivered. His attention was on

the house in the distance and Ryder saw the same determination to get inside reflected in the sleek lines of Murphy's quivering frame.

But it was the sound of a shot—muffled from inside the house—that put them on the move.

Ryder gave the order to Murphy, who took off like a shot, then moved, hollering to his partners at the same time. "I'm going in!"

Arden kept her tight hold on Statler's back, the limited benefit she got by leaping on him fading quickly as he moved around, trying to shake her off with all the strength of a bucking bronco. Blood bloomed on Shayne's cheek but her own shock at Rick's brutality shifted quickly as she moved in to help Arden.

Both of them punched and kicked, using whatever collective strength they could muster against the man, and in the heat of it all Arden forgot about the gun. But as Rick tossed her off, her body falling hard against the floor headfirst, she saw him move. The fall had her seeing double, but both Ricks in her line of vision were equally bad. He had a gun out of the waistband of his jeans and pointed toward Shayne.

Gathering every bit of strength she still had and praying she'd be fast enough, Arden launched herself at Rick. She hit him as the sound of the gun echoed around the room, falling over him in the rush of movement.

Shayne screamed again but Arden took heart in the sound, hoping it meant the shot had gone wide of her friend. She used her position to slam a hand into Rick's head, trying to disorient him, even as her own head still rang with the hit to the floor. Shayne leaped on Rick's downed hand with a heavy stomp of her foot at the same time as Arden's palm connected with the man's ear and she heard a heavy groan as he again struggled to buck her off.

Try as she might, she was no match for his bigger frame, nor could she hold her position as he got an arm free and swung it against her body. They were wild moves, but the two of them were so intertwined that Statler landed a few blows and as soon as he felt some slack in her grasp he used it to his advantage, arching his back to push her off.

Arden fell once more, the thin layer of carpet over the concrete foundation slab doing little to break her fall. Statler swung at Shayne as well, his professional training serving him well as she fell to the ground in a heap. From her periphery Arden saw Statler turning on her and struggled against the spinning room.

Breathing hard, Arden knew the truth. Their only hope was to keep working together to overpower him. Her head throbbed and her vision was wobbly, but she refused to give up.

Or give in.

Willing every ounce of strength into her limbs, she rolled just out of reach and scrabbled for purchase to get to her feet. She'd much rather take her chances standing than lying down and was nearly up when Rick moved, looming over her. His cold, empty eyes glittered down at her, flashing with something so dark and insidious that she actually stilled for a moment.

That involuntary pause gave Rick the room to get closer. He was already leaning down, his hands on her shoulders when a heavy growl filled the room. A streak of dark fur leaped over Arden's head, knocking Statler down and away from her.

Murphy!

Arden rolled out of range as the dog attacked Statler, the full force of his body and snapping jaws occupying Statler's full attention.

The room still spun but Arden fought through the disorientation to get to Shayne. Her friend was huddled on the floor in a heap and Arden touched her shoulder, turning her gently.

Murphy's growls continued in unison with Statler's grunts and it was only as she heard a hard yip from the dog that she turned. Again, the man's training did him well and he had the dog pinned on the floor. Well aware that Ryder had to be close by but unwilling to wait another second, Arden's gaze landed on the gun still on the floor. Leaping for it, she picked it up and prayed a lifetime of training around guns would serve her well, especially since she was still seeing double.

Lifting the gun, she aimed for Statler's head, hoping that even if her shot went a little wild she was far enough away from Murphy to avoid hitting him.

Arden lined up her shot, aimed and fired, the kickback immediately reverberating through her arms. She knew immediately that her shot didn't hit its mark, but Statler's loud cry confirmed that she'd done some damage. Despite her wavering vision, she kept her arms lifted. Pain rippled through her head but she lined up her shot once more.

Statler's gaze was no less harsh—no less vicious— but even in her wavering view, she saw it.

Defeat.

And then the view shifted as the man took off for the edge of the room, Murphy in hot pursuit.

Ryder pushed harder, his heart pounding as he swept the back room of the safe house. Noah's contact in Dallas had remotely unlocked the doors so they'd had an easy in to the house and Murphy had moved in as advanced attack. Ryder heard his partner's heavy growls and the fight from a distance and even though they'd believed Statler worked alone, he couldn't break protocol or the support of his team to ignore the need to clear each room as they went.

Shouting an all clear, he moved from what was a mudroom slash laundry room and on into a kitchen.

He followed the steps.

Worked the room just as he'd been trained.

It was only as he heard the second shot that he ignored it all and moved.

Chaos greeted him as he breached the living room. Arden stood, her arms extended with the gun in hand, even as the room before her was empty. Murphy barked and whined as he scratched at a door on the opposite side of the room. And the woman he recognized as Shayne Erickson lay on her side about ten feet from Arden.

"Arden!"

Her arms still trembled as she turned and Ryder rushed forward, focused on removing the gun before adrenaline or the confusion of the moment could cause her to fire. Her arms shook but she lowered them as he came closer, confirming for him that she was in control of the situation.

In control of herself.

He took the gun dangling from her fingers, setting the safety before laying it down on the floor, and then pulling her close.

"You're here," she whispered against him, her arms tight around his waist.

"You're safe now."

They stood like that as her brothers swarmed in behind Noah and were still standing like that when the MPPD showed up a few minutes behind.

Ryder ignored the rest of the room, only making room for Murphy when he nosed his way between the two of them.

"Murphy saved Shayne and me," Arden whispered, before she rested a hand over the dog's head.

Ryder laid his hand over hers as his faithful friend leaned his large body against their legs. The dog had earned himself about a week of rest and Ryder knew there was no way he could ever repay the loyalty the animal had shown.

Her brothers moved in, gentle but all eager to pull her close in a hug. And it was Ace's offer to Murphy of the largest steak in the freezer that had his faithful companion's tail thumping hard and in clear understanding of his upcoming reward.

Arden hugged Ace, then Tate and Hoyt in turn, before returning to Ryder's arms. As her brothers moved off to help Noah, Arden spoke. "He escaped, didn't he? Statler? No one's saying it, which has to mean he's gone."

Ryder pressed his lips to her forehead. "You can thank your brilliant sister-in-law. He not only didn't escape, but her crack team of MPPD officers were waiting for him as he exited the house."

Relief seemed to swamp her at the news, tension fleeing her body in a rush. "He set this up. He set this place up."

"He did." A fact he and his colleagues had to live with. "And we'll deal with it. Maybe not tonight. But we will."

Arden stared up at him. He didn't miss the vaguely unfocused gaze and already had plans to call over the medics when she lifted up on her toes and pressed her lips to his. "I love you, Ryder Durant. I'm sorry I had to get kidnapped to tell you."

Ryder sank into the kiss, a mixture of gratitude and the simple awe of having her safely back with him filling him up and chasing away the bleakness that had been his constant companion since they'd discovered her gone. A few whispers of unease still lingered, but they were nothing now that he had her in his arms.

When he finally pulled away, he whispered back the words he'd been so eager to say. "I love you, too."

She smiled at him, her gaze still vague even as something sure and solid sat behind the smile. "And there's one more thing."

"What's that?"

"I want a puppy. Newman, to be exact."

Those last whispers that swirled in his chest faded away.

She might be hurt, but she would heal.

They had a whole future in front of them and he was going to spend every single day showing her how much he loved her.

And starting tomorrow, it looked like his life was about to get a lot more dog fur in it.

He was exactly where he belonged.

Epilogue

Arden breathed deeply before pressing a kiss to the crown of William's head as he slowly wiggled awake against Hoyt's shoulder. Newman struggled in her arms to add one of his own puppy kisses, but she held him back, not ready to subject her two-week-old nephew to the slobber.

There would be time enough for that.

She already envisioned the two of them rolling around on the floor, along with Newman's future half sibling. Hoyt and Reese had already put in their request with Brennan Gabriel to secure her next puppy who didn't pass training.

"That dog will never learn if you spoil him like that." Ryder came into the living room, Murphy at his side. "*Especially* if you spoil him like that." He shot Murphy a look and added a long-suffering sigh. "Holding him like a baby."

Reese waved an airy hand at Ryder before taking her rapidly waking son in her arms. As Hoyt had already joked as he settled into fatherhood, his son went from full-on sleep to full-on hungry and screaming in less than eight seconds.

Arden had clocked him at six but kept the news to herself.

Besides, Newman had already chewed the toe on one of Hoyt's boots and she wanted him in a good mood when he found it.

"There's no such thing as too spoiled," Reese added as she settled her son at her breast. "Or there shouldn't be."

Arden set Newman down beside Murphy and the two nestled in beside each other. Although Newman hadn't succeeded in K-9 training, he was coming along nicely with the older, wiser canine tutelage Murphy provided and Arden loved seeing the way the small puppy snuggled up against his alpha.

Satisfied there were no stray shoes lying around and ripe for attack, she took a seat beside Ryder, settling in herself against his chest.

The past two weeks had passed in a blur. Despite working relentlessly, Ryder and Noah and the rest of the team hadn't succeeded in finding all of Statler's contacts or the depths of his crimes. She'd reached out to Shayne a few times but her friend obviously needed some alone time. After all, Shayne wasn't just processing the pain of the kidnapping, but Rick Statler's emotional betrayal as well.

Arden was finally starting to feel better. The headaches that had come on the heels of her concussion diagnosis had finally begun to subside and the doctor was pleased with her progress. Ryder had been patient with her—infuriatingly so—refusing to do anything more than hold her against him each night in bed.

But she had plans for this evening.

She'd waited long enough and had damn near asked for a doctor's note to convince him.

In the end, though, it was hard to stay miffed. Arden knew that care and consideration were a hallmark of the man she loved. The man she was making a life with. And those late-night snuggles had produced a lot of conversation, including discussion about their future.

Together.

Just like her brothers, it seemed love had found her, too. Reynolds Station was teeming with life and love and a beautiful future. Although she would always mourn the loss of her child, it was good and happy and deeply fulfilling to look at William and see a great-great-grandchild of William "Wildhorse" Reynolds in their midst. It was even better to know that others would follow him.

She'd always wondered if her great-grandfather had looked out over the land and seen the future. But as she looked around the room, at Belle and Tate; Hoyt, Reese and William; Ace and Veronica and then to Ryder, Arden understood something else.

The future was something made in the present.

With loved ones.

With friends.

And with the confident—and hopeful—understanding that you could face anything with the people you loved.

* * * * *

#2171 SNOWED IN WITH A COLTON
The Coltons of Colorado • by Lisa Childs

Certain her new guest at the dude ranch she co-owns is hiding something, Aubrey Colton fights her attraction to him. Luke Bishop is hiding something—his true identity: Luca Rossi, an Italian journalist on the run from the mob.

#2172 CAVANAUGH JUSTICE: THE BABY TRAIL
Cavanaugh Justice • by Marie Ferrarella

Brand-new police detective partners Korinna Kennedy and Brodie Cavanaugh investigate a missing infant case and uncover a complicated conspiracy while Korinna is slowly drawn into Brodie's life and family—causing her to reevaluate her priorities in life.

#2173 DANGER AT CLEARWATER CROSSING
Lost Legacy • by Colleen Thompson

After his beloved twins are returned from the grandparents who've held them for years, widowed resort owner Mac Hale-Walker finds his long-anticipated reunion threatened by a beautiful social worker sent to assess his fitness to parent—and a plot to forcibly separate him from his children forever.

#2174 TROUBLE IN BLUE
Heroes of the Pacific Northwest • by Beverly Long

Interim police chief Marcus Price is captivated by newcomer Erin McGarry, who has come to Knoware to help her sick sister. But he has his hands full with a string of robberies and a credible terrorist threat, and he's not confident that Erin didn't bring the danger to the small community or that either one of them will survive it.

HRSCNM0122B

Marcus watched as she got to her feet. He was grateful to
see that she was steady.

"Can we have a minute?" Marcus asked Blade.

"Yeah. Hang on to her good arm," his friend replied.
Then he walked away, taking Dawson with him.

"What?" she asked, offering him a sweet smile.

"I'm going to find who did this. I promise you. And
you're going to be okay. Jamie Weathers is the best
emergency physician this side of the Colorado River.
Hell, this side of the Missouri River. He'll fix you up.
But don't leave the hospital until you hear from me. You
understand?"

"I got it," she said. "I'm going to be fine. It's all going to be fine. I barely had twenty bucks in my bag. He didn't even get my phone. I had that in my back pocket. Nor my keys. Those were in my hand. So he basically got nothing except the cash and my driver's license."

Things didn't matter. "You want me to let Brian and Morgan know?"

"Oh, God, no. Please don't do that." She looked panicked. "Morgan can't have stress right now. I'm grateful that her room is on the other side of the building. Otherwise, she could be watching this spectacle."

They would want to know. But it was her decision. And she was in pain. "Okay," he said, giving in easily.

"Thank you," she said.

"Go get fixed up. I'll talk to you soon."

She nodded.

"And, Erin…" he added.

"Yeah."

"I'm really glad that you're okay."

Don't miss
Trouble in Blue *by Beverly Long,*
available March 2022 wherever
Harlequin Romantic Suspense
books and ebooks are sold.

Harlequin.com

Get 4 FREE REWARDS!

We'll send you 2 FREE Books plus 2 FREE Mystery Gifts.

Harlequin Romantic Suspense books are heart-racing page-turners with unexpected plot twists and irresistible chemistry that will keep you guessing to the very end.

FREE Value Over **$20**